A SPECIFIC DESTINY

ROBERT ALLEN SENTER

SenArc Publishing
Orlando, Florida

Cover design: Juanita Arce
Editing: Juanita Arce

ISBN 978-0-9833783-3-4

I would like to dedicate this book to the loving memory of my mother, Flora Senter, and of my younger brother, Ben Senter. Also, to every man, woman, and child who has suffered as a result of war.

CHAPTERS

INTRODUCTION

DO YOU FEAR being alone? Are you afraid of never finding true love? Do you fail more than you succeed? When you look back, does your life have the meaning you desire? These are the questions we all confront and deal with in our quest for understanding who we are.

Did you ever wonder about things like the purpose of life and what is your part in it? Did you ever feel that maybe there is a specific destiny waiting for you? Have you wondered about death and dying? How about the big question, "Is there a God?"

Well, I know someone who had the same questions and this is the story of how he found his own answers. I was riding on the rear platform of the last car on a Long Island railroad train watching the tracks speeding off into the past in parallel lines, not being able to see what's coming, only what had just passed, and hearing the clickety clack of the wheels against the track. This had a strange and hypnotic effect on me and always put me into a contemplative mood. That's where Joe first appeared.

Joe was an average-looking man; he seemed the sort that would make for a good friend. As a casual conversation started, we both exchanged personal facts about each other. I worked at the World Trade Center and he was visiting his family on Long Island. He said he had been a soldier in the Army. I couldn't help but wonder where he had traveled and what he had experienced, so I asked him. He said he had been to places where time didn't exist and had seen many wonders in the world. This really spurred my curiosity, but my next question was for my own benefit. I wanted to find out if seeing the world and experiencing its wonders could fulfill a man's dreams and satisfy his quest for adventure.

"Are you happy?" I asked.

"Happiness is a fleeting thing," he said; "the best you can hope for is contentment."

Again I questioned him, "How do you find contentment?"

"I have a story to tell and it will answer all your questions, even questions you haven't asked yet."

Full of curiosity, I agreed to listen. Throughout many encounters and conversations, I learned of this man's quest for adventure and enlightenment through the telling of his life's experiences.

This is Joe's story. This is the story of an American who happened to be a soldier, but he was also a son, a brother, a friend, a lover. It is the story of an average person whose experiences lead to an awakening. As his young mind becomes aware of the world he lives in, the people around him, and his own individuality, Joe unwittingly searches for answers while seeking love and adventure and exploring the boundaries of his world, his mind and his soul. What he finds is completely unexpected and far more profound. Every life's journey is a chain of events for the most part not affected by you until you make an individual decision. Even then, though you think you are in control, there are greater forces at work that can alter the outcome.

Joe's story dramatizes how the difference between dreams and reality molds a man's character, and reflects on how a man's specific destiny unfolds.

IN A SMALL SOUTHERN FARM

JOE WAS WALKING down a long country dirt road, not far from the farm where he lived in the South. He was a young boy and it was a beautiful, sunny day; the sun was bright but not too hot. The air was fresh and clean and the smell of honeysuckle was everywhere. What a glorious, eternal day it was! He was beginning to have his first feelings of individuality, realizing there was a place in the world for him, and he was on the right road to finding it. This was the first day of the rest of his life and he knew it. All of a sudden he had a very strange sensation. He felt as though he was being watched. The strange thing was that he knew who was watching him. He could feel himself as an adult looking back on himself from years into the future. He could feel the man he would become wanting to return to the boy he presently was. The feeling was so strong he yelled out, "You stay where you are, you don't belong here, this is my time!" With that, the strange ghostly sensation faded and was gone. Joe wondered what would cause his future self to look back so far with such a woeful yearning. He knew he would remember this day for the rest of his life, but he didn't know why. It was okay with him, though, because this was a beautiful day and he was full of life.

A popular song of the time was "Que Será, Será." Joe's mom used to sing this song while washing the dishes. The song went like this: "*Que será, sera! Whatever will be, will be! The future's not ours to see. Que será, será.*" Joe used to ponder a lot on those words, being a young boy with no idea of what his future would be. Those words consoled him and relieved him of the burden of ever worrying about his future, and he never did.

Naturally, being a little boy, Joe thought the whole world was a small farm in the South. That was okay too, because there was always something to play with, or a new place to explore. Like the time when Joe and his older brother Chad were exploring the barn and they found a 50-gallon drum in a dark corner. Chad tossed Joe a book of matches and said, "See what's inside." Joe lit the match and looked in; there was a dark fluid inside. When the match burned out, Joe threw it into the drum. After a second try, Joe reported that he couldn't see anything but this dark fluid, so Chad took the matches and decided to see for himself. No sooner had Chad lit his match than there was an explosion that sounded like kingdom come, followed by a quick ball of fire and billowing smoke. Joe saw his brother blown clear to the back of the barn like a rag doll. The sight was so odd it brought instant laughter from Joe until his brother began screaming in pain. His face was completely burned red and blistered. Upon hearing the explosion their mother came to the rescue. She grabbed Chad and ran into the house where she hit him in the face with butter and steaks. Would you believe that he never even had a scar from that? A lifetime later, Joe asked Chad what it had been like for him. Chad said he saw a small flame rising up in slow motion and that was all he remembered.

Another interesting place to explore was the unknown and uncharted woods across the street from the house. These woods were awesome in their scope. They had a prehistoric smell to them and the thick canopy of moss-covered trees made for a haunting dark challenge, especially for a young boy. But no one in his right mind would go into those woods alone. No one had ever been in those woods before, probably not even the ancient Indians. In the Deep South, things grew really quite large in swampy areas—of course they would, with all the abundance of sunshine and just enough rain. Everything in those woods, plant or animal, had nothing else to do but grow! Joe and his older sister Myra had decided it was time for a quick strike into the unknown. They would, side by side, go slowly into the woods, prepared to evacuate at even the slightest movement of a branch or a leaf. That was the plan. Upon getting deeper into the woods and nothing happening, there was quite a relief that fell over Joe. After all the fear and anxiety, after having all his senses on high alert and his eyes wide open with a relentless attention to detail and movement, it turned out to be just a walk in the woods. He could now relax; all the horrible imaginings about the woods were false.

The two courageous children came upon a pile of logs and decided to take a short rest. The logs were evidence of human intervention, providing more proof that all was well; these woods had been explored! Joe lay back against the logs with his hands behind his head. As he stared into the deep blue sky, he realized the investment of his courage had secured a new playground. Just at that moment Myra screamed, "Joe!!! Run!!!" Myra didn't wait another second before she started running herself; Joe had never seen Myra run so fast. In fact, he had never seen anyone run that fast before. Myra was double-jointed in the knees, so it appeared as though her legs were doing revolutions when she ran, like a cartoon character. It also appeared as though her feet never touched the ground. Myra was back at the house before Joe could ask what's wrong. Joe was not impressed by Myra's alarm, as she had given so many false alarms in the past just trying to make life a little more exciting. So he lay back to enjoy the serenity of the puffy white clouds that his imagination was sailing away with. Just then, something streaked across Joe's vision and in an instant returned to where it came from. It looked like a thick dark line that forked at the end. Joe, too lazy to get up, arched his head backwards to investigate. He found himself face to face with the biggest green lizard he ever saw! This monster was longer than Joe was tall and as big as a small dog. As the lizard stuck its forked tongue out again, Joe rose straight into the air and ran so fast he almost left his body behind. He reached the door of the house before Myra. Needless to say, those woods were never trespassed again. Joe swore he would return to those woods someday with the biggest gun he could find, and he would walk freely through those woods without fear. Because if something did move, he would blast the damn thing back to hell in pieces.

Well, if you're a kid you can make a toy out of anything, especially a stick; the bigger the stick, the better the toy. A stick can be a sword to do battle with or an extension of the arm to get fruit out of trees. A stick can be used as a walking aid or a spear. Joe had spied a recently fallen stick that arched over the foot-tall grass in the back yard. This stick was thick and had a good shape; it could easily provide hours of entertainment. As Joe approached the stick his older brother Chad grabbed his arm and almost ripped it out of the socket. Chad said, "Wait and be still." Joe was annoyed at the pain Chad was causing to his arm and was pulling back to get loose from his grip. But when Joe looked back at the stick, it was moving! There was a great behemoth rising up and down in the tall grass, and it wasn't a stick—it was a snake! This was the finest example of impossible that Joe had ever seen. It was simply impossible for a snake to be that big, yet it was. The sight of it as it arched its back, making several rippling waves over the tall grass, took Joe's breath and speech away. It had a slow, flowing, and silent movement to it as it moved towards the house.

It was time to sound the alarm and call out the guard! Joe ran for Dad—Dad had the gun—while Chad kept an eye on the snake. When Joe reached his dad, he was trembling from head to toe and unable to speak. All he could do was grab his dad's clothes and start pulling. Dad got the message and he had his rifle and flashlight ready in no time. Joe wondered if Dad's rifle was big enough to do the job. They ran to where Chad was but the snake had gone under the house by this time. Back then, the houses in that part of the country were built off the ground on stilts to provide for flooding. Dad attached the flashlight to the barrel of the rifle; a few minutes into the search the flashlight zeroed in to the snake's eyes—they were two glowing red balls of reflected light against the pitch-black darkness. Dad took aim and hit that nightmarish obscenity right between those glowing eyes. Joe was proud of his father for shooting the darn thing, but could not believe this creature was really dead with just one shot. Well, it was really dead and, as was the custom, Dad skinned the snake and displayed it out front of the house for non-believers. Joe always thought twice before picking up another stick after that.

Joe had some cousins in the Great White North, and during one summer they came down for a visit. There were five of them and they were about the same ages as Joe and his siblings, so this made for more diverse playtime. One day, they all decided to go fishing. It was quite a hike deep into the woods and Joe was really too young to keep up with the older ones. But go he must; Joe was not going to stay behind and miss out on all the fun.

After following the tribe as long as he could, Joe began to fall behind and found himself alone in a wide-open field. He began to scream out for the others to wait, but they didn't. He could hear the echoes of their voices fading into the woods up ahead. Joe had gone farther from home than ever before and had no idea of his location. This represented more than one wrong thing. The first was being alone in the wild, the second was being lost, and the third was not knowing what to do about it. If answers didn't come soon, Joe could fall victim to a pack of wild dogs or worse, and that was the only thing he did know. Joe looked around for even the smallest clue to his whereabouts, searching every detail. Then the fourth wrong thing happened: he panicked! Fear overwhelmed him as he screamed for help in a state of hysteria. His eyes filled with water. That was great, just great—now he couldn't see! He eventually fell to his knees crying in defeat, realizing his fate would be horrible. He desperately tried to think of what to do. If he waited, then maybe the others would return. But if they took a different route home, then daylight would run out, and so would all rational hope. Massive tears still made it impossible to see anything. Then he remembered something his mother said to him. She said, "If you're ever in trouble, you could ask God for help."

Well, Joe had already gone past the point of no return and was now wide open to any given options. So he called upon God. "God," he prayed, "please help me! I am lost in the woods and I'm afraid. Oh God, please help me, 'cause my mom said you would."

At that moment, he saw a glint of red light through his tear-soaked eyes. Red! There is no red here! There is green for the trees, brown for the ground, blue for the sky, and not a damn thing in tarnation that should be red! Whatever this was, it could be a threat and Joe thought he better clear his eyes in a hurry. This red color was being reflected off a far-away object, and when Joe was finally able to focus somewhat on it, he could see it was not moving. That was good! The object was pretty far off but did not appear to go with the surrounding area at all. Upon further observation it appeared to be pretty good-sized. This investigation was at least distracting Joe from his fear as he headed for the unidentified object. Suddenly, he recognized what it was: it was a broken-down old tractor. Joe thought how funny, it looked just like the broken-down old tractor he had seen when his dad had taken him to town. It was a long shot because broken-down tractors were commonplace, but if there was a dirt road on the other side then it would be the same one that he had seen before with his father. And that would be the road that would take him home. Shaking with fear, he ran around to the other side of the tractor, and there it was—the same dirt road. Triumphantly, he marched home, forgetting to thank God for answering his prayer.

In the heritage of the Deep South, it was commonplace for a father to take his sons hunting. For that purpose, Joe's dad had handcrafted 22-caliber rifles for each of the boys. Of course kids will be kids, and one day Chad and Myra were playing target practice inside the house. Myra was holding a pie tin with both hands, about six inches in front of her chest; Chad was aiming the rifle at her, no more than three feet away. Joe was in the next room, but could see the whole thing as it was happening. Before Joe could yell "Stop!!!" the shot was fired. Joe looked at his sister and saw she was just standing there; he thought she would fall dead any second. But what he saw when he ran into the room was truly a miracle—the entire pie tin was bent inward and had a deep groove in it. The pie tin had actually deflected the bullet! Joe could not help but think how lucky they all had been.

Little children's common sense is born out of basic logic. Joe's mom had become ill and there was a lot of medicine around. This was a chance for the kids to do something good for Mom. Now, in a child's mind, if one medicine is good for you, then combining all the medicines would surely be the cure. So a cauldron of medicine was assembled in a large pot, and then cooked because you can't give raw medicine to anyone without cooking it—it might make the patient sick. The mixture turned into a dark tar-like substance with an odor that could drop a fly out of mid-air. It was decided that when the "cure" reached boiling it would be safe to drink. That was good thinking because boiling kills bacteria—doesn't it? Then came time for the testing of the newly formed concoction. Fortunately, the fumes and the smell were so intense that no one wanted to go first. That's when Mom came in; you should have seen the look on her face! Mom got well real fast after that, without ever trying the cure.

Living in the South there was never a dull moment. Let's take the weather as a fine example. There were thunderstorms with lightning and thunder that compared to the worst episodes of war. There were cracks of thunderous explosions that sounded as though the fabric of time and space was being ripped apart. During one of these storms, Joe found himself in his usual place of refuge: under the bed. For some strange reason, even if an atomic bomb fell Joe would feel safe under the bed. Peering out from under it, Joe saw his dad sitting on the porch. Despite the hellish noise, the blinding flashes of lightning, the relentless winds and the driving rain, there sat his dad, cool as a cucumber. Joe looked at him as though he were crazy; why the heck wasn't Dad running for cover? Joe knew that if he wanted to keep his dad, he would have to venture out from under the bed and go save him. So mustering up all his courage, he left the only safe place he knew.

It was difficult to reach Dad because every clap of thunder would cause Joe's reflexes to slam his body into the floor. Upon reaching his dad, he pleaded for him to come into the house. Dad just laughed and said, "You're not afraid of a little storm, are ya, son?" Ka Boom!!! There was another flash of lightning strong enough to cause temporary blindness, and another clap of thunder that caused every nerve in Joe's body to cringe. That's it! Joe had done his duty, now it was time to get the heck out of Dodge. Joe dove to the floor and crawled back to his fortress of security under the bed. Again he watched his dad from there. Joe was in awe of his dad's fearlessness. What manner of man was this, to face nature's fury so calmly without blinking an eye? Was he not afraid to die? How could you not be afraid to die?

When the family decided to move out of this country setting, Joe made a solemn vow to himself that no matter how long it took he would return. He would return to see, with the eyes of the man he would later become, the truth of his very own beginnings. This vow was solemn because he made it to himself alone, and it still stands. "I will return to this place someday, and confront the huge wild creatures I encountered; I will remember to bring the biggest gun I can find. I will also stand in the fury of one of those thunderstorms without fear, and fear no death, just like Dad."

Moving to a new neighborhood with lots of people and buildings certainly reduced the hazards of wild animals, and this was good. But it didn't have one bit of effect on the weather. That became strikingly apparent when a tornado hit. What was in the mind of God when he came up with tornadoes? It is a giant black finger that comes down from the heavens, to suck innocent souls up into the sky, in a never-ending swirl of death. Joe knew there would be no relief from this fear because there was no defense against it. Like everything else, he knew he would eventually come face to face with it too.

Now that day was here; he knew it was here by all the signs. Even in daytime everything turns black as night and the thunder and lightning become intense beyond belief; the hail hits the roof with an ocean-like roar, and then everything becomes calm just before the tornado hits. Joe sought refuge in his usual sanctuary, wrapped up in a ball with his brothers and sister under the bed. His mother was trying to put a blanket over the window so the children would not see the funnel cloud coming. But she couldn't hide the train-like sound it made. The sound of a great unfathomable beast claiming ownership of the world was right outside the door. All the sounds came together in a tumultuous crescendo drowning out the screams of frightened children and their prayers—then it was over! It was over as quickly as it started. It wouldn't be until morning light that the whole story would be told.

Upon opening the front door the next day, Joe's eyes witnessed destruction beyond his worst imaginings. Everything on his side of the street was okay. But there was no other side to the street. There was rubble clear to the horizon! Half of the neighborhood was leveled to the ground. Joe went for a walk to survey what his own eyes couldn't believe. He saw cars standing upright against telephone poles, mattresses atop the few remaining trees. There was a lady sitting on her couch in the living room; all the furniture was neatly in place, even the TV and lamps were there. But she had no walls or roof. There was so much rubble it covered all evidence that streets were ever there at all. Joe realized then that there were forces at work in this world even more powerful than adults could handle.

LIFE IN THE GREAT WHITE NORTH

EVENTS WERE SOON to change in a big way. Joe's mom and dad had been fighting for some time. His dad was a tall, dark-haired, blue-eyed, man of the world. His good looks and quiet manner were nothing but an attractant to other women. So the end result was inevitable: they would go their separate ways. Dad would follow his basic instincts after a younger woman. Mom would gather the children and depart for the Great White North; she had kin in a place called New York City.

The children had seen pictures of this place with buildings reaching into the sky. They were informed that people actually lived in those buildings. New York City was also a place that didn't have any snakes and no mosquitoes. Most fascinating of all, it snowed there! Joe couldn't imagine what manner of place this was, with people living in the sky. Also, what the heck was snow like? Well, no sooner than more questions could be asked than they were on their way. The family traveled by train, bus, and taxi to this far-away land.

First sight of this new place called New York City was at night. There were lights, thousands of lights; the children were informed that every light stood for people living there. There was snow, piles of it everywhere; it was the blizzard of 1960. How fascinating this was! It was cold! It was white! It was like the stuff you would find in your refrigerator! But the real introduction came when Joe was getting out of the taxi. Never having seen anything like this before, he thought you could walk on top of it. Taking his first footstep out onto the top of the snow, he quickly sank and fell face down and sprawled eagle deep into it. Shocked and confused, he lay there trying to gather his wits. Just then he was jerked up and planted square on his feet by his new kin, his namesake Uncle

Joe. So this was snow, and another face-to-face encounter with the unknown.

Well, children belong in school. Upon Joe's first day in school he was introduced to the class. The teacher explained that Joe was from a far-away place where things were done differently, that the class should be kind and understand his different ways. When his teacher asked him a question, Joe would stand up and say, "Yes, Ma'am." This was not done in the Great White North, and when it drew much attention from the others, Joe was at a loss. On breaks, the other kids would surround Joe and ask him to repeat certain words like "chocolate." When he said the word, they would all laugh. Joe thought this was a northern game and didn't really see what was so funny. After all, he could barely understand what they were saying to him most of the time. The other children sounded very funny to him, too, but he would never have laughed at them like they were doing to him.

   Then Joe saw her: her name was Dolores. She had long, light-brown hair and olive skin. Her eyes had a sad tone to them, and he found himself staring at her. When their eyes finally met, Joe was awestruck! His insides went completely berserk; he fizzled like a 4th of July sparkler. There were sensations of unexpected delight. What manner of girl was this to steal his voice away and paralyze his motion with just one look? How could he get to know her when he couldn't speak in her presence? Joe would catch a glimpse of her every once in a while in the crowd and would try to follow her or even just try to get close. Joe noticed that she had a best friend, so he decided this was his best way for an approach. He would send a message to Dolores through her best friend; if the feedback were positive then he would act. The message came back that it was not possible for them to get together. Joe asked why. "Am I not good enough for her?" The answer was a religious one. She was a Jehovah's Witness and wasn't allowed to have a boyfriend. Joe didn't understand the meaning of this, but was willing to adopt her religion if that's what it took to meet her.

One day he had his chance; there was a big event at school and crowds of people were there. While standing in a crowded room, suddenly the crowd parted and opened up right up to her. There she was. Their eyes met again. This time neither one looked away and the same thing happened to Joe: his voice left, his heart pounded, his insides fizzled, and he was paralyzed again. This time, they were locked into a stare that neither could break. And for a short time Joe had the sensation that she felt the same way about him. He knew it was now or never. He was going to get to know her at any cost, even if it meant hurtful rejection. Even if his first words to her were complete babble, he was compelled by the thought of a future of self-condemnation if he didn't try. So he took his first steps toward her while their eyes were still locked together in a timeless hypnotic trance. It was as though that stare was bringing them together; it was a bond between them and if it broke all would be lost.

Suddenly his arm was pulled back with a sudden, hard jerk that turned his whole body around. A friend was trying to get his attention, and when Joe turned to her again—she was gone! The bond had been broken and she disappeared. Joe didn't see her at school anymore after that; it seemed like she vanished, never to be seen again. Joe knew he would never forget her and would think about her for the rest of his life. He knew that if the world had just left them alone, they would have known a love like no one had ever known before, a love that would laugh at time. He knew this because he would always love her. He knew throughout life that she was out there, somewhere, and this comforted him. Maybe, if fate had justice, or kindness, or pity, by some unknown force it would bring them together again. If not, it would mean a love unlived, a chance for happiness never realized, and a soul left lost and searching. What manner of fate is this?

Of course, school days would not be complete without an ultimate character-building, face-to-face conflict. It all started in the cafeteria with Joe's younger brother, Burney. He had worn a "net" t-shirt to school. This was a fashion concept years before its time. In other words, if you were going to wear something like that in public back then, you sure better know how to fight. Joe could beat his younger brother in a fight with one hand. Well, this day the entire cafeteria surrounded Burney and was laughing and poking at him. Joe came upon the scene and let this go on for a short while to make his brother pay for embarrassing him. But when enough was enough, Joe stood up and said so,

"All right, enough is enough! Will everyone please return to your seats!" The crowd dispersed and they all sat down, except for one. Joe would later come to know this guy as Kale.

Kale said, "If you want me to sit down, then make me." A slap fight ensued, punches were thrown and Joe made out pretty well. Joe was not a proponent for fighting; in fact he was a coward. But this could be used as a chance to set an example for his brother on how to stand up and face your fears like a man. Teachers came and broke up the fight. Kale threatened, "This is not over!" From that point on, whenever Joe and Kale made eye contact, they would run at each other with a reckless fury and attack, attack, attack! Most of the combat occurred within the halls of the school. Each time, Joe inflicted more damage than he received, and a confidence was building in Joe that he could teach this menace to cease and desist with all hostilities.

After their last flash fight, Kale made a request; he requested the matter be completely resolved after school, that day, in the back schoolyard. It was to be—literally—the mother of all battles. Throughout the entire day, the rumor mill was working with a fever pitch; some 3,000 kids had received notification of the Olympic event. Some kids approached Joe and warned him not to fight, telling him that Kale was the champion school wrestler. Joe said he had done okay before and expected to do the same in the upcoming event. Secretly, Joe knew he was a coward and had no desire to fight.

At the end of the day, it had snowed just enough to cover the ground. Joe figured he could go to his locker and slip out the side door, avoiding any distasteful conflict. That's when he discovered that Kale's locker was just a couple of feet away from his own. A strange, nauseous, sinking feeling occurred in Joe's stomach as he hurriedly turned to leave and found himself face to face with Kale. From the expression on Kale's face, Joe had the feeling that Kale had no interest in this Armageddon, either. But by this time there were 3,000 entertainment-starved students standing by, literally blocking the wide halls. They were promised a fight, and after a long, boring day at school they were drooling for it. Surprisingly, Kale turned to Joe and asked, "Are you sure you want to go on with this?" Joe knew there was no backing out now and responded, "Let's get this over with."

The crowd parted, just as if Moses was parting the sea. The two unwilling gladiators marched side by side to the agreed-upon location, with the crowd behind them. It seemed like everyone was on Kale's side, rooting for him. Upon reaching the site, the crowd engulfed the two, forming a circle with no escape.

The fight began with a combat-like dance and an occasional jabbing for weakness. Kale took a few strikes and missed; Joe responded and hit! Joe was turning out to be a bit of a skilled boxer. Kale would make a suicide dive into Joe's stomach; Joe would hold onto him and throw all the punches he could, while he could. This happened several times and Joe didn't understand what Kale was doing. These constant dives were leaving Kale somewhat bloody and you could hear the shock and disbelief from the crowd. A southern hick was beating the school champion! On his last kamikaze attack,

Kale finally managed to bring Joe to the ground. This is where a champion wrestler is at home. Kale proceeded to climb on top of Joe and held him down. He then rained down punches on Joe's face until Joe could hear the bones in his face breaking. Being completely pinned, all Joe could do was turn his face so the other side could take up some of the punishment. This was a real fine example of turning the other cheek. Kale kept yelling, "Give up! Give up! Give up!" and kept punching Joe's face like insanity had taken over. The crowd began to make sounds of horror and tried to pull Kale off Joe, but to no avail. Kale kept it up, as though there were other forces at work that were driving him on.

Inasmuch as Joe refused to give in, it proved only to infuriate Kale more. Joe was beaten badly and he knew it. During the fight there was a broken glass bottle under Joe's back that was cutting deep into his flesh. Joe realized that he could not win and the next best thing to do was to get this madman off him before permanent damage was done. So he did: with both eyes swollen closed, he reached out his hand in blinded defeat. The fight was over, Joe had lost, and he was bleeding from the mouth and from his back. His shirt was torn to shreds and he had lost his shoes. That was great, simply great—he only had two miles to walk home through snow, with no shoes!

When Joe finally made the cold bloody trek back home, his family gasped in horror at the sight of him: he was unrecognizable! Joe walked straight through the house to the bedroom. His brother Burney didn't stay for the fight and had gotten home early. As Joe passed him, he could see the shock in his brother's face. Joe threw one more solid punch and decked Burney, while falling unto the bed. Chad came in the room and demanded to know who did this. When Joe told his older brother what happened, Chad set off looking for vengeance. Chad reached Kale's house and banged on the door. It turned out that Kale had a big brother too, much bigger than Chad. So Chad let him off with a warning. Joe would always have a good feeling about that fight, though, in that he faced his fear despite overwhelming odds and had overcome his cowardice with nothing but sheer heroism. What manner of human was Kale, though? Where Joe came from in the South, a man was beat when he was down. What manner of man keeps beating another after the fight is over?

This all may sound like a hard-luck picture of Joe, but this is actually not the case. Joe was a happy sort and usually enjoyed the companionship of a close buddy, not to mention the many happy times he enjoyed with his close-knit family. There were Christmases and summers and all sorts of holidays, when he enjoyed being out of school and playing till the sun went down. Joe was just able to get passing grades in school due to his busy social life, which left him little time to study.

Joe really didn't care much about school anyway. He knew there was a world of interest out there for him and he wanted to discover it. Instead they were teaching him things that he really didn't care to learn. Because of this he could never gage his own intelligence. He compared himself to others and always came out normal. So one time he decided to find out the answer to his question, once and for all: "How smart am I, really?" It would be a self-evaluation, a very personal challenge. He was going to use an upcoming and very difficult test to measure his intelligence. He was going to try something he never attempted before: he would study. This was the test to end all tests. This effort would tell him what his true capabilities were.

Joe studied the print right off the pages. When I say he studied, I mean he studied up a blue streak. He never really understood school. The teachers would tell you something and ask you to repeat it in a test, like a parrot. That didn't really mean that you learned it. Instead of testing, why didn't they just move on to new and undiscovered subjects? That way everyone had a chance of learning something they were really interested in.

And so he studied. He memorized concepts, theories, and details. Joe had made this a personal challenge and failure was not an option. When he was done studying, he could actually feel his brain hurting. But he felt ready, ready to pass the most difficult test of all, a test of self. The day was here, the day was long, and the test was said to be just as hard and long. Joe found himself answering questions as fast as a speed-reader. He saw the others struggling on every question as his pencil was filling up the space on his paper. He was sure his teacher would suspect deceit at Joe's speed and accuracy. After all, this behavior had never been seen from him before. Done! Joe handed his paper in, light years ahead of the others and with an alien-like confidence. Yes, he knew all the answers, and he knew he was correct too. The teacher handed the test back to Joe and asked him to put his name on top. Okay, no problem! Yet there was a problem. He didn't remember his name! Okay, all Joe had to do was relax; he was sure he could do this without any embarrassment. Because who in blazes would believe you could forget your own name? Hmm!

But the answer wasn't immediately forthcoming. Joe had to take some remedial action. "My books! My name has to be in my books," he thought. No go; the books were clean of any indication of identity. Okay, don't panic! Pockets! There had to be something in his pockets that would provide immediate relief from this absurd and unheard of situation. No go; there were the few odds and ends that a boy would normally have in his pockets, but no name. As a last resort, Joe turned to the kid next to him and asked, "What's my name?" The kid said, "Oh, stop joking around!" Now Joe was becoming concerned, so this time he went to the teacher. He admitted to her that for some strange reason his name wasn't coming to mind, and asked her to please tell him what his name was. The teacher—not wanting to fall for a possible trick from a deviant youth—said, "Why don't you check your books." Joe could clearly see this was going nowhere fast; it was time to go home anyway. As he was leaving, the teacher told him she would take points off for not having his name on the paper.

As he started off, he thought he would remember his name once he got home. Home? Great, just great! Where in the tarnation was home? This crap was getting deeper and deeper with every turn. "Okay! For Pete's sake, just don't panic!!!" Joe thought if he were to walk completely around the school maybe a landmark would key his memory. So that is what he did. He did see something that made him head in that uncertain direction. Figuring that one landmark would lead to another, and being the only lead he had, he went that way, knowing that if he were wrong, things would only get worse. Worse! I mean, how much worse could it get, when you forget your name and where you live? This was sort of like another test. Joe did follow one landmark to the next. When he saw his home, he recognized it; then he remembered his name. "My name is Joe!" Even though he really didn't identify with the sound of it yet, he was sure it was right. The emergency was over! Later he became aware of something called temporary hysterical amnesia, which could be caused by the stress of studying too hard. Funny thing is, Joe never studied again.

Well, at least he found out he was intelligent. But he still didn't know how intelligent he was just because he aced the test; that only meant that he could be even more intelligent than what the test measured. Now he surmised there was really no test invented yet that could measure that, and if it can't be measured or weighed, then what manner of thing is this intelligence?

By this time, Joe was feeling older and wiser and demanding of more privileges at home, one being to stay up later at night.

When his mother flatly refused, Joe put forth an ultimatum: "Either I get my way or I'll leave!" What his mother said next took Joe by surprise. "Go ahead, leave! It will be one less mouth to feed!" Joe had always known his mother to be loving and compassionate towards him and he was shocked by her reply. He felt challenged and willing to call her bluff. He bid his mother a cordial good-bye and said he would not be returning. His mother wished him well without so much as looking up from her cooking.

Joe got on his bike and put all the anger and frustration he was feeling into pedaling. He figured he would only stop when he didn't recognize the surroundings. With each mile, he thought about how much his family would miss him and regret being so cruel. After what seemed like hours of traveling, Joe pulled over and asked a passerby what town he was in; the passerby said Levittown. Joe thought that was impossible; he had ridden all afternoon and into the evening and had not left the town he lived in!

By now, Joe was exhausted and hungry. He realized that the world was a much bigger place than he had ever imagined. He also recognized defeat when it became abundantly clear, as it was right now. The only logical course of action was to return with his tail between his legs and accept the fact that he was still a boy. It was very dark outside when he made it back home. He returned to find his family calling his name and searching for him all over the neighborhood. In seeing their distress, he decided they had suffered enough for their inequities and he could now return with some degree of honor. He envisioned that someday he would be able to expand his boundaries without limitations but now was not that day.

Joe, having a devilish character, was always playing tricks on Burney and was always prepared for Burney's return vengeance, as Burney was so predictable. In this particular night, Burney had fallen asleep before Joe. Feeling somewhat mischievous, Joe wanted to see if he could get away with stealing the blanket and pillow from his brother. This would take a light and stealthy touch. But since time was on Joe's side, he decided to give it a try. Holding his breath and pulling slightly on the pillow inch by inch, he managed to free the pillow from under Burney's head. Taking the covers off was the easy part. He knew Burney would be extremely annoyed when he found out and it would be a gut-wrenching laugh for Joe.

So in the middle of the night when Burney started saying in a cautious and soft voice that the house was on fire, Joe's first thought was that Burney was trying to get back at him for the missing sleeping comforts. Joe heard Burney's continuing cries but found it very difficult to fully wake up until Burney shook him intensely. When Joe was finally able to open his eyes, all he could see was a smoke-filled room; he then realized why he couldn't wake up—he was almost completely unconscious from smoke inhalation. This was very bad! Then Burney said the words that would live in infamy, "Should we tell Mom?" Joe responded, "Unless you want her to burn, you idiot!" They went to their mother's room and after telling her what was happening, she responded in the usual fashion: she panicked! She gathered all of her children into the living room and held them tight in her arms as she screamed for help. The neighbors saw smoke billowing out of the windows and called the fire department. The firemen punched holes in all the walls of the house and in the ceiling, too. They said they did this just to let all the smoke out, but they actually did more damage than the smoke ever could. They found out that the smoke was caused by a fan belt overheating on the water pump downstairs, but with the degree of smoke that filled the house, it was very much a life-threatening situation.

The truth is that Burney saved the entire family from dying that night. He never got credit or a hero's reward. Years later when Joe and Burney were talking about the event, Burney admitted that the only reason why he woke up that night was because Joe stole his pillow. Imagine five lives were saved because of a stolen pillow. Who should be credited for saving the family in this case, Joe or Burney? Joe still thinks that Burney was the unsung hero.

Well, it was time to move again. The next rented house was a real case for the books. It was a box-like structure that looked like every other house on the block. In fact, one day Joe came home from school and, as he walked in the house, he saw several strangers sitting on the couch. Joe said hello and asked where Mom was. The strangers pointed towards the kitchen. When Joe walked into the kitchen there was a motherly looking lady in there. But it was the wrong motherly looking lady. Joe said to the woman, "You are not my mother." The woman said she knew that. Joe asked, "Where is my mother?" The woman said she didn't know where his mother was and that he must have the wrong address. Joe ran to the front door to check the number on the house and discovered it was indeed the wrong house. How strange it was, to walk in off the street into a complete stranger's home and talk to everyone there before realizing his mistake. He left in a hurry, scared and embarrassed.

This box-like house looked somewhat humble, and you could pass it by without taking notice. However, as you may know, not all is as it appears. What I am about to say may seem strange. It all started one afternoon, when Myra started screaming from the bedroom. Joe was in the next room, and on the second scream he burst through the door. Myra was sitting on the bed in a hysterical crying mess. Joe didn't see any immediate threat and figured she had had a bad dream. Myra said it wasn't a dream—she said she saw a shadow, on the wall, of a man. She told Joe she was giving it orders like "forward march" and "about face." When the "shadow man" started following her orders, she realized this was not a game and started screaming. She told Joe that when he came into the room, the shadow man went behind the door. Joe checked behind the door and didn't see anything. He didn't want to alarm her any further, but the truth is that when he first came through the door he did notice—out of the corner of his eye—a flicker of a shadow going behind it. Okay, no damage done and no way to verify, so case closed. Myra never saw the shadow again.

Then there was the "cold spot" incident. It was 90 degrees outside, but in the hallway of the house there was a cold spot. When I say cold, I mean you could see the frost from your breath. It was an area from the ceiling to the floor about six inches wide that was absolutely freezing cold. Touching it was like putting your hand in the refrigerator. No cause was found for this effect and it didn't last; it was there one day and gone the next. Okay, no harm done, no way to verify, case closed. But that was surely interesting.

The next event happened to Joe while searching in the bottom of a closet for an old pair of shoes. There were many old and smelly shoes in there, and Joe had to dig deep to find his shoes. While deep in the midst of this smelly nightmare, suddenly the smell of roses filled the closet. It was a profound and overwhelming smell of heaven. The divine scent engulfed Joe; it was all around him and on him. It was so strong that it couldn't be ignored. Joe crawled out of the closet to see if a window was open; maybe there was a rose bush outside working overtime. But the windows were closed. Joe went to tell his mother, but he no sooner spoke a word than she asked, "Why do you smell like roses?" Joe told her about what happened in the closet and she went to investigate but no cause was found for the smell. Okay, no harm done, no way to verify, case closed. This turned out to be another unsolved mystery.

Many other happenings occurred for which there was no explanation. Most of them happened at night when everyone was asleep, like the chairs under the kitchen table that would be found scattered all over the kitchen in the morning, and nobody knew how; other nights, footsteps were heard in the attic, like a person pacing back and forth. For several nights in a row, there was the sound of something rattling up and down against the banister on the stairs leading to the attic; the next morning, things like a shoe or a stick that wasn't there the night before would be found at the base of the stairs. There was no intruder ever found, no human intervention ever detected, that could explain these occurrences.

Now, Joe considered himself to be a junior scientist, knowing that every cause has an effect, every action has an equal and opposite reaction, and everything has a beginning and an end, a purpose and a reason. There had to be an explanation for everything that happened. The "unknown" was just something not known yet. Through observation, analysis, and experimentation, he could obtain the answers. But after many a watchful night and many failed attempts to collect evidence, he was left with the idea that this reality might not be the only reality—or be real at all—and that not everything can be understood or explained. Joe's mind was exposed to the notion that there are unknown forces in the universe that we cannot conceive of but that can sometimes touch our lives. After three years of these bizarre incidents, lost sleep, and calls to the police, it was time to move again.

By this time, the question of the year was "what are you going to be when you grow up?" Joe knew that most guys turned out to be whatever their father was. All Joe knew about his father was that he was a merchant marine and had left the home when Joe was four years old. Joe didn't see his father again until he was ten when, one day while playing in the front yard, a cab pulled up to the front gate. A tall, slender man with gray hair got out. Joe thought the man looked familiar. Joe walked up to the man and said, "Can I help you?" The man said, "Don't you recognize me?" With the sound of his voice Joe knew! It had been so many years, and the memory of his father was nothing but a vague shadow. Now he was looking square into the piercing blue eyes of the father he had always needed. Joe felt as if he were meeting God.

His father had come to see his children one last time. Joe didn't know this at the time but found out later in life that his father had a terminal illness and would eventually die from it. Joe asked his father if he was coming back to stay. When his father answered no, Joe ran off crying, feeling all the lost love welling up in his eyes and the need for his father choking him. He was going to lose his father again. When Myra stopped him in the hallway, she asked Joe why he was crying. Joe looked at her as though she should know. Myra said, "Don't waste your tears on him; he is not worth it." With that, Joe understood that in many ways she was right and he stopped crying. He then felt strong enough to return and ask his father why; his father said, "Son, you will understand someday." But this was not enough to comfort a young boy's crying heart. All Joe wanted was to wrap his arms around his father and hold him tight. A simple hug would have made up for all the lost years. A crying confession of love would have then burst forth from Joe's heart. But the opportunity was missed and completely lost. It was like missing a chance to hug God. Once again, Joe was left with questions not asked and answers not given.

Well, his father stayed for only one day; he bought presents for all the kids and had dinner with them. Then the tall slender man with the gray hair and piercing blue eyes was gone again, this time forever. Once again, Joe was left without a father.

Back to the question that bothered Joe. How was he supposed to know what he would turn out to be? So he decided to fight this eternal question with a little sarcasm, something that would give him a little return, possibly some shock value. He told others he wanted to be a hobo and ride trains. When that story wore out, he told them he just wanted to sit back and have the money just come to him in the mail. But his search for this answer was honest and true. Joe didn't recognize any special talents or qualities he had that would make him excel. He was average in his grades, fair in sports, not mechanically inclined, and had no leadership skills. Until one day, when Joe watched an Army movie—now he had his answer. He wanted to become a soldier! Better even—a marine! They wore distinguished uniforms! They had adventure and saw the world! They faced the ultimate test of manhood: combat! So Joe would watch every war story ever made for television. He would learn every trick of combat. He decided he would join up right after high school. Besides, being from a poor family that couldn't afford college, the military made the promise of benefits very alluring. Joe thought it would be better to die for his country than make another hamburger for that place he worked at; he had made so many hamburgers that the smell of them was coming out of his skin and wouldn't wash off.

Oh yes! Joe could see himself charging bravely up the hill conquering his foes. He could see parades and medals being pinned on his gallant chest. He could see women falling at his feet because he would look so debonair in his polished brass button uniform. It would be a chance to help the family too. There would be one less mouth to feed, and he could send money home, too. The military made some kind of promise about being able to help Joe buy a house. Joe didn't really understand how that worked, but it sure sounded good. The family had to move every time the rent went up. After moving about 40 times, the sound of the word "move" made Joe nauseous. The military said something about being able to send Joe to college, too. Altogether, it seemed like the only way to go. So there it was, the real and only choice for a poor boy. Joe's mother knew this, too, without ever saying it. She knew this because she was from a poor family also and had lost a brother in the Korean War. Joe's uncle was the only real hero the family had. He was awarded many medals posthumously. Would you just believe he happened to be a marine? She also knew that her son Chad had made the same choice and had joined the Army a couple of years before; he was now risking his life in Vietnam.

Finally, high-school graduation day was here! Joe asked his mother to wake him in time for the ceremony. After four years of high school and being denied sunny days, which he viewed through the school windows, he wanted to step up and claim that paper that would give him freedom. Now it was time for freedom from the tyranny of oddball teachers that were just doing their 8-to-5 to get by; freedom from the walls that blocked the sun and from all the stolen personal time called homework. Joe knew that after learning how to read, write, and do math, they had nothing else to teach him. This was all done by 6th grade. The rest of the time was used to keep the kids off the streets and out of trouble through institutionalized baby-sitting called high school.

Would you believe that Mom failed to heed Joe's request and didn't wake him up on time? He got up and rushed to the school, just in time to see everyone leaving. No matter; he still had a chance for freedom with no encumbrances. He was young, and all the sunny days ahead were his. And that's all that truly mattered!

YOU'RE IN THE ARMY NOW!

IT WAS ONE of those sunny summer days that Joe found himself alone. This was a rare occurrence, being that family or friends were always around. Whenever he got bored, he would get on a bus and ride until he was completely lost. Then he would get off and hitch his way back home. This always proved to be a good way to meet new people, have interesting adventures, and broaden the boundaries of his horizon. He could also go to the beach and have his soul cleansed with ocean water. The sun would renew his spirit and the wide-open spaces would allow his imagination to soar. Joe would stand at the edge of the water and focus his eyes on the line between ocean and sky. Joe knew there were people on the other side of that ocean. He wondered how different they would be from him. He knew European people were like him, but oriental people were something else. The oriental women were alluring and mysterious, the culture was strange, and they looked so different. He yelled out to the sky and the sea as an invincible young man, "I will go there!" He didn't know how or when, but he knew his words were not hollow. He felt that the ocean and the sky had heard him and would bow to his indomitable spirit. Now all he had to do was conquer time.

On this sunny day, Joe boarded the bus undecided about the best thing to do. He would decide while on the way. Maybe he would just ride the bus all day as a tour. After all, having been incarcerated for so long by the educational system, freedom took some getting used to. While on the way, Joe thought he needed a new source of entertainment. He decided he would get off at the next stop and look around. So he pulled the cord and took his position for exit at the door. The bus pulled over and the doors opened; he got off and was struck motionless with what stood before him. The United

States Marine Corps Recruiting Station was right there. This was a monumental challenge to his childhood dreams. Could he do this now? Why not? He was of age and finished with high school. This was an important decision; it scared him like the loud band of his first dance. He had learned not to act on his first impulse because he usually screwed it up, so he decided to have a cup of coffee at a nearby café and take some time to ponder about the possibilities.

He would be mature about this and not have his mind set on one branch of the military. He would give them all an equal chance to influence him, while secretly knowing the Marine Corps was the one. All the recruiting stations were little separate houses in a row. He would give the Marines first crack at it just for an interview, though. Joe put his hand on the doorknob of the Marine house. He heard loud yelling coming from inside. Joe looked through the window to see what was up, and saw a massive Marine soldier. His shoulders were as broad as a bridge and his body looked like it was made of stone. He was yelling at this scrawny recruit in a hellish way. Joe thought that after growing up with a bully for an older brother he had enough of that.

Hmm, maybe now would be a good time to check the Air Force. Flying a jet would be a pisser. Joe asked the Air Force guy, "Could I fly one of your planes?" He responded by asking Joe, "Do you have a college degree?" Joe said no; the Air Force guy said no. That made it time for the Navy. Joe sat there listening to others being interviewed by the Navy guy. One question being asked was, "How long can you tread water?" Joe got up and left. He felt that the Navy didn't have any confidence in its own ships.

The Army was last at bat. The Army had been watching Joe's actions from a distance and they were ready with a warm handshake and a hot cup of coffee. Joe thought, "Now this is the way to handle business." The Army guy asked, "What kind of job do you want?" Joe thought a soldier was just a soldier and he was caught by surprise. All Joe knew was what his brother Chad did: Chad was an Army Security Agent. Joe didn't know what that meant, but one job was as good as another. As long as Joe could become a soldier that would be okay. So he told the recruiter he wanted to be a security agent. Sold! Joe had done it—he had joined the United States Army!

Upon leaving the recruiting station, every bell within 50 miles went off. It was probably just 12 o'clock, but Joe took it as a sign. It was a sign of the birth of a new destiny. The bells made Joe feel as though the heavens were in approval and were wishing him well. He was feeling overwhelmingly excited and scared at the same time. This was the first decision he had ever made completely on his own without consulting with family or friends, but he had a feeling that the timing would determine his entire future. How odd it was to betray fate and not become a marine! What ramifications was this going to have? Was this predetermined? The country was presently involved in the Vietnam war and that was the destination for most of the troops. Would he survive unscathed or be injured in some life-altering way? Now it was done. The "stuff" was about to hit the fan! Joe had set into motion a chain of circumstances far beyond his wildest imagination circumstances that could not be calculated, controlled, or predicted.

Joe was scheduled to leave in four months; that gave him enough time to say his goodbyes to all he knew. But it also gave him plenty of time to think about the right or wrong of killing. The Vietnam war had been going on for nine years now; Joe felt that this was his war and he was missing it. It was his last chance to be the soldier he always wanted to be; he could see future technology taking the glory and the heroism out of war and reducing it to the push of a button. On the other hand, this meant that the possibility of taking another life, or even losing his own, was real. Up to this time, his decision to enlist had been based on immature dreams: wearing a soldier's uniform, traveling to exotic lands, and meeting alluring women. Now he was facing the hard truth of it all: he could not kill another human being. Killing was wrong, no matter what, and he would not do it. He had to find the way to fulfill his obligation without killing another human and hopefully his good intentions would keep him from being killed himself.

The Army came to get him in a car at night. Joe tried to clear the frost off the car window with his hand. He wanted one last glance at his loved ones, but the bright streetlights and the frosted window denied him this one last look. He was off and away, like being pulled to another universe by unseen forces. It was like watching things happen to yourself and you're not making them happen.

Joe's first stop was some kind of bus station. This was a chance to catch some shut-eye. That way he could be awake and alert for whatever the Army had in mind. While in a deep sleep, suddenly Joe was jabbed in the arm. This stranger told him that his bus was about to leave. Joe stood up, still groggy with sleep. The stranger put something in Joe's hand, pushed him towards the bus, and said, "God Bless You." While on the bus, Joe regained his wits and found he was holding a small bible. "Oh, for heavens sake, what am I going to do with this?" Joe was an agnostic, which meant he didn't really know one way or the other about God. Joe didn't throw the book away, just in case. Little did he know it would become his source of strength to endure the upcoming tests.

Joe looked around at the other "boys" on the bus. The sense of fear was thick as syrup in the air. Instantaneous conversations would spring up. Joe thought these boys would be linked with him in the upcoming ordeals. His eyes searched the faces of each, searching for signs of courage or leadership. Joe thought this would be a good time to take out some insurance. He started a prayer. It went something like this: "Oh God, I don't know if you're real or not, but if you are, then I hope you hear me. I feel alone and I am aware that I am heading into danger. I ask for your protection from harm, and make me worthy of this great test. Amen." Just in case.

The bus pulled through a brightly lit archway with stiff, serious-looking soldiers on either side. This was Fort Dix. A white-gloved hand made a stiff pointing motion signaling forward, and the bus proceeded. When the bus rolled to a slow stop and the doors opened, the sounds of guttural screaming could be heard outside. A man with a "Smokey the Bear" hat boarded and started throwing bodies off the bus, while shouting how we maggots made him sick. This caused a stampede, and one busload joined another until 200 men were running, falling, and being yelled into oblivion by Smokey the Bears on both sides. Joe was confused by all the excitement, because he didn't see any reason for it. So, if there was no real threat, Joe preferred to walk. He walked by one of these yelling freaks and asked what all the yelling was about. The freak yelled at Joe, "Who do you think you are, maggot? Do you think you are something special, maggot? I'm going to remember you, maggot! You better start running, maggot, or you will need surgery to get my boot out of your ass, maggot!" Joe started running just to get away from that freak. Hey, Joe thought, I am a volunteer! What manner of welcome is this?

Well, the "herd" was finally put to bed. The sun had set over the maggots' world. Joe noticed the blankets had an unfamiliar smell but they were warm. As he fell asleep, he heard the whimpers of a few surrounding scared souls. Morning came with the same kind of fervor. This freak came into the barracks at 4am kicking a garbage pail and yelling for the maggots to get their maggot asses outside and lined up. Oh yeah! Joe thought, I remember now: the Army. It occurred to Joe that even the squirrels were not up yet. He vowed to himself that he would kick or bang a tree with his rifle every chance he got; if he had to be up so early, then so would the damn squirrels, too.

Joe decided to take a look around for a bit while waiting for further instructions. It was just then that Joe saw his first real soldiers. They marched by in perfect step, while calling cadence like mechanical people. Not one turned his head or blinked an eye. Joe wondered what manner of events could cause this strange behavior. What could cause men to become machines? Joe passed a man wearing little eagles on his collar. Joe wanted to be polite and said, "How ya doing?" This man went off like all the fireworks on the fourth of July. He started screaming like he was out of Prozac. "I am a colonel and you will salute me! What is your name, rank and unit?" Joe said he didn't know, but if all he wanted was a salute, then that was okay with him, so why all the fuss? The colonel resumed his course of abusive language. "You mean 'That is okay with me, Sir'!" Joe said, "Okay, yes, Sir." The Colonel asked, "How long have you been in the Army?" Joe looked at his watch and said, "About three hours now." The colonel screamed again, "You mean 'About three hours, Sir'!" Joe replied, "Oh, yes. Yes, Sir." After a few minutes of being berated to non-existence, Joe gently walked away, thinking that there must be lunatics walking all over this place. Better get back to the barracks and to safety.

Joe learned pretty quickly what life in the Army was like. A regular Army day went something like this: You were woken up at 4am and in 15 minutes had to get dressed and line up outside for a head count. You had to run two miles and do six laps on this monkey bar thing, hand over hand, before breakfast. You only had three minutes to eat breakfast after you sat down. The first meal was three scoops of very bad smelling white stuff, which Joe couldn't bring himself to eat. Next was the 15-mile hike through sand to the training area while carrying a heavy backpack, a rifle, and a helmet. The extra weight caused your boots to sink deeper into the sand making every step more difficult. By the time you started training, you were already exhausted.

A day of bayonet training was eight hours of yelling "kill mother" to the top of your lungs, while thrusting a bayonet into a dummy. Then the drill instructor would demonstrate technique. This man truly scared Joe to the core, even from a distance. Joe knew if he ever came up against a man like that on the battlefield, he would throw his weapon to the ground and run! This man was an artistic killing machine, no wasted movement. This sergeant was later to become known as "Sir Yes Sir." He was a short, black man with black leather skin. When his eyes were glassy, the maggots knew they would barely survive the day. When his eyes cleared up, there was no chance at all. The maggots would suffer the fury resulting from a lifetime of discrimination in one day.

After a lunch of swill-like soup served from 50-gallon drums, the afternoon had some little surprises. One of them was the "gas chamber." This was a cement block room with no windows and just one door. In the middle of the room was a device with a burner and some chemicals in it that were burning and making smoke. All the soldiers wore gas masks as they entered the darkly lit chamber. Joe thought that as long as he was wearing the mask this exercise would be a breeze. To his surprise, when there was enough smoke in the room that you couldn't see the man in front of you, the maggots were ordered to remove their masks. Upon one sniff of this gas all the fluids in your lungs and nasal passages started to flow out of your nose and mouth. The purpose of this exercise was to demonstrate the effects of a gas attack. As Joe ran for the door in panic, he knew he could never survive a similar situation in real life.

The day naturally ended with the 15-mile hike back. But you couldn't eat until you ran another two miles and did another six laps on the monkey bars. Then back to the barracks to shine shoes and wax floors or do kitchen duty. Joe's first kitchen duty was washing pots and pans in scalding hot water—the cold water had been turned off. After 13 hours of doing this, Joe could play with the skin and meat of his hands like silly putty. The whole time Joe thought about his bunk. That is what made it bearable; he could imagine placing his head on a pillow and smelling the clean sheets. He could imagine sleeping even if it were for just a few hours. Daydreaming eased the pain and made him keep going. Since this was the first assignment the Army gave Joe, he was determined to do the best job a man could do. In fact, since he did such a good job, it came to the attention of the kitchen sergeant. He was so impressed with all those shiny pots and pans that he requested Joe be assigned to him on a more permanent basis. Joe realized he screwed up in reverse. He learned it might be wiser to choose a better time and a better job before he displayed his good intentions.

When the ordeal was over, Joe ran for his bed. He ran for his bed like a man on the desert that just discovered water. When he got back to his room, his bunk was stacked on top of all the other bunks reaching to the ceiling. The other seven men in the room were waxing the floor. Joe tried to explain what he had been through and why it was so imperative that he gets some sleep. They told him they were under orders to have the floors waxed. Joe said, "This is bullshit!" He then told the men he was going to get his bed down and go to sleep, and nobody better get in his way. All seven had formed into a small crowd by then and were taking an offensive posture. Joe's eyes turned glowing red and his voice had the tone of a wild junkyard dog. He would not betray the desires of his dreams: the bed and the beautiful sleep. He had something to fight for now and he really meant business.

Two men took a step towards Joe. Then Joe took a step towards them without hesitation; Joe was ready and his crazed eyes and fearless stance said so. Any normal man would not even think of testing such obvious resolve. As to invite them to attack, Joe turned his back to them. He climbed the mountain of beds and single-handedly lifted his bunk and threw it to the floor. He then jumped into it and pulled the covers over his shoulders. Yes, there was some follow-up static from the other men, but not enough to disturb Joe's sleep. Completely unarmed, he had faced down seven men and won because he really, really meant business! Besides, if they had disturbed him, Joe would have simply attacked all seven of them if need be! Even if a fight had ensued, my money would have been on Joe.

The next time Joe was to pull "KP" (kitchen police) he hid under the sign-in desk the whole time, not caring about the repercussions. Would you believe he never got caught for that?

Joe's first screw up came with rifle cleaning. Sir-Yes-Sir had instructed the class not to use the wrong bore brush on the rifle. Joe only had one bore brush: the wrong one. So he jammed it down the barrel. When it didn't go fully through, Joe turned the rifle upside down and banged the bore brush on the floor until it was deep inside the weapon, making it impossible to remove it. Several men tried to help Joe before inspection but no one could move the brush an inch. Great! Just great! Now it was too late: Sir-Yes-Sir called everyone to attention. Each man stood motionless as Sir-Yes-Sir went down the line, inspecting each one at a time. Joe stood at attention with his bore brush sticking out of the barrel of his weapon. When Sir-Yes-Sir got to Joe, he grabbed the weapon from Joe's hand. Sir-Yes-Sir put his nose to the tip of Joe's nose. Then while he slowly removed the bore brush with his bare hands, he told Joe in a very low guttural voice that only Joe could hear, "I'm going to kill you."

Shortly after that, someone did die. You see, during training it is not recommended to become sick. If you become sick then you are diagnosed by the drill instructor as a malingerer. On this day, a soldier fell out. That means for some reason he hit the ground face first. The sergeant was going to teach that malingerer a lesson, so he marched the entire company of 200 men over him. It was later found that the soldier had had a heart attack, but too much time had been lost to save him.

As if there wasn't enough conflict going around, this one guy asked Joe, "Where are you from?" Joe replied, "I'm from New York." This guy—for lack of a name I'll call him the "V-shaped man"—had his shirt off and his body was really V-shaped. His muscles were tightly packed and he stood several feet taller than Joe. His shoulders were wider, too, by about a foot and a half. He was a black man from Philadelphia. He said he loved to kick the shit out of New York boys. He walked up to Joe in a hostile manner and stood face to face with him. Joe knew he was going to have to do something special to get out of this; he knew he couldn't beat such a massive physical specimen. Joe told the V-shaped man that if he threw even one punch he would drag him through every court inside and outside of the Army. Joe told him that he better enjoy himself now, because after that he would be pursued for the rest of his days. To Joe's amazement, the V-shaped man backed off.

Joe later found out that this man had had some experience with the court system. He had been sent to the Army after stabbing four men and shooting another. It must have been divine intervention that saved Joe's butt that day.

By now, Joe could see that he was living in a world without mercy, reason, or compassion. To survive in this world he had to jettison those things himself. He learned that if he wanted something, he had to fight for it; I mean fight without hesitation and to completion. So when the server in the chow line didn't put enough food in Joe's plate to feed a bird, Joe requested more. When he was denied and told to move on, Joe told the man, "Put more fucking eggs on this plate or I'm coming over the counter." The man pulled out a large kitchen knife; Joe put one foot up in the rails where the trays go and was attempting to go over. At this point, the cook intervened and instructed the server to give Joe more eggs. Joe had never behaved like this before; he was wondering what was happening to him and what this could lead to, because he knew he was willing to go all the way.

As a soldier, your rifle is considered to be another part of your body. As such, it was highly recommended that you do not to leave it on a log and forget about it. Needless to say, Joe did this, and as a reprimand he was handed a toothbrush and told to paint a latrine the size of Grand Central Station. That was not so bad, because after a while, other toothbrushes came in for similar offenses. A lot of toothbrushes can be better than one. While painting, Joe noticed he wasn't feeling well, but he painted on. After a while, things became blurry and he fell out almost unconscious. Joe was sent to the hospital; he was completely exhausted and sick and lay in bed for two weeks, not even strong enough to eat. He would only leave his bed occasionally to stumble to the Kool-Aid fountain for a drink. He was really getting no medical care, as they believed that every soldier that claimed to be sick was faking it just to get out of duty. He was still grateful for the bed. After loosing like 40 pounds, the doctors suspected that something was really wrong.

It turned out that Joe had pneumonia, probably from all the strip searches in the snow; they were always searching to make sure no ammo was brought back from the field. This was done as insurance against a possible assassination attempt against Sir-Yes-Sir. So they gave Joe a little blue pill so small that Joe almost lost it in his hand. He thought they must be kidding, he had never seen a pill so small. He took the pill anyway, and about 20 minutes later he was doing song and dance numbers from Broadway shows on his bed. When the effect wore off, he asked for another one. Another eight hours of solid show-tune entertainment followed.

During this time, Joe went to the men's room and was surprised to hear a commotion right outside the window. That was strange because he was on the 8th floor. Upon looking out the window, Joe saw a helicopter landing by the hospital entrance beneath. They were pulling out some wounded children from the chopper. Joe could see straight down into the action. He saw these children with "bloody lakes" where their faces used to be. Joe was so overcome by the horror that he immediately passed out. He later learned that the children had found a grenade on the firing range where training was held and had pulled the pin. To Joe, this proved he was not prepared for a real war and to become a real soldier he would have to change in ways that not even he would approve of.

Even though he was still sick, time came for Joe to sign himself out of the hospital; otherwise, he would be recycled to the beginning of training again for missing too much training time. During his stay, Joe had made a friend in the bed next to his. His name was Murphy; he and Joe spent hours talking and laughing and just getting to know each other. Murphy got to leave one day before Joe. When Joe was on the way out the next day, the hospital doors swung open and Joe was severely blinded by the sun, not having seen it for over two weeks. A new incoming patient was blocking Joe's exit. This man had a completely mutilated face; his cheeks were hanging shredded meat. Joe looked away as fast as he could. Just then, this monster face called out, "Joe!" It was Murphy! Murphy's first return assignment was guard duty at the motor pool. Occasionally, civilians would break into the motor pool to steal automotive parts. If caught, they could be pretty brutal, and they were to Murphy. This was a dangerous assignment, especially since they were given just a small stick for self-defense. Soldiers chosen for this duty screamed for mercy as they were pushed off the truck delivering them to their posts.

Unfortunately for Murphy, this assignment proved to be a case of bad timing.

Well, Joe finally returned to his Charlie Company unit but the records showed that he had been transferred. He had lost so much weight that nobody recognized him. Technically, he could have gone home, and the Army wouldn't have had any record of his existence. Charlie Company couldn't take Joe back, though, because he missed too much time. So without doing a complete recycle to the beginning, they sent him to Delta Company. They were behind Charlie Company in training and were at the point where Joe left off anyway.

A few days later, his new sergeant woke Joe up at 3:30am. Before his eyes opened, he was handed a broom and told to sweep the street out in front of the barracks. The sergeant told Joe the general's car was going to take this route. Since you just don't question orders, Joe took the broom and swept the street, even in the dark. The whole time, Joe thought about the tires on the general's car. Didn't the general know that tires are supposed to get dirty? When daylight came, Joe could see the damn street was already clean enough to eat off of. The next thought Joe had was what the general could do with that broom.

For some time after arriving at Delta Company, Joe was still sick. This didn't make the training any easier either. Then, when returning from the field one day, he found his family had come to see him. Joe sneaked off base to get his family settled in a hotel. But when Myra was driving him back, she broadsided a Volkswagen. The Volkswagen was knocked clear to the telephone pole on the far corner of the street. Fortunately no one was hurt. When Joe reported in to his new sergeant and tried to explain what had happened, he found he had lost the ability to speak coherently. Nothing came out but unrelated sounds. The sergeant tried to calm him down until he was able to talk. This was an apparent case of temporary hysteria—Joe had been in the front passenger seat and he was sure he was going to be a dead man that night.

When Joe finally got back to the peaceful barracks, he found a friend that was all "drugged out" on guard duty. If caught, the entire Company of 200 men would pay for it. So Joe took the duty and stayed up all night to cover. When Joe asked what the training was for the next day, he was informed in one word: grenades. Great! Just great! Let's add up all these mishaps: Sick would be #1, shock from car accident would be #2, no sleep would be #3. This combination is not recommended by the Surgeon General for throwing grenades, and could be extremely hazardous to your health.

Now, in most training exercises the Army would bring out one priest. In grenade training they would bring out a truckload of priests. I guess this would be to bless the many parts you are about to become. The Army would make you empty your pockets and give you a chance to change your will. Even the contents of your pockets would go to the next of kin. It was a very scary scenario. That wasn't the worst part, though; the worst part was hearing the thunderous explosions and feeling the ground shake under your feet from miles away. Joe had a bad feeling about this. The feeling was so bad that he went to his sergeant and asked to be excused. The reply was to be expected, "Get your maggot ass out there!"

There were three cement block pits next to each other. Joe took his position in pit #1. He was handed a rather large grenade that more than filled his large hand. He was instructed to pull the pin, draw the grenade back behind his head, and the lever would be released upon throwing it; then, dive into the ground behind the wall. It is not a well-known fact, but the killing radius of a grenade is farther than you can throw it. He did so, and to his surprise, all went well. He was relieved, thinking it was over. But when he stood up again, he was handed another one. Just then the sergeant in pit #2 yelled at

Joe. He said, "Who the hell do you think you are, John Wayne?" He yelled, "Get that goddamn scarf off your neck!" It was wintertime and Joe was wearing a scarf to keep warm. He took the scarf off, then pulled the pin and threw the grenade. It rolled off the side of his hand. He saw it rise high into the sky and arch its trajectory in the direction of pit #2. When it came falling back to earth, Joe hit the ground. He was convinced he had just killed a sergeant and a troop in pit #2. All Joe could hear was the thunderous roar of a very close explosion. Believing he had killed them, he started crying and laughing at the same time, a real authentic nervous breakdown. As things turned out, the sergeant and the troop did make it out of pit #2 just in time. Joe's sergeant grabbed Joe by the back of the collar with one hand and planted Joe square on his feet. He started laughing at Joe. Joe screamed at him, "Why are you laughing? I almost killed them!" The sergeant told him that the sergeant in pit #2 said he "would never mess with you again!"

Joe was forced to run back behind the lines with the soldier he almost killed. During that run, the man called Joe every name in the book. When Joe got behind the lines he saw the entire Company of 200 men was staring at him; they had all seen what happened. No one said a word. Joe felt a great watermelon grow in his throat and ran off into the woods to cry. A priest followed Joe into the woods and put his hand on Joe's shoulder. Joe thought finally, a word of comfort to relieve him of his great suffering. The priest said, "Son, this wouldn't have happened if you had followed instructions." Joe knocked the hand of the priest off his shoulder and told him to get out of his sight. Later, they took Joe to a station house to be charged for attempted manslaughter because the accident appeared to be done on purpose. They believed that Joe tried to get back at the sergeant for yelling at him. After Joe told his side of the story, the sergeants in charge realized it was all an unfortunate accident and let him go. Afterwards, they all had a drink together to celebrate the near-death experience. Still to this very day, Joe is not sure how much of the incident was really an accident.

By the time this day was over, Joe was completely sapped of energy, dignity, strength, and hope. He saw the little bible sitting in his locker and reached for it figuring it couldn't do any harm to check out a few words—the promise of "no harm" seemed like a desirable state. He also figured that he couldn't be disappointed by the words that brought peace to so many others. He opened the book to a random page and started reading. The message he read was one that caused a surge of strength deep from within the core of his soul; he suddenly felt invincible, that no creation of man or conception of hell could touch him. Then he looked back at this little book and thought, "This little bitch has power." He also thought that if he should ever weaken again he now had a defense.

The next day, Joe asked what the training was. The answer came back in two words: grenade launcher. Great! Just great! Joe thought the Army could not possibly be that stupid to put another grenade into his hands. There was no way on God's green earth that they would let Joe get near another grenade, unless they were crazy or had some sort of death wish. Well, they were and they did. A grenade launcher is an attachment to your rifle. Once attached, it slides open to receive a grenade-like shell. Then the entire rifle works like a mortar that has to be pointed into the sky, because if you hold it like you normally would the grenade would hit the ground a few feet in front of you. This would be a very bad thing. Joe was holding the rifle like he normally did, which was the wrong way. He thought that was okay, as he was not going to fire it until an instructor came to check on him. When the instructor saw Joe holding the rifle the wrong way, he repeatedly beat Joe over the helmet with a nightstick. Joe felt he was unjustly punished. Then, aiming properly, Joe proceeded to completely destroy one target tank, two target half-tracks, and one target two-ton truck. With five grenades he completely destroyed an entire convoy. How strange it was to find that the thing you are most expert in was in launching grenades. Not a lot of call for this in the civilian world, though.

No day went by without discovering a deeper part of yourself. As was the traditional ritual, you had to conquer the monkey bars. The monkey bars was a horizontal wood ladder pretty high off the ground, about 20 feet long. You had to jump to catch it and swing from rung to rung across the length, and then go back and forth about four times, all this before breakfast. The individual rungs had been smoothed by the hands of thousands of soldiers that had gone before. At the beginning of his training, Joe had tried it for several days and never went for more than a few rungs before falling to the ground. Then the sergeant, in a disgusted tone of voice, would say, "Go to breakfast."

On this particular day, Joe figured that it would be like all the other days, but it wasn't. This time, Joe did one lap on the monkey bars and found Sir-Yes-Sir standing right below him. Sir-Yes-Sir told Joe that if he fell he would kill him and make it look like an accident. Joe had thoughts about falling on top of him and getting at least a few good shots in, but that was not enough to show the hatred he had for Sir-Yes-Sir. So Joe growled like a demon from hell, completely shocking his drill sergeant and leaving him in awe as he took the monkey bars like he was born there. Joe continued to go from rung to rung without stopping and then started to do extra laps, holding the entire company up for breakfast. Even upon orders to come down, Joe screamed, "No, drill sergeant, I won't," as he continued. Upon a second demand to come down, Joe finally did slip and fell to the ground. Upon standing up he looked his drill sergeant in the eye with a killer's intent; he was readily dismissed to breakfast. Joe saw the first sign that he had an inner strength that he had never used or conceived of, and it was for real and forever. That made him feel akin to the beasts of the earth. He felt that he was one step closer to awareness.

Something unusual happened on the pop-up target course, too. This course was in the shape of an S. The sergeant made the mistake of going ahead, into the line of fire. Joe realized that he was in a good position to shoot his drill sergeant, so he took aim. It was a funny thing to see the sergeant at Joe's disposal. But even funnier was that the sergeant looked so small in Joe's sight that he couldn't bring himself to shoot. Had the sergeant appeared to be a little larger, he would have been a dead sergeant. If you train someone to be a killer, then what do you think you get?

Joe had enough of being treated like an animal. He found himself acting like one too. One day the drill sergeant stole Joe's gloves. This was part of being a drill sergeant: he would steal your gloves, then declare severe punishment for not having them. Joe was at the raw edge and couldn't take any more punishment. So he stole his friends' gloves and let his friend take the punishment. Another time, while in the field, the sergeant ordered Joe not to give the troops any noodles from the soup. The sergeant then told Joe that he and Joe would eat the noodles later. What made this really bad was that the men were cold, tired, and hungry. Joe still did as he was told. That's how the Army knew they broke him.

Joe knew he was broken, too. The only thing left to do was to run and go AWOL; maybe he could run to Canada where so many other smart boys went to avoid the war. Joe slipped out one night and headed to within visual range of the front gate. The floodlights were bright all over the place, but there were no guards! Joe could not figure why there were no guards. He could just walk through that gate if he wanted to. Then he thought the only reason why there were no guards was that they wanted you to run just so they could hunt you down like a dog. This would give purpose and job security to the MP's. So Joe returned to the barracks. During formation the next day, one hundred men were missing. That is exactly half of the entire Company. The MP's, the C.I.D., and local authorities hunted these men down like dogs; all were captured and severely punished. Joe was glad he was not one of them.

By now, all the boys that Joe was training with didn't look like boys anymore. They looked like hardened killers. If told to run in front of a machine gun, they would do so without hesitation. All of them—including Joe—had become soulless killing machines that would attack any obstacle if signaled to do so.

On one running exercise, Joe had an epiphany. As tired and beat as he was, without having one ounce of strength left, someone yelled, "Alright, men! Let's go!" And Joe started running, like he was an early-rising spring chicken. It was as though he had discovered some unknown energy deep within himself. He knew they could not hurt him anymore, that the worst was over! If anyone so much as bothered him, he would just toss them a grenade, and problem solved. In fact, everyone in the unit was turning into some kind of crazed killing thing. They were feeling invincible and indestructible. Until one day in the field, when another company ran past. This company must have been some sort of Army secret weapon: each man was over six feet tall and each one was as muscular as a giant gorilla. These men appeared to be some kind of scientific experiment; they made a normal man appear to be the size of a small boy next to them. It was a very humbling experience for all. Joe was glad they were on our side and hoped the enemy didn't have a unit like that.,

During another time when they were running, Joe began to cough up blood. His sergeant asked Joe what was wrong. Joe said he thought he was sick. The sergeant asked, "How long have you been sick?" Joe replied, "Sergeant, I have been sick from the day I joined the Army." Joe then was told to report to the captain's office. "Private Joe, reporting as ordered sir!" Captain Moseby asked, "What is the problem, troop?" Joe replied, "Sir, I started coughing up blood while running, sir." The Captain said, "I have the answer to that, troop: you need to run it off. You're dismissed." "Sir, yes, Sir." And with that, the matter was closed.

After another hard, cold, and miserable day, it was again time for the 15-mile trek back through sand with heavy equipment. A convoy of cattle trucks was coming down the road. If the sergeant could stop the truck, then each one of the 200 men would give the driver a dollar and they would be able to catch a ride back instead. This was a real break, the first sign of any kind of humanity Joe had seen for some time. Okay, so there was only enough room for 50 men in the truck. However, if you piled them on top of each other, they would fit. Joe learned humanity costs 200 dollars to travel animal class. Just like the cattle the driver had just dropped off, they were going to the slaughterhouse. That is the way it was, all 200 men stacked on top of each other. Their arms and legs were so entangled you couldn't tell what belonged to whom. Joe had some guy's boot on his shoulder but that's the way it had to be, so he took it without rebuttal. When the guy started to apply pressure by pushing harder on Joe's shoulder, that's all it took: Joe knocked the trooper's foot off his shoulder. The soldier said to Joe, "I'll get you later for that." Without pause, Joe replied, "Bring it on."

When the journey was over, Joe returned to an empty barracks. He walked to the far end of the room to watch the rain out the window. When Joe turned around, there was a soldier in the doorway holding a knife, pointed at Joe. It was the soldier from the truck with the heavy boot. When the soldier started walking slowly toward Joe without saying a word, Joe started screaming for help. Joe then picked up a mattress and held it in front of him, all the while still screaming for help. The threat was still approaching slowly, so in a hurry Joe tried to explain how painful it was to have that boot digging into his shoulder and how sorry he was for causing him any inconvenience. When another soldier showed up at the door, the attacker put his knife away. Then he said to Joe he was just trying to scare him as repayment. Joe had no doubt that it worked. At that moment, Joe realized that even your fellow soldiers could be your enemy. This meant having to watch behind you as you watch ahead.

Now I must talk to you about women. Joe always took women for granted because there were so many of them. I mean half the darn world is filled up with women, maybe more than that. So the last thing Joe expected was a shortage. For three months, Joe didn't see so much as one visually pleasing, poetry-in-motion, shapely creation of God. The world had turned into one cold, stone-hard, miserable place in the universe. He felt as though the life experience without them was just not worth it. He couldn't believe how much he missed women, even just the sight of one.

One cold miserable day, Delta Company was in the field when the rumor blazed across the countryside that women were handing out cough syrup from the Red Cross truck. Joe could not believe his ears! "You mean real women?" he asked. This started a stampede for two reasons. One reason was the women, and the second was the cough syrup; most of the men were sick with colds and needed the syrup. You could get drunk on the syrup if you drank enough of it, so even if the women weren't there as promised you really couldn't lose. You could still get drunk enough to kill the pain. It was a sorry sight to see hundreds of men surrounding that truck. Yeah, those women had Army uniforms on, and the Army had done real hack jobs on their hair. But there they were and they were real! Hundreds of men just trying to get close to the truck and maybe even just say hello. Some soldiers were happy to watch from a distance in silence. After all, they did move like women, and if one smiled at you that was better than getting mail from home. Joe did both: first he watched from a distance; every move they made was majestic poetry. Then he was able to get up close. One actually smiled at him and Oh, what a feeling! That wasn't really a lot to go on, but it was enough to trigger memories of soft skin and laughter and sweet days that seemed long passed. Thank you, God, for women!

Another time, towards the end of training, the company was returning from another tough day in the field. The barracks were in sight, just one more road to cross. Then, there she was: another real woman. She was in a car. Joe's eyes fixed on her, like a pilot's radar locks on to a target. In fact, he found he couldn't get his eyes off her. Not seeing the wire coming down from the telephone pole, Joe's foot got caught. Joe's face and body slammed into the mud, spread-eagle, right in front of this woman. Joe's helmet flew off, with his pack and rifle going in different directions. When he looked back at this heavenly creature, she was laughing out of control at him. Joe was in severe pain but gathered his belongings and his dignity, then caught up with his unit.

Hip! Hip! Hurray! This was their first day off. Joe had never seen the Army take a day off. This was an event that he could plan for. There would be wine, women and song, enough to drown out the memories and stress of the preceding months. For this event, every button would be polished and shoes shined to a high gloss; in other words, "standing tall." Joe was now ready for the "Flamingo Club." This was the only and well-known watering hole for maggots only. Joe asked his comrades, "Are you sure there are going to be women there?" The answer was "Yes." That was all Joe needed for his spirits to soar. He could dream of the way they comb their hair or put their make-up on. Their movements would restore his lost faith in everything. He could learn how to smile again. That was something that he hadn't done for the last three months. Joe also had plans to drink himself into oblivion.

The night finally came, and Joe looked better than a recruiting poster. He and a small group of friends descended on the Flamingo Club like invading paratroopers. Joe flung open the doors and stood primed in the doorway. His eyes scanned the entire playing field. When his scan was completed, his heart sank like the Titanic: there were hundreds of soldiers and only two women. The two women looked very much like each other. They both were fat and had blonde choppy hair and were not very attractive. Men surrounded them both. At this crushing sight, Joe figured it would be best to just drown his sorrows. He was going to drink until all the pain and disappointment of the recent past days was completely neutralized.

At that moment of decision, one of the blondes approached Joe and asked him to dance. In a disgusted voice, he said no. After all his suffering, he felt as though he deserved better. What he didn't expect was that after 30 beers those two unsavory blondes would start to look pretty good. He thought that if he had an opportunity over all those hundreds of soldiers, he might as well take it. So he decided to ask one to dance. Imagine Joe's surprise when she said no in a disgusted voice. Joe knew this was just a payback, but this was also a crushing defeat to his ego and just one more letdown to add to his despair. He started to believe that all he had the right to expect out of life was disappointment.

The next day Joe pulled inside guard duty. This only happened because the drill sergeant met and wanted to date his sister Myra. Inside guard duty was considered choice duty when the only other choice was all night guard at a frozen lake in the woods. He was to guard the vault at Fort Dix. The vault was underground and held all the money for every soldier at the fort. It was the only guard duty assignment that called for five rounds of live ammo. This assignment also came with explicit orders. "If anyone tries to gain access, then blow their fuckin' heads off." These were the first "real" Army orders Joe had ever received. Joe knew that the chances of the vault being robbed on the same night he had guard duty were astronomical. He took comfort in this.

The vault was made up of two metal covered rooms. One was the guard station and the other was the vault room with iron bars, like a jail. It had a huge vault inside. One man would be locked behind the bars, where the vault was. The other would be blocking the door at the guard station; that was Joe's assignment. You had to walk down a flight of stairs to get to the door. Since no one was authorized to walk down those stairs, this meant an easy night, which was long overdue, was finally here. This would be a night with casual conversation and many hours of vacation from the Army.

Just as Joe was leaning back to take his first relaxed breath, he heard footsteps coming down the stairs. There was now a man standing at the door. He wore an Army uniform with a white helmet. This man tried to open the door. Joe's heart began to race, thoughts of what to do were pounding in his head. Joe didn't want to kill anyone. So he yelled, "You better get away from that door or I will shoot!" The man in the white helmet tried to open the door again. Joe remembered his orders and pointed his loaded rifle at the door with the safety off. Joe yelled one more time, "You better get away from that door!" Joe figured if anybody was going to rob the vault, he would do it dressed as a military policeman with a white helmet. Joe turned his head away so he wouldn't see the outcome, as he pointed the weapon and began to squeeze the trigger. Thank the Good Lord that the man got the message in time! He saw the rifle pointed straight at him and he ran. All Joe saw was a streak of a white helmet and heard the fading sound of cursing words ascending the stairs. Taking a deep breath and without thinking, Joe leaned his weapon against the wall, and before he could stop it the rifle began to fall. A loaded weapon off safety falling onto a metal floor could easily go off. The bullet would bounce off every metal wall until it hit you. Realizing what could happen, all Joe had time to do was hold his ears. Luckily, the weapon didn't fire when it hit the floor, and Joe concluded that was enough excitement for one night. He never found out who the man was or what he wanted.

Did I tell you about the "take the hill" training? It seems there is more to taking a hill than Joe knew about. Otherwise, training wouldn't be necessary. The instructions were simple: charge this hill while firing your weapon with live ammo. Of course, when it came to live ammo, red flags went up all over in Joe's head. He decided to hold firing his weapon until the end of the course. Then he would fire the live ammo into the woods at the top of the hill. This would prevent the possibility of an accident. Upon charging the hill, Joe's thoughts were of the heavy equipment he was carrying, and how it brought him to a slow crawl. He also thought there was no glory in this. It was obvious to see that if the enemy commanded the top of the hill then Joe was nothing but a big slow-moving target. Upon conquering the crest of the undefended hill, Joe looked out over a vast wasteland of trees or what used to be trees. Good, now it was Joe's chance to rid himself of the ammo in his M-16. He raised the weapon to his hip and proceeded to mow the forest down with automatic fire. Of course, this was not acceptable by drill sergeant standards. The drill sergeant walked up to Joe and repeatedly banged on his helmet with a nightstick; this was the sergeant's usual expression of disapproval. Being a brave soldier was far from what Joe expected.

Another day off was coming and this time Joe knew what to expect. So he scaled down his hopes and dreams of meeting a woman. He would go to the club with the simple and sole purpose of getting drunk. This would reduce any disappointment and could not fail. The plan was to drink so much until he forgot where he was. That was a good plan, too.

This time no attention would be paid to detail. No extra effort would be put forth other than to concentrate on the purpose at hand: getting blind and stinking drunk! Would you believe that a woman showed up! She walked over to Joe's table and asked to sit down. Joe had not known a happy moment for some time. He figured fate was setting him up for another "rip the heart out through your nose" experience.

This woman had red hair—which was ruined by the Army—and she wore a uniform, too. On a scale of one to ten, she was blurry because Joe was drunk. Joe told her he hadn't seen a woman for months. He told her he had forgotten what human kindness was like. He told her how much he wanted to kiss her. He told her he just wanted a kiss and if not that would be okay, too. She stood up and held out her hand. Joe reached for her hand not knowing what to expect. He reached for her hand like an abused animal, half afraid of rejection and the other half hoping for pity. She took him out back by the lake and made love to him. Upon returning from being renewed, she asked him, "Did you get what you wanted?" Joe said yes, and she left. Joe thought maybe the worst was over; finally, something good had happened. In fact, he said it to himself again, "Something good happened," with complete and total disbelief! Okay, it wasn't a long or meaningful relationship, but he got mercy and pity, and a sensitive moment of kindness. Joe felt as though he could walk back into hell now and take whatever came, because of her. "Oh God, hear my prayer! Thank you for women!"

Did you ever just want to say no, I mean like no to a teacher or a policeman or some other authority figure? You know you really can't say no but you really want to. Well, Joe was resting in his bunk when a corporal came to tell him to wax the floors. Joe felt he deserved some rest and didn't want to be disturbed. So he thanked the corporal for his offer and said no.

The corporal explained how this wasn't an offer; it was more like an order. Joe, while still trying to be polite, replied, "No, thank you. Please, I'm really not interested." The corporal left the room in a huff. Joe went back to rest, thinking that if he had known saying no was that easy he would have said it a long time ago, and many times too. Minutes later the corporal returned with a low-ranking sergeant. Joe felt that his rest was surely being interrupted and this was becoming somewhat annoying. The lowly sergeant ordered Joe to wax the floor. Joe explained that he had already declined the order from the corporal because he really didn't feel like waxing floors. Since he still felt the same way, Joe told the sergeant not to take it personal, but the answer was still no. Now the sergeant and the corporal left in a huff.

Would you believe that the Army doesn't understand the meaning of the word no? This was proven when the corporal, the lowly sergeant, and now the Top Sergeant returned to tell Joe to wax the floors. When Joe saw that now there were three of them, he wondered how high he would have to go in the chain of command to have them understand that he didn't want to wax the floors. It was explained to Joe that he could be arrested, sent to Leavenworth Military Prison, and dishonorably discharged for refusing to follow an order. Joe realized that his rest had already been disrupted anyway, so he reluctantly got up, grabbed a mop and started waxing the floors. When the entire cadre was satisfied that orders were being followed, they left. Guess what Joe did then? He went back to bed! They never came back to check if the job was completed. Joe was surprised to realize that he got his own way after all, when he should have been arrested after he said his first no. For a moment in time, he had been insubordinate and the system failed to punish him. That made him think he was going to have to start thinking for himself. He couldn't depend on a system that was not reliable and that could leave him vulnerable.

The end of basic training was almost here. That's when the "white glove test" was scheduled. The sergeant would lay a white glove down. You would take your rifle apart, and the sergeant would scrape his knife over the parts of your rifle. If anything came off onto that white glove, it would mean no weekend and three more days of cleaning your rifle. Well, Joe failed the test and had to clean his rifle for three more days. Not only that, but someone had to clean all the rifles of all the men that were in the hospital due to training accidents. Of course, Joe was ordered to do so by another sergeant named Riker. Joe had never seen this sergeant before.

Enough was enough, though; Joe had plans to skip this. Joe looked like any other soldier and figured he could get lost in the crowd. That is what is called "fading back into the green." So he quietly stepped out the back door and back to his barracks. Joe knew that Sergeant Riker would be an old man by the time he found him again. Finally, Joe was fighting back in his own way. Be dammed if it didn't work too, with no penalty paid!

Things of an odd nature kept happening to Joe even just walking down the street. While passing the motor pool, a sergeant ordered Joe to move this large truck up to the gas pump. Joe didn't have a driver's license; in fact he had never driven before. So Joe did the right thing and informed the sergeant of this fact. He said, "Sergeant, I don't know how to drive and have no driver license." The sergeant must have gone to sergeant's school, because he replied with the only thing that sergeants say, "Get your maggot ass up there, troop!" Joe thought, "Okay, now the Army is going to get exactly what they ask for. After all, 'fair is fair,' right?"

Joe climbed up into this monstrously large truck and started looking for the key, but there was none. The sergeant pointed out in his most sophisticated manner that this vehicle started by push button. When Joe pushed the button there was a great roar of a giant engine starting. This scared the living daylights out of him. He then threw it in gear and smashed the gas pedal. The great and massive truck leaped into the air with a mighty roar. It occurred to Joe he didn't know how to stop this thing. The massive truck landed on its rear wheels and stalled right in front of the gas pump. Joe got out of the vehicle—somewhat shaken—and said, "Okay, sergeant, the truck is now in front of the pump." The sergeants' eyes were bugged out, his cigar was bitten in half, and he was speechless. Joe walked away thinking another mission accomplished.

Not everything the Army had to offer was scary or painful. Like the night of "night fire," which was actually quite a beautiful thing. Hundreds of men lined up for about two miles, all of them firing tracer bullets at a hill. The whole scene was like a waterfall of streaking lights with a background of thunderous explosions. The deafening noise and the lights hypnotized you, and for a timeless moment you were a child again and it was the 4th of July back home.

Another example of awesome was a tank. Joe got a short ride on top of one and oh, what a feeling! He had this mighty feeling of power and a sense that nothing would stand in the way of this incredible killing machine. Joe had seen heroes on TV that would jump on top of a tank and throw a grenade down the hatch. In reality, this is not a likely event. But you have to love the movies! Joe wondered why a machine that was two stories high with inch-thick steel, machine guns all around, and a cannon, was needed to kill flesh-and-bone men.

Graduation day! Now Joe really knew what it meant to be a soldier. He saw blocks of 200 men at a time being shipped off to Vietnam. It was no different than cows being herded, counted, and then sent to slaughter. Joe could see the production line and saw his place in it too. He saw 200, then another 200, and there were still more; real people marching bravely and headlong into the insatiable meat grinder. If you survive, then you have a right to live.

While the ceremonies and parades were proceeding, Joe had tears in his eyes. Not out of pride, but because he saw what he had become and he was ashamed. He had been stripped of any human decency and had been shown the horrible animal that lived within him. He could now kill without question or conscience. He was crying for his own broken soul while knowing he too was nothing but cattle going to slaughter, the final processing. The men of Charlie Company all got Vietnam; so bravely they marched off! Now Joe and all of Delta Company were standing on the block awaiting their assignments. Joe felt disgusted at being a part of this hideous ritual. It was just then that Joe decided not to kill; no matter what, he swore he would not kill. That was the only way to stop this insanity and to save his very soul.

Just at that moment the base commander interrupted the ceremonies in a most unusual way. He grabbed the microphone and announced the war was over. "Dear Lord, thank you for saving my unworthy ass!" Joe prayed.

Joe's next assignment was at Fort Devens in Massachusetts. That was "The Army Security Agency Training Center and School." But first things first: Joe got a month's leave before starting school. This meant going home to a hero's welcome. He wanted to get his maggot ass off that base he was on as soon as possible, so he ran to his room and started quickly packing his gear. With no delay he threw all his possessions into a duffle bag, and without looking back he headed for the door. Would you believe the door was blocked by an imposing figure squarely planted in the threshold—Joe could not believe that hell would not release him! It was Sergeant Riker, who had been looking for Joe ever since he bugged out of rifle cleaning.

The conversation that followed was a bit one-sided. It went something like this: "Maggot, you are mine! You will clean rifles until the parts are so small they don't fit together. You can forget about going home, and unpack your gear now, maggot! You are mine now and I will teach you the full meaning of pain and suffering!" Joe's sergeant heard the commotion and arrived at the scene. He told Riker he had no authority over his troops. His sergeant ordered Joe to leave, and he did—so fast that even his shadow was confused about which way he went. Joe swore he would not even fly over New Jersey for fear the plane would fall on that forsaken place.

When Joe finally got to within eyesight of his home, again his eyes filled with water. This time it was for a joyous moment. He knew his family would greet him with tears of joy and a hero's welcome. He dried his eyes and stood tall as he walked through the door. He walked into the living room and announced, "Hey everybody, I'm home!" The cat slowly walked up to Joe and licked his boots, and that was the extent of his welcome home. The entire family had left to go see Joe at the base. They wanted to surprise him with an unexpected visit. Joe wanted to surprise them and didn't tell them that he was coming. They must have passed each other en route. Joe wondered if life had anything else to offer other than one anti-climax after another.

This was a period of transition for Joe. He had been told the worst was over. He was informed that the Army would be just like a regular job from now on. His next assignment was to report to A.I.T. (Advanced Individual Training) in Fort Devens. This meant nine months of job training. All Joe knew was that he was tired, his spirit was broken, and it would take every ounce of courage for him to return from leave. So far he had not traveled far from home. New Jersey is certainly not far from his Long Island home. Now he was being sent to Massachusetts, which was only three or four hours away. Joe wanted to see the rest of the world, not just the surrounding area where he grew up, so this left him somewhat disappointed.

After a month at home, it was time to go back. The bus trip to Fort Devens was long and boring, leaving Joe even more tired than he was before. Arriving at his new base, Joe wondered what form of torture they would have to offer. It was the last snowfall of 1973. The base looked like a regular Army base. Joe found an unclaimed bunk and, without unpacking or taking off his clothes, he crashed into it. He would officially check in after getting some rest. What happened was that Joe wound up sleeping for two days. He figured the Army could wait before they had another crack at him. Besides the Army didn't really know who you were until you checked in and Joe wanted to delay that inevitable reunion for as long as possible, but now the time had come. When Joe finally woke up he found himself surrounded by seven other men sharing the room. They had all seen Joe sleeping for that long period and had been wondering who he was and why he wasn't getting up. Joe didn't know it at the time, but all of these men would become closer than brothers to him.

The introductions were short before it was decided to go to the mess hall. That is the place where the slop was served. At least that was all Joe had ever experienced before. Holy Moses! It was real food and it was good, too! And when the cook went to each table and asked how the meal was being enjoyed, Joe thought this couldn't be real. What is the Army doing, setting us up for a big nasty payback? Joe figured he would eat and enjoy while he could, before the Army took its pound of flesh. There was no running two miles before every meal or even doing that monkey bar thing. You could even take as long as you liked to eat. Not like the three minutes you had before. What the hell was going on here? This place was run like a college campus. All you had to do was spend the entire day in school and that was it!

School was somewhat strange, though. Training was held in a classroom with a vault door, just like in a bank. They were teaching how to use the first computers. This was how Joe came to know and hate Mr. Samuel B. Morse, the inventor of the Morse code. Everyone had a computer they would use to learn international speeds for Morse code. There was a keyboard on the screen and whenever you made a mistake the keyboard would light up. First they started out slow and as you passed each speed, the computer would get faster. The speed that they intended you to reach was incredible. The individual tones sped through your ears so fast as to not allow even a single thought process. In fact, to be good at this you had to be in a semi-conscious state, half-awake and half-asleep. The object was to keep five letters in your head at all times. One letter consisted of several tones. When one letter came in, you let one letter go out.

After eight hours of this every day, Joe realized the truth. The Army was no longer attacking his body and his emotions—now they were going for his mind! Every once in a while a student would stand up, start screaming, and throw his computer against the wall. Joe didn't know what was happening to those people but he hoped it wouldn't happen to him.

After a while, Joe wasn't keeping up with the speed; in fact, he was falling behind. If you fell too far behind your name would go onto a drop list. This would piss the Army off bad because they had a lot of money invested in each soldier. When your name hit the top of the drop list, they would reassign you to a regular Army unit. Then the Army would send you to one of two places. One place was to the southern states where you would dig ditches in the swamp. The second place was to dig ditches in Alaska. Joe was not up to either assignment. Joe even took No Doze to try and speed up his response time. It helped, but not enough to turn things around.

When Joe didn't pass a speed in one day he was given homework of a tedious nature. He was told to write the alphabet 10,000 times with its Morse code equivalent. Each letter had to be a quarter of an inch high in block letters. It took exactly the amount of time from the end of one school day to the start of the next school day to do this. Guess the Army figured Joe would do better with no sleep. The next day, when he turned his paper in, they tore the exercise up in front of him without checking it. Joe realized that this had been an exercise in mental abuse and was left feeling numb and detached from any sense of fair play or sanity.

Things were getting bad again. Joe's name rose closer to the top on the drop list. Then it happened: while punching away in a half-awake state, Joe saw it. The computer screen turned into another world. There was a large room with a giant fireplace, there were people dressed in formal attire. There was a rope hanging from the curtains, the kind of rope you pull to call for the butler. The hostess of this party was a very attractive woman with auburn hair and was serving hors d'oeuvres from a silver platter. She walked up to Joe and asked, "Are you enjoying the party?"

It was the sound of his own voice replying yes that brought him back to reality. Joe realized that his mind had created the whole thing. That scared him worse than anything he had ever experienced. Joe pulled his headphones off and covered his eyes. He prayed that this apparition would be gone when he looked up again, because if it were still there then he would know he was truly crazy beyond repair. When he looked again, it was gone. Thank heaven! The sergeant in the control booth could tell when a computer had stopped receiving input; Joe could see the sergeant was standing in the isle looking at him. Joe was so shaken that all he could do was point to the computer and shake his head in a "no" gesture. The sergeant appeared to understand. So this is what happens! This is what causes people to start screaming like madmen!

Maybe someone else's illusion was not of a party; maybe their innermost horrors became real. Joe thought that if you can't trust your own mind, then what in the known universe could you trust?

Joe realized he needed a vacation, and that was all there was to it. A plan was needed and a plan was developed. Joe had found a very unusual place in the woods. It was an abandoned military post. It was perfect for camping. There was a crystal clear lake surrounded by tall sharp mountains on all sides with small waterfalls feeding the lake. It was the perfect place to be alone, and to commune with nature; a place where he could recharge his soul and return refreshed. Joe could use the time to try to remember happier days—even normal days would be fine.

The weekend came and Joe was packed and ready. The military had lots of good stuff for camping; you might even call them camping experts. So off he went into the woods. It took a long time to find the place again, but when he did there was still enough time for a swim and to set up camp. Since he was sure he was completely alone, he decided to go skinny-dipping.

He took off all his clothes and jumped into the crystal clear lake. The water was so clear, you could see a hundred feet deep, and swimming was like flying. That is until Joe felt something give him a pretty intense bite. A small fish with adult teeth had just taken a pretty healthy chomp on Joe's leg. Then another fish bit his toe, and another bit his arm. When one bit his penis, you could hear the screaming all the way back to shore. In fact, Joe swam so fast he could have beaten Tarzan swimming. Okay, swimming was out of the question! Joe set up a "pup tent" as dark began to fall.

As he started to snack on a sandwich, he noticed the mosquitoes where getting a little thick and becoming annoying. Too dark now to see, Joe pulled out his flashlight. All he could see was a thick blanket of mosquitoes. They began biting him and getting in his mouth and nose. Joe waved his arms furiously to no avail. Even though it was dark, it was time to abandon ship and get the hell out of there. The one thing Joe forgot to pack was bug spray. Even though he wasn't sure he could find his way back, he packed up and left faster than the mosquitoes could suck his blood.

The way back was pretty brutal too. Joe tripped and fell into sticker bushes, which scratched him up pretty bad. Then he wandered into a swamp and fell into some thick black mud. By the time he made it back to the gates of camp, he looked like "Rambo" in shock. Oh, well, the vacation must have been successful in a way, because during the entire day Joe didn't think once about the Army or Morse code.

Outside of school there wasn't really much to do except sit around and worry about the drop list. Joe heard about this Army marching unit that would march in all the surrounding town's parades. After a parade, the town would throw a big party. Now that sounded like an interesting diversion, so he joined. Each man would hold a flag representing a different state. Joe would always carry the flag from New York. The unit would twirl the flags and do impressive tricks to please the crowds. Joe must have marched in over 50 parades, enjoying the corresponding parties afterwards.

One day, after one such parade in Jaffrey, New Hampshire, Joe noticed a local town girl who was sitting at the bleachers near the buses. Joe struck up a conversation with her and she invited him on a sightseeing trip of the area. She led him to her secret place in the mountains—it was a beautiful place with a river and waterfalls. Joe expected to get lucky, and told the girl he was going overseas soon, hoping that she would take pity on him. She said no, but that if he ever returned they could try again. Joe had to write this campaign off as a loss, and bid a hasty retreat. By the time they got back to town, the bus that would return him to base had already left and Joe spent the rest of the night hitching rides to get back before roll call in the morning or he would be counted as AWOL. Not a good ending for a disappointing day.

None of this was doing any good for the "drop list." Joe's name had now risen to second from the top. That's when the Army first let women into class. In fact, Joe got to sit right next to one. That was the answer for Joe. First some teasing went on, and then things got more seductive—she placed her hand on Joe's leg, massaging him in an erotic way. All of a sudden, Joe passed three code speeds in one day. "God, thank you for, and please bless, all women."

Before much time went by, Joe was really punching out those "dits." That means taking Morse code by keyboard. He noticed his hands were typing by themselves, without Joe telling them what to do. His hands were responding to the sound of code coming into his ears. It was the strangest thing to see his very own hands dancing over the keyboard, as though they were a separate entity. This was a fine example of the "Pavlov's' dogs" theory. When the scientist fed the dogs he would ring a bell. Then one day he just rang the bell without feeding them. The dogs' mouths watered as a result of an involuntary reaction. It seems that dogs and humans have a lot in common.

One day, when Joe got back from class, there was something strange going on at the barracks. There were men standing at attention at every door, even at the latrine. The floors were waxed to a high gloss shine. Joe asked if a general was coming for inspection. It turned out that all this hoopla was for a simple captain named Morgan. Joe was tired from school and was not about to play games for some lowly captain. So he jumped into his bunk and went to sleep. When the captain caught Joe sleeping, all hell broke loose. This captain yelled at Joe for a solid half hour. Joe thought this called for some payback.

Joe learned that it was really the little man that ran the show in the Army; it was the lowly private that got the job done. Joe came up with a plan. When soldiers failed school they were temporarily assigned to different jobs until their next orders came through. Some of Joe's friends that had failed were placed in payroll. So all it would take was a simple call and pay records could be lost. Joe called payroll and requested Captain Morgan's records be sent to the shredder. If pay records were lost it would take the major part of six months to get paid again. It so happened there were two captains by the name of Morgan; which one did he want? To be sure Joe got the right one, he told payroll to do them both. He never saw the captain again, but heard about a Captain Morgan that had been demoted. Yes, Joe was fighting back again now. The unwritten law states, "Never mess with someone who has nothing to lose."

Every base had a nightclub nearby where soldiers gathered; in this case it was the Mohawk Club. Joe knew it would be filled with GI's, so you don't go there looking for women. Joe had a need to kill the Morse code that was beeping in his head. If you drank enough, the beeps would go away. That's all Joe had in mind. When he walked into the club, he saw something he just could not believe. It was a beautiful woman. Naturally, soldiers surrounded her. That was okay, because at least Joe could look at her from a distance. After a few hours the crowd dissipated and Joe found himself standing right next to her. Joe told this woman he would honestly cut his right arm off just for the chance of a date with her. She was amused and said for Joe to keep his arm, that she would date him anyway. She was a doll, short light brown hair that curved around her head. Her skin was olive and her eyes were sultry. Joe's spirit rose to new heights; he felt as though he could put an eagle's soaring flight to shame. Then he had to break the bad news to the beautiful woman: Joe didn't have a car and could not pick her up. She said she would drive but there was one condition. Under no circumstances was Joe to cancel, because others had stood her up before. Joe couldn't imagine anything that would keep him from this sweet destiny, so he agreed.

Come the day of the date and Joe's family showed up for a visit. They had traveled all the way from Long Island and only had the weekend to spend with him before they had to return. Joe tried to explain to his family about his date, but they just wouldn't understand. He was starting to think that fate was nothing more than a stupid bitch. So Joe made the call: he called the girl with the news and begged for her understanding. She hung up on him. Joe screamed to the top of his lungs: "For the love of God, when is something going to go right?" Or is life just being stuck between a rock and a hard place?

During one quiet weekend, the Army decided that the men needed something to do. News came of a general wanting to have lunch in the wooded area across the street from the barracks. Now, in order for the general to have lunch in the woods, the woods had to be cleaned. Every rock, stick, leaf, and thing not attached to the ground had to be picked up. Joe didn't really understand what the hell was wrong with the general, but orders were orders. Joe calculated this was not a situation for fighting back directly. Instead, something like this might call for a little passive resistance. Since his uniform conveniently matched the surrounding background, the plan became one of camouflage: if you couldn't see him then he's not there. So that is what Joe did, not wanting to be a part of such foolishness. He watched from a distance as 199 buttheads picked up leaves in the woods. During that time he thought about what it meant to think for yourself. He thought about how lemmings will run off a cliff following each other. He knew the time would come when he might have to use this skill of independent thought to save his own life. Mainly, he thought about how his mother didn't raise a big slow moving target or a lemming either. Would you believe that the general cancelled? Would you believe that everything had to be put back in the woods, every leaf, every stick? To Joe, this was evidence that he was right, and the general was a raving lunatic.

There were so many other childish things going on in one place or another. Like the new guys, or "nugs," who were often told to spend the night on the roof of the barracks on helicopter watch. The orders were to count and record the numbers of all passing helicopters. The thing was that there wasn't a helicopter within 500 miles of the place. At least Joe didn't fall for that one.

To a soldier, one general looks like another, with the same uniforms and star insignias. Well, one of the biggest events of Joe's life was coming. His class was going to be inspected by not just any general, but the general of all generals: General Omar Bradley. He was the only general that had risen up through the ranks of private (or maggot) to a five-star general. He wasn't privileged by wealth or status. He picked his battles wisely and seriously cared about the soldiers under his command. His contributions to winning World War II are too many to mention. He was justly and affectionately known as "the Soldier's General." His name would be respected throughout time and be linked with other giants such as Generals Patton and Montgomery and McArthur. I mean, this was going to be a real special event in Joe's life. The day of the inspection, everyone was sitting at the computers as usual. Joe just couldn't wait to see real history walk right in front of him. This man was not only history himself but he made history happen.

The computer room sergeant came in and briefed the class on how to act. The instructions were to look forward while keeping your hands on your keyboard. Under no circumstances was anyone to move their heads or attempt to look at the general. The following is Joe's sequence of thoughts about this matter: "This is bullshit, and I've had enough of this Army bullshit!!! Does the Army have to suck the life out of every uplifting thought? Okay! If they don't want me to look at their sacred cow general, then they can have him all to themselves!!!" Joe did exactly as he was told. He sat straight up in his chair, eyes front, and hands on the keyboard. As the general came in, everyone in the class looked, except Joe. Everyone in class was sitting relaxed knowing they were immune from discipline while the general was there. Joe sat statue-like as he had been instructed. Joe was facing the door and through the corner of his eye he saw an old man come in the room surrounded by colonels. But he still could not see over the computers.

After a few minutes of sitting like this, Joe felt a tap on his shoulder. He thought he was in trouble again. He thought, "For God's sake, man, I was following instructions! Isn't that enough?" As he remained in position without responding, he felt the tap on his shoulder again. As he turned ready to defend himself, he saw it wasn't the sergeant. It was a colonel. Colonel Green was one of Omar Bradley's staff. Joe said with great surprise, "You're a colonel sir." The colonel said he was sorry about the surprise, and just wanted to ask Joe a few questions. The colonel said Joe didn't have to worry about military protocol. The idea was just to have a man-to-man chat. The first question from Colonel Green was, "Why are you sitting like this?" Joe explained he was just following orders and he really wanted to see the general. The colonel wanted to know how Joe liked the Army. Joe said, "You have your good days and you have your bad." The colonel then asked, "How do you like your job?" Joe handed his headsets to the colonel and typed out a few dits for him. Joe asked the colonel, "How would you like to do that for eight hours a day?" The colonel said he understood; he then asked Joe where he would like to be assigned after he finished school. Joe explained his curiosity about the oriental people and how he had heard a lot about Thailand. Besides all else, Thailand was directly on the other side of the world, where Joe had promised himself to go some day. He told the colonel that if the Army didn't send him there, he would go there after he got out. The colonel replied that he would see to it that Joe got his wish. Joe thanked the colonel and assured him that if by any chance he forgot it would be okay with him.

During this whole conversation, Joe could see the concern of several sergeants at a distance. Joe told the colonel that he thought he was in trouble now for talking to him. The colonel told Joe not to worry, that all would be well, and thanked Joe for his time. After the meeting, Joe found himself being surrounded and questioned by three or four sergeants. They all had this dumbfounded look on their faces. They asked Joe how he knew Colonel Green. Joe said he didn't know the man and it was just a casual conversation. Joe couldn't help but notice the fear they showed in their eyes. Joe really didn't care much about the whole affair, except that he still didn't get to see the general, and he knew the colonel would not remember him. Joe noticed he was treated with cautious concern by the sergeants after that.

As far as school was going, Joe was coming in 13th out of a class of 14. It was only the number one student that got his choice of assignment. Many months had gone by, and Joe had forgotten the colonel and the conversation. One day in school Joe was having a bad day and never looked so bad with his unkempt uniform and shoes not shined. Stress was catching up to him. Now he stood before a great wall of buttons and blinking lights. The instructions were to synchronize the equipment, then close it down in proper sequence. This took all of Joe's concentration. He was well into the synchronization part when his sergeant called him. Joe was not authorized to leave his post with equipment still active. In fact, you're not allowed to leave your post until all procedures were complete, right to proper sequence of shutdown. Joe signaled to his sergeant he would be there as soon as proper procedures were followed. He noticed his sergeant was standing with a man that was wearing a really nice civilian suit. Joe kept working so hard he forgot his sergeant had beckoned him.

Upon the second request for his attendance, Joe realized he was in deep now. So he pulled his headsets off, hit the main power switch, and attended to the sergeant's call, expecting a reprimand. Before Joe could apologize, the man in the suit said, "Don't you remember me?" Joe was intrigued. "You look familiar, sir." The man announced himself as Colonel Green and said he knew he looked different out of uniform. The colonel informed Joe that he had just stopped by to let Joe know that he was approved for Thailand. Joe was shocked that the colonel had remembered a lowly private first-class after all this time. Again, the sergeant's mouth hit the floor in disbelief. The entire class was listening with their headsets half off, and they looked at Joe as if he had just stepped off a spaceship. Joe had come into contact with many colonels in his short military career, with no special fascination in regard to them. But for some unknown reason, this Colonel Green was some kind of special honcho. Joe thanked him with all his heart and returned to his duties.

"Imagine," Joe thought to himself, "I am going clear to the other side of the world." From where he was, if you dug a hole right at your feet and went straight through the earth, you would come out in Thailand. You couldn't get farther away unless you left the planet. At the young and tender age of almost 21, Joe just got the green light for this ideal adventure and the fulfillment of his childhood dreams, all at once. He would meet the people he had promised himself that day on the beach. Joe would even have the opportunity to "discover" the mystery of the orient. He was at the perfect age, this was the perfect adventure, and nothing could stop it. He was also going to see many of his roommates and friends that had gotten there before him. The only missing element was Joe. He had been reduced to 139 pounds by basic training and was in doubt about his own mental health after taking Morse code for the last nine months. Oh well, what I mean to say is: whatever was left of Joe was being sent to Thailand.

Towards the end of school certain students were chosen to play taps for the whole camp. Joe was one of them. Joe often heard the beautiful sound of that sad, longing bugle. He knew he could never play it that well, so he said so. The sergeant said, "Oh, yes, you can and you will do it! That's an order and you'll do just fine." For heaven's sake, they don't even give you a chance to practice, Joe thought. Okay, again the Army is going to get exactly what they ask for. Joe did not want to dishonor all those that had gone before and done well. After all, the tune represents the sunset of the day and the sunset of life. It was the big goodnight and goodbye for a soldier. Come Joe's time to sound out those beautiful round notes on the bugle, he knew he couldn't do it. He was terrified. The sergeant took Joe into a room and opened a small closet. He ordered Joe to push a button on some electronic equipment. When Joe did, he heard taps being played for the whole camp in beautiful round tones. It was a reel-to-reel tape player! The Army didn't even use a real man for this job! Joe wondered if they had 21 gun salutes on tape too. He thought that when it came to be his time to receive taps they better offer him the real thing. Joe had all that anxiety for nothing! Nice guy, that sergeant.

Graduation time! Joe was really amazed that he had completed training with just an average IQ, especially when the IQ level of his fellow classmates was well above 110. Joe had seen one man make a radio out of stuff he got from a garbage can. Another guy could look at a computer the size of a wall and diagnose and repair it in an instant. Joe was average in almost everyway, including his IQ. He knew he slipped in because the war was going badly and they needed replacements no matter what. Joe graduated with the help of No Doze and the girl next to him rubbing his leg.

There was just one little obstacle that had to be dealt with first. The passing speed for Morse code interception was 18 groups per minute with no more that three errors. A "group" is five letters with each letter having multi-tones. To graduate you had to reach 19 groups per minute. Joe's first try was 18 groups per minute. It took special permission to take the test again, but Joe was allowed to take it one more time, and he scored 18 groups per minute again! The chances of that happening were astronomical, but it happened.

Since it was obvious the effort was there, they offered Joe another job in teletype interception. This job entailed enormous responsibility as many people could either be saved or be killed. This was the procedure: first, upon interception of a hostile signal, sound shots (or bearing shots) were sent out from three separate locations; the beams of sound would all cross at the origin of the enemy's location. The coordinates of enemy location were then given to the Air Force. The Air Force would send high altitude bombers to reduce the area to "level" within a three-mile radius of target.

Joe knew if they threw him out of school it would be off to the swamps of the South or to frigid Alaska. The choice was easy: Joe accepted the job. Now his dreams could come true.

After finally being awarded his new World-Wide Interceptor insignia, Joe was returning to his barracks feeling like a heavy burden had been lifted from his shoulders. The sharply crisp air filled his lungs like a first breath. The previous night there had been an ice storm that had left every individual tree branch coated with sparkling ice. The sound of the branches as the wind passed made a chime-like sound that could enchant one's spirit. The snow was pristine and untrodden, reflecting sunlight like a field of glimmering diamonds. It was such a rare experience that Joe took it as a sign of approval, an award for completing the most difficult task that he had ever embarked upon.

THE MYSTERY OF THE ORIENT

NEXT STOP: THAILAND (previously known as Siam). This was the land of oriental mystery and adventure. It was a country that had not yet been affected by the American culture. In fact, in some parts of the country they had never even seen a white man. After all his trials and tribulations, now it was wish- and dream-fulfillment time. This was really something for a guy who had never been out of his backyard before. Now he was being sent to the exact opposite side of the world. Officially, the war was over, and Thailand—even though it was close to Vietnam—was not supposed to be a dangerous place. Joe figured all would be safe and okay.

En route, Joe had a stop at Travis Air Force Base in California. There, he was to change planes for his first time leaving the United States. All stops after that where going to be strange and exotic places. Joe had several hours to kill and decided to spend them at the nearest watering hole. He didn't like flying so he thought the trip might go better if his senses were numb. He ordered a rum and coke and was flatly refused. Joe asked, "Why in heaven's name would you refuse a soldier a drink before he goes overseas?" The bartender explained that he could not serve anyone under the age of 21 by law. Joe, not wanting to cause a scene, calmly held out his ID proving that he would be 21 in a few days. The bartender told Joe to come back then. Joe said that in a few days he would be in a dangerous part of the world defending this country. The bartender, in an apologetic way, told him that the law was the law and there was nothing he could do about it. Joe left, wondering what manner of a country is this that sends a young man off to a war zone but considers him too young to serve him a drink.

Then an announcement came over the loudspeaker at the airport. "All flights to Thailand are cancelled!" The troop quota for that country had been reached; no more troops were being sent there. Great! Just great!!! Now Joe was stuck in California with no place to go, no orders, and no assignment. Joe thought this would be a good time to leave the Army. They would never even know he was gone. Just then an MP (military police) noticed Joe's nametag. He told Joe they were looking for him, and he was to get on the plane right away. Amazed, Joe suspected that Colonel Green had something to do with it; only an order from the highest level could make this possible. Okay, the show was back on the road again.

Instead of flying straight across the ocean, the pilot went by way of Alaska. While flying over Alaska, Joe saw the scariest, most desolate expanse of mountains. There were thousands of miles of shadowy, dark, snow-covered mountains with howling winds. Joe knew if the plane went down in that part of the world, they would never be found, even with a transponder signal. The pilot made an announcement that they were headed into rough weather and needed to land in Fairbanks to refuel. It was nighttime when the plane pulled up to a cinderblock box structure. There was snow in the air, on the ground, everywhere. A man came out wearing a coat that covered even his face. He refueled the plane and off it went again. After seeing the sun come up and go down a couple of times, they were still flying. Joe had developed a case of claustrophobia from the cattle truck incident. By now, Joe was crawling out of his skin and didn't care anymore if the plane went down just so he could get off. Finally, the plane landed in the Philippines at Clark Air Force Base. When he got off, he could feel the scorching heat of the sun. All he wanted was a shower and a cold beer or both at the same time. This was an overnight stop and Joe would have both.

After checking into a hotel, a native asked Joe if there was anything he wanted. Joe told the man to please send one beer at a time to his room until there was no answer at the door. After a few beer deliveries were made, the young man bringing the beer asked Joe if he wanted a woman. Joe asked, "You mean a real woman?" He then said "Okay, but she must be pretty." A few minutes later a woman knocked on the door. She was pretty all right—pretty damn ugly. Joe sent her back. Hours went by and so did the beers; one after another they were brought to the room as instructed until Joe's eyes got a little blurry. Then another woman showed up at the door. Joe could not tell if she was good looking or not; all he could see now was a blurry woman's face. But that was okay, so he let her in. She said that the price of "paradise" was 25 pesos. Okay, what the hell is a peso? Being too drunk to care about the exchange rate, Joe just reached into his pocket and pulled out 25 dollars and handed it to her. The girl looked like she had never seen that much money in one place before. As he later discovered, 25 pesos was about 5 dollars. So handing this woman 25 dollars was five times more than she expected. In any case, no sleep was the order of the night.

When the sun finally came up the next day, Joe thought he would take a break. Just a quick nap was all that was needed. Six hours went by and Joe woke up to find the plane was long gone. Great, just great! Now he was stuck in an island country on the other side of the world. Making arrangements for a new flight was not difficult but it meant he would be AWOL. Joe really didn't care, though, because he felt great. He would just tell the commanding officer some "bull" story about missing the plane.

Since this whole affair meant an overnight stay, Joe went looking for the nightlife. The Philippines was a really "party animal" kind of place. The clubs were rocking right up until curfew and so did Joe. Later on, Joe found a bunk at the barracks on base to crash in. No sooner did he lie down than someone brought a woman into the barracks to save a few bucks on a hotel room. Those old Army cots sure have noisy springs. Since it wasn't Joe who was making the noise, he got up and packed; the plane was leaving in a few hours anyway.

The next plane out of the Philippines was a real military looking thing. It was a C-130 cargo plane; the entire back end of it opened up to receive cargo. Joe was impressed by its size. It had no windows and the only view was of the cargo. When it took off, the engines sent a thunderous roar that vibrated the plane like the devil was walking past right outside. After a quick moment of fear, they were airborne and all was well. Joe struck up a conversation with the guy next to him. After talking awhile, he discovered that this guy lived on the next street over behind Joe's house. How strange it was to meet your neighbor while traveling to the other side of the world.

The pilot announced that the plane was now flying over Vietnam. The next and last stop was Thailand. As the dream got closer, the reality became clearer: Thailand—a completely primitive and basically unknown land of strange customs, a place where a young man could explore and have the adventure of his life. Just one more short plane hop and the yearning to meet the people on the other side of the world would be realized. The farthest horizon would be breached for a guy who once couldn't find his way out of Levittown, USA. Joe thought it was a good thing to have avoided the war and still have his dream come true.

As the final destination was approaching, Joe's imagination started to go wild. He wondered if this experience would live up to his expectations or would it be just another shocking disappointment. Suddenly the plane took a steep dive as though the pilot was doing some kind of evasive maneuver. Joe felt sick as his insides came up against his throat. Then the plane leveled out just before touching down. When the wheels bumped against the ground, Joe knew he was there, "there" being an alien world that was as far away from home as he could get. Just then it occurred to him that once you've been to the other side of the world it would not be possible to ever get lost again. That was okay with Joe because getting lost was never his favorite thing anyway.

As the plane taxied to a stop, Joe could still not see anything. Then the entire tail of the plane started to open, revealing a hazy, very bright landscape with a thick tree line in the background. This was his first look at his new world and his new home. So far it looked like a regular military airbase. There were certain exceptions, like the phantom aircraft fighters surrounded by bunkers. There were many machine gun nests surrounded by sand bags. Joe and several other guys were herded into a van with caged windows. The drive to the Army post was very revealing. Joe's nose was glued to the window of the van the whole time. Joe saw women walking down the street in robes and carrying large bundles on their heads. The sounds and smells were all so different, unique, and unexpected that Joe was left in complete awe.

Joe was delivered to a very small but well-manicured communications center in the middle of the jungle. There were only about 1,000 men on this post. The whole place looked like a Little America. There was a movie theater, a bowling alley, a PX; it was a real home away from home. When Joe got out of the van, he ran into Bill, a buddy from Fort Devens. Bill didn't look the same though; he was riding a bicycle and had golden skin from the sun. They made arrangements to get together later after Joe checked in. The truth of the matter was that Joe was looking for the first open gate that went off base. All he wanted to do was see and meet these people of this new land, to fulfill the dreams and imaginings he had since childhood. Just to step foot onto that foreign world was tantamount to visiting another planet. This event would escalate Joe's status to that of adventurer and explorer all at the same time. This was a country that had been in existence long before America had ever even been discovered.

It was Joe's 21st birthday and he was going to celebrate with new adventure and exciting discovery. It was a long way to the main gate and he made a dash for it. On the way there, his stomach started to make funny gurgling noises. It was probably the food he ate in the Philippines; after all, his stomach wasn't used to the bacteria on this side of the world. It felt as though he had to pass gas, and why not, there was no one around to offend. But it wasn't gas; just then and in a split second his pants filled up to his knees with shit. Great, just great! His first act as a grown man was to shit in his pants! Standing right there with the main gate in sight, Joe could see the people of this land off in the distance, but he surely was in no condition to meet them. He realized the dawn of adventure would have to wait just a while longer, as this problem required immediate attention. This was not a defeat, though; this was just a temporary delay, an invasion rescheduled. He looked like a man doing the space walk back to the barracks. Heading straight for the shower he dropped his uniform and cleaned himself. The houseboy asked what to do with the soiled uniform; Joe said, "Burn it!"

Upon donning a new uniform, a second assault was put into motion. When you are this close to a lifetime dream you just don't let a little personal setback stop you. The guards at the main gate weren't stopping anyone from leaving the post. So Joe walked right on through, but still felt quite surprised that no act of man or nature was stopping him. There it was, right in front of him: the village. This was a row of shack-like buildings that looked very much like they were straight out of the old Wild West. His eyes and ears filled with the sights and sounds that were all around him. Oh, my God! There was poverty everywhere he looked! Was this the mystery of the Far East? This place was even more poverty stricken than his early years in Texas!

For the first three days Joe could not close his mouth for the shock of it. He could not believe that he would have to spend a year of his life in this rundown garbage heap. All his life Joe had seen newsreels of the war in Vietnam and had had glimpses of the grass hut villages. It never occurred to him that Thailand would be just like that. It seemed to Joe as though he was in the middle of one of those newsreels now.

It was really odd when Joe met his friends, the clean-cut American boys he had trained with at Fort Devens. They had arrived in Thailand months before Joe did. They were all so very different now. Their skin was yellow from the sun and the change of diet. They were speaking fluently in the Thai language. They all lived in bungalows and had "t-locks," which meant girlfriends. Each one had found a woman that perfectly fit their personalities. They sat cross-legged on the floor and ate with chopsticks, and even wore native clothing. In other words, they were not recognizable by any stretch of the imagination. Joe calculated that all these changes took just months to occur. Joe didn't know how these changes could happen so fast. As hard as it was for Joe to understand and believe, he knew that somehow in just months he would have to become the same as his friends just to survive. He would survive by paying attention to those that went before him and not assume that anything would be the same as he had ever known.

After the major shock of the poverty was over, it was time to get settled in. The first day on the job was very interesting. This was a large, windowless bunker-like building surrounded by two eight-foot electrified chain link fences. On each corner was a guard tower and it was patrolled 24 hours a day by guards with attack dogs. It took a security badge, guard check, and combination to a security lock just to get in the front door.

Joe discovered very fast that, in the real world of high-speed enemy communications, what he was taught in school did not apply in the field. For example, it was now necessary to learn the names of every city in China. You had to learn everything from Xingloi to Myping. Another sorely needed skill was the ability to identify unknown signals. Joe did not exactly excel in either of these areas. All ineptitude could be forgiven if you had another particular or invaluable skill. Like being able to open and repair a large computer. This too was another skill Joe was not the slightest bit familiar with. This lack of experience, knowledge and ability made Joe about as useful as tits on a hog. So they assigned Joe to the weather intercept station. Again, he felt humbled into obscurity because it surely would be hard to excel from that position.

Joe knew that weather is important and has affected the course of history in the past, but this was not the contribution he had envisioned himself making. He wanted to make a noteworthy contribution, something that would deserve a little recognition. Joe decided that he would learn everything he could about the high-priority signals. So during his breaks he would use his equipment to search for, identify, and try to capture one of those signals, like the one named "Ark." This signal was at the top of the most-wanted list, and represented a leap in progress for the enemy.

The Ark didn't stay on air for longer than ten seconds and could come up on any frequency at any time of the day. The Ark was noteworthy because it could transmit a library's worth of information in that ten-second period. This information was critical to the security of the United States. That meant the interceptor would have less than ten seconds to identify the signal, tune and calibrate his equipment, call for bearing shots, and record the signal. It took Joe damn near ten seconds just to identify a signal.

His work days were eight-hour shifts of boring weather intercept and shooting in the dark during breaks. Either way, it was an endless flow of static, beeping sounds, and oriental chatter that would not even allow for a private thought. That wasn't the only thing to contend with either. Some of the guys had gone a little "Asiatic." They would put black ink on your headsets or stick the perforated end of the computer paper down the back of your pants and set fire to it. They would do things like hand you a beautifully wrapped present; inside would be the shit they just took. There was this book that had the complete Chinese language in it and every dialect too. It weighed about 30 pounds and was rather large. They would order you to take it to the other side of camp to show to some sergeant. The sergeant would open the book and pretend to read some and then would send you somewhere else, and so on. Joe's favorite one was the ticker tape message that came out of the urgent response computer. They had a prefabricated message that read the United States was being attacked with nuclear weapons and several cities were burning. They would let the new guy get the message and run around in a panic, screaming "It's war! It's war!"

Joe had found that life was easier if he had something to look forward to. All day at work he would imagine a cold beer waiting for him after work. He could see the golden brew with a nice head of foam on top. It would be served in a frosty mug and when it went down it would burn and chill his throat at the same time. This beer would cool him down on a hot day while quenching his thirst. Right after work, Joe would grab his bicycle and make a mad dash, heading right for that beer. Then there it was, just as he imagined it. The sun was shining through it, giving it a golden yellow glow, with the white foam head slightly dripping over the side. It was served in a frosty mug too, just like he imagined it.

On this particular day, as he began to sip on this heavenly brew, a woman approached him with an offer to go upstairs. Joe explained that he was there just for the beer and had no interest in anything but that. Joe returned to concentrating on his beer. He was amazed that his imagination didn't let him down. In fact, this beer was even better than he expected. Just then another woman approached with the same offer. Joe again explained how he didn't wish to offend, but the beer was all he wanted. When the brew was half finished, a third woman approached. When Joe looked up to relay the same message again, he saw one hell of a beautiful woman. She was half French and half Thai. Her look was alluring and exotic. Her breasts were full and firm. She asked Joe if he wanted to go upstairs. Without hesitation, he betrayed his beer fantasies and followed her up the stairs. She took off her blouse and Joe was awestruck: her breasts defied gravity. She then unbuttoned the top of her jeans and lay back onto the bed. Joe sat on the side of the bed and reached out and placed his hand on her breast. She made a very seductive moan. When he climbed on top of her, she felt like she was more of a woman than he was a man. As he began to make love, she signaled him to stop. Joe thought, "Great, just great! Another control freak!" Then she took over the entire process and, in doing so, she made Joe have an orgasm before he was even ready. He didn't even know that was possible. He did know he had been unexpectedly and completely conquered. He would have married this woman for the sex alone.

When all was said and done, Joe wanted to express how grateful he was for an experience he would never forget. He couldn't speak the language, so he kneeled down before her; he took her hand and kissed it gently as though she was a princess and he was her knight. He knew right then he would never again meet another woman that would make him feel that way again. She was the illusive fantasy of every man's secret passion and desires realized. Joe felt as though she had just set him free from the search for what he was looking for in a woman. Now he knew this was the once-in-a-lifetime experience that he would carry with him forever. He wondered if maybe she was the true mystery of the orient. He was grateful to learn what the best really was. The experience was so incredible he didn't desire another woman for weeks. But since she was a working woman, this meant she would not be suitable for a meaningful or a long-term relationship. Man! So close but so far! Joe thought that maybe what every man really wants is a beautiful woman, schooled in the art of sexual pleasure, and devoted to just him alone. Now, that wouldn't be asking for too much, would it?

After work, Joe took time to find his place in this new world. Although the Army provided proper accommodations, living with the villagers was preferred. This was the best way to learn the customs, culture, attitudes, and beliefs of these strange-looking and strange-sounding people. Joe got together with a couple of friends and shared rent on a bungalow on the outskirts of the village. It was a beautiful house with three bedrooms, two baths, a patio, a balcony, and even a carport— imagine the place having a carport when there were no cars. All the windows had wooden shutters and the floors were made of marble; there was a teakwood staircase leading to the upstairs bedrooms. The view was unobstructed over the virgin green rice fields clear to the mountains lined with purple, blue and gold hues. The front of the house had colored stones embedded in the wall that made the scene of a palm tree and the setting sun. This place even had a tall white picket fence around it. Best of all, it had a tin roof; the rain falling on a tin roof would carry Joe away to a timeless sleep.

On his first morning of awakening in his new home, Joe went in search of coffee. A fire was started in a large thick ceramic pot, the water was boiling, and all was going well. Joe decided to throw open the wooden shutters and breathe the unpolluted air. When he opened the window, Joe's eyes were filled with an image that his brain registered as not real. There was a large hairy face with horns, pointed ears, big black eyes with long black eyelashes, and a long snout filling the entire window frame. Joe's first thought was that he was face to face with the devil himself. His lungs gasped for air as he grabbed his chest and fell backwards across the kitchen. The shock of the matter was that this apparition was truly alive. This wasn't an illusion, a mirage, or a hallucination. This thing had eyes that moved and it had a mouth that was chewing on something. This demonic looking thing was truly alive! As fast as Joe's eyes were sending messages to his brain, his brain only responded with "not real." But this hideous looking creature did not disappear in a puff of smoke; it stayed. Slowly he realized what it was. To this very day Joe is still amazed at how much a water buffalo looks just like the devil! He wonders how many years of his life were scared right out of him because of this event.

As the truth became known, Joe found out that they use water buffalo to chew up the grass around the house. He thought about his lawnmower back home and how smart it was to use animals to do this job.

Joe still didn't have a woman to live with like the other guys. It was suggested that Joe see the papa-san of the village for advice. The papa-san was the father image for the village. His wisdom was supposed to be beyond that of the common man. All Joe saw was an old oriental guy. But since he had nothing to lose, Joe decided to give it a shot. He told the wise man that he wanted an intelligent woman with a good sense of humor. She could not be too plain or too pretty. Joe saw the papa-san's eyes go into a distant stare as though he were surveying the possibilities. Then he smiled and said, "I know the one of which you speak." He said he would arrange the meeting, and if Joe were deemed suitable, he would be approved for the match. Joe had always been the one who did the approving; now he was made to feel like some native girl was going to pass judgment on him.

The day of the meeting Joe was there on time and standing tall. His hopes were high, as this would complete another difficult adjustment. Several women came in; Joe was not sure which one was intended for him. They kind of all looked the same: olive skin color, long black hair. None of them spoke English so an interpreter was used. After introductions were made, Joe realized that it was the girl who sat in the middle. She was young, timid and average looking. The questions went like this: can you provide food, shelter, and above all be kind to this woman? Joe responded yes. Then a lot of negative-sounding oriental chatter took place among them.

It didn't look like all was going well, so Joe decided to take matters into his own hands. He requested to speak to the woman alone. Joe went outside with her and wasn't sure what he was going to say. After all they didn't even speak the same language. Joe thought that if she could hear the sad longing tones in his voice, they might transcend mere language barriers. They were sitting on the steps together and Joe said, "I know you don't understand me, but I have never been so alone in my whole life. I promise to be good to you and make you happy." The tones in his voice and the sound of his sincerity made the difference. She accepted him and told the others of her decision. They left hand in hand, on their way to consummate their union.

That night she prepared the sleeping area at her house by lighting candles and coils that would keep the mosquitoes away. Just before going to sleep, all hell broke loose. There were two packs of wild dogs that had a border dispute under the house. All the houses were built high off the ground to provide for the rainy season. These dogs weren't playing either. It was a matter of life or death to them, and that is the way they fought each other, too. The continuing sounds of the ferocious battle went on. The dogs were growling and screaming as they tore each other apart. That wasn't all either: that little coil was not keeping the blood-sucking mosquitoes away. After two hours of this Joe couldn't stand it anymore. He told the girl he had to go back to his bungalow to get some sleep and would be back the next day. Since she didn't understand a word of what he said, she thought Joe was leaving her, but he was calm and caring and tried hard to explain. Oh, by the way, her name was Yome Moon, and so far she was just the woman the papa-san had promised. She was pretty but not too pretty, that's all Joe knew for now. Joe returned the next day to take his new woman home to his own house.

No matter where you live or how, eventually life takes on some kind of routine. Joe was finding he was learning something new everyday. So that is what turned out to be the routine. On the job and at home, every action had a new flavor and a twist of new meaning. Joe did have one thing going for him: he was relentless in his pursuit to make a noteworthy contribution, mainly because while growing up all he ever wanted to be was a soldier. It's logical to think that if you set your goals to be reasonably obtainable, you will obtain them.

This day was going to be another eight hours of surrendering his mind to the onslaught of sounds he would intercept. Until he heard it—it was a signal like no other. It was a combination of warbles, sirens, blips and chirps. It was the Ark! Joe was somewhat taken back by surprise. He had heard the description of the signal before by other guys, and this was a dead-on match. He jumped to his feet and started the tape recorder and that's all he had time for. The signal was gone! Joe had spent too much time listening to it, and failed to tune his receiver properly or even to get bearing shots. He did manage to get about three seconds of Ark recorded, but that wasn't enough to claim capture. That was enough for the others to determine it was the Ark, but nothing else was learned like the location or the coded information. Joe felt as though he had just won the lottery and the winning ticket was destroyed. He made a solemn vow to himself: if the Ark ever returned he would be ready. He kept all of his equipment tuned and calibrated. He contacted every station throughout the Far East and established not a minute-man method but a second-man method of intercept so that, with the push of one button, Joe could call three different stations in three different countries in one second. He even had his tape recorder stripped down to a one-button operation. He was ready now, and if Ark ever made so much as a blip again, Joe would be on it like white on rice.

Another day on his job, Joe was notified that a general was coming for inspection. The sergeant didn't want Joe around because Joe was new and inexperienced. The sergeant didn't want the general asking Joe any questions, so he handed Joe a pair of scissors and ordered him to go outside and cut the grass. This pissed Joe off to no extent; he said to himself, "If they want me to cut the grass, then that's what I'll do." Joe went outside and positioned himself where he knew the general would have to pass by. Joe got down on the ground and picked out one blade of grass that was now slated for a hair cut. He cut the first blade of grass to form a point at the top. Then he went on to the next one, making a rounded design this time. This ordeal was turning out to be a rather pleasant break from the constant flow of noise that assaulted Joe's ears and mind inside the operations building. Then, just as predicted, the general passed by. The general couldn't help but notice Joe lying on his stomach with a pair of scissors cutting one blade of grass at a time. The general seemed somewhat curious about what was going on and stopped to talk to Joe. When he was questioned, Joe explained he was following orders. The general told Joe to resume his regular duties. Joe never had to cut the grass again.

On his way home that day, Joe turned a corner at the edge of town. He then found himself in the middle of and completely surrounded by a pack of wild dogs. These wild dogs were very lean and had the mange really bad. Joe saw the leader of the pack begin to signal the others, and they all stood up. These dogs would surround their prey and attack one at a time from behind, until the prey would fall to the ground; then they all would move in for the kill. Joe bent down slowly and picked up a big stick. The fight was on; as they attacked, Joe started to fight like he was a wild dog himself. He swung that stick hard and hit one dog in the head. Another one jumped him from behind and Joe beat him off. Joe was terrified and couldn't figure a way out. Then he thought if he could open a hole in the circle, he might be able to break free and make a run for it. So that is what he did: instead of waiting for them to attack, Joe decided to start an attack of his own. He noticed a weak link in the circle and pounced on it. Joe started swinging that stick and growling louder than the dogs. Joe didn't recognize this part of himself; it was akin to being a caveman.

By now all civilized behavior was gone; Joe had reverted to the vicious animal instincts that exist within us all. As Joe increased his efforts so did the dogs; they were coming at him two and three at a time now. The dogs attacked with striking bites to Joe's legs to bring him down. Joe kicked and swung that stick making several very successful hits, causing some of the dogs to think twice about moving in. When the dogs hesitated, Joe took the strategic advantage and broke a hole in the circle; he then ran through the break and didn't take a second to look back. He was glad when he made it home. Funny how a lazy walk home turned into a lesson in survival.

Joe was trying to get used to having Yome around. She didn't look or sound happy. One night, when Joe asked why, she communicated through a friend that she was responsible for supporting her parents and needed some money for them. Joe's reply was, "I'm not sleeping with them." He told Yome that she alone was his responsibility and not her parents, and that half his income was going home to his own family for support. This caused a long stretch of arguments and general discontentment. Joe figured he had made a mistake and was considering ending the newly formed relationship. Just then several loud explosions came from the direction of the camp. There were flashes of light and what sounded like gunfire. Bill, Joe's roommate, came running down the stairs and asked Joe what they should do. Joe said that since they weren't given weapons, the Army couldn't expect them to fight. The choices were to immediately leave and head south through the jungle or to get a closer evaluation of the situation.

Maybe now is a good time to clarify a few things about the rules of war. Upon arrival to the country, all soldiers were informed that carrying a weapon was not authorized by the Geneva Convention—something about not being in an identified combat zone. They were also informed that if the enemy attacked the camp, it would take the enemy just 30 minutes to break through the defenses but it would take the weapons room sergeant 45 minutes to hand out the weapons. So the instructions were to run into the jungle and head south. That was not all either: several hundred miles south was an American air base. On this base was aircraft designated to destroy everything should the base be overrun, whether Americans were on it or not. The idea behind all this was to not let classified information fall into enemy hands. It also gave credence to the word "expendable." Most people didn't know this, but even though the war was technically over for the United States, it appeared as though someone forgot to tell the enemy. There were about a dozen factions that would love to kill the American invaders. Yet Joe was walking around as though he were on a Far East vacation.

The decision Bill and Joe made was to get a closer evaluation. Now Joe's mind was filled with "real war" and how do you fight a war without a gun? Were all his friends being slaughtered because they were unarmed also? One mistake or hesitation and Joe would lose the "being alive" that he loved so much. After all, he was a coward. They would know what to do after getting a closer look. Bill and Joe were doing a low crawl as they neared the camp. The sounds were getting louder and there were bright bursts of light. The heroes were beginning to have second thoughts about their ill-advised undertaking, when they discovered the cause for the threatening commotion. It was a transformer that was exploding! It was a fucking electrical transformer!!! Joe knew he should be thanking God that this was not a real emergency. But he also knew that that fucking transformer took years off his life, and now part of him would never really be at rest again. Mainly because Joe knew the real war would eventually find him, too. He also knew better men than him had already been killed.

This became more of a reality on another occasion when Joe and Yome were walking through the heart of downtown Udorn. There was a large gathering and a man was standing on a truck using a megaphone, talking a mile a minute. Joe thought it was nice that all these people seemed to agree on something. Yome told him it was a "Kill the Americans" rally. If Joe had been in his uniform they would have decorated one of their street lights with him. Since they thought he was a European they didn't pay much attention.

There was another time when Joe underestimated the circumstances. He was in the process of cheating on his t-lock in the local brothel when his fellow soldiers stormed through the door with an urgent message. The village three miles up the road had been hit by the communists and the leaders of that village were all shot dead. Thailand had only one road running from north to south, making this village the next stop on the road. The camp was on high alert. As Joe ran through the bar pulling up his pants, he couldn't help but think how he had sworn that this would never happen to him: the enemy would never catch him with his pants down—and yet they did. When it turned out that the enemy had decided to turn around and go home, Joe and a couple of the guys set out to check the scene of this war crime.

By the time they entered the village most of the mess had been cleaned up and the bodies removed, but there was still blood everywhere. The hair stood up on Joe's arms like there was an electrical charge in the air. His senses went on high alert when he smelled the sickening sweet syrup of human death; it was thick in the air. This was the smell of life given up too soon and unwillingly. This was the smell of the last essence of sweet souls that hadn't completely left yet.

Suddenly, he had the acute knowing that eyes were on him now, and he couldn't see from where. The feeling was so real that Joe did not question it and felt compelled to act on it by making a hasty withdrawal. Not because he was a coward (which he was) or because he didn't have a gun (which he didn't), but because he could feel the crosshairs of a gun on him. He signaled the other guys to do the same. You do not fight a war without a gun, that is all there is to it. Luckily, Joe and the others made it back safely.

The saga continued back at the home front, as Joe and Yome continued arguing over support for her parents. Joe decided to give Yome to his friend Bill, as it was the custom that when a man became dissatisfied with his woman he could give her up to another man. Bill questioned Joe, making sure that he was serious about it. The deal was done and done, and Bill took Yome to his room. Joe was leaving the house just to make sure that he wouldn't have time to change his mind. But on his way out he heard hysterical crying coming from Bill's room. You see, Yome had fallen in love with Joe. For her, it was a fate worse than death to be given up by the man she loved to a man she didn't love. It also meant that she had failed her only and original purpose in life: to serve her man. This failure was a terrible disgrace among her people.

Yome's crying was that of a soul trapped in hell. Joe couldn't take it anymore; he kicked open the door and apologized to Bill, saying that he just couldn't go through with it. Joe then reclaimed his woman. As he dried her tears, Joe assured her everything was okay. He even asked how much her family needed for support. When she responded $15 dollars a month, Joe told her he had said no before because he thought she was talking about hundreds of dollars. Of course they can have $15 dollars a month. Joe and Yome became somewhat famously happy together after that. Life was beautiful, sunny, timeless, and full of laughter.

The next real-life experience happened on a beautiful sunny day. Joe was walking home to the woman he was happy with. He was thinking about how they would have a campfire on the front lawn and have dinner under the night sky; they would stare at the stars while in each other's arms. At that moment a shot rang out! Joe knew he was the target instantly. When a gun is fired directly at you, it will sound much louder. Joe could hear the bullet coming like a switch cutting through the air. He didn't know which way to move so he stood perfectly still. The bullet touched Joe's right ear as it passed and popped his eardrum as it sucked all the air out of his ear. Joe grabbed his head as though he had been shot and fell lifeless to the ground. That was his only and entire plan for survival: playing dead just like he learned from the movies he saw as a kid, just like the war games he played as a boy. This time it was for real and Joe was nothing but scared.

All options were very open now and mostly depended on his attacker. If this sniper decided to check his prey, then Joe would have to do a really good act as a dead man. Joe remained perfectly still in the middle of the road. He was greatly relieved when he heard the sound of footsteps running away thru the leaves in the distance. Joe still waited for a while before crawling the rest of the way home. For about 24 hours after the incident, he could not hear out of his right ear. Joe had realized a long time before that the enemy could kill him at any time, at their own convenience, but he couldn't understand why they would want to kill him when he was just doing his job and minding his own business. Then he remembered he was a soldier in a danger zone, something he would not forget again.

So basically that's the way life was going; Joe was getting all the excitement and adventure he had always wanted and needed. He learned that adventure is anything that makes your heart go from 0-100 instantaneously. Like when Joe reached in around the doorway to turn on a light and he put his hand on something that was coarse and bumpy. Not being able to identify what it was, he gave it a squeeze. When the leather-like thing moved, Joe's heart hit 100: it was one of the lizards they call geckos! He had heard about these lizards in Thailand that are about a foot long, and they look and feel like a small alligator. These lizards are considered lucky because they eat their weight in mosquitoes. Joe let out a guttural groan and didn't wait around for the creature's reaction.

Joe would suffer trauma after trauma. For instance, the people in Thailand use wooden glasses for drinking. Joe got a glass of water from the refrigerator. As he was drinking the water he felt something bumping up against his upper lip. Upon looking in the glass he saw a huge floating leach. His stomach twisted and part of his mind broke from the shear grossness.

Another time, at Joe's house during a beer party, Yome got curious about the taste of beer. Joe saw this as an opportunity to have some fun. He convinced her that beer has to be drunk quickly. She took the beer and drank it down as fast as she could. Joe had never seen an oriental girl turn green before, but she did, and immediately passed out. Joe put her to bed and put a glass of water by her bedside. He then returned to the party. Hours later when going to bed, Joe laughed when he saw Yome was in the same position as when he left her. Joe picked up the glass of water and drank it half down before he realized something was wrong. Joe looked in the wooden glass, and the smell and taste of puke hit him at the same time. Yome had drunk the water and had thrown up in the glass. He grabbed a beam on the wall and held on tight until the worst had passed.

Joe learned his lesson after that: he looked in his boots in the morning, checked all light switches before touching, looked in the glass before drinking, and so on. He didn't want any more surprises.

Not all was distasteful, though. Joe and Yome would laugh themselves to sleep almost every night. Then they would listen to taps being played from camp. Joe would never let Yome talk while taps was playing, because it made Joe feel like the sound of the bugle was being played for him. Every once in a while it was pretty funny to pull something over Yome. She was a real smart girl; she learned the English language in three months. But every once in a while Joe would find a weak spot. Like the time Joe convinced Yome that men have periods just like women do. Or another time while they were both looking at the moon, Joe asked, "What is that?" Yome asked, "You mean the moon?" Joe said, "Is that what that is?" He then told her that the moon does not appear over the United States and that he had never seen it before, and she believed him. Joe also had a lot of fun when he convinced her it was a sign of respect for her to call him "master" and in return he would call her "slave." It was days before she caught on to him for that. She chased him around the house with a big stick for that one.

Work was still going on and Joe kept trying to find the Ark signal again. Every once in a while he would test the system for readiness, always making improvements where time was concerned. There was one sergeant that really didn't care for Joe. This sergeant would push Joe to the edge on every conversation. This sergeant (let's call him Sgt. Butthead) really got off on his authority over another human being. On the next to the last conversation they had, Sgt. Butthead succeeded in pissing Joe off to the max. Joe had had enough and was willing to give up his military career rather than suffer one more minute of this relentless pig.

Sgt. Butthead gave Joe an order to pick something up at his feet. Joe never thought he could abandon the oath he took to God and country to follow the orders of his superiors, right or wrong. Putting aside all the Army training and discipline for years embedded into his soul—that above all, you follow orders—Joe looked at Sgt. Butthead and said, "Fuck you!" Sgt. Butthead's eyes opened wide and he asked Joe in a concerned voice, "What did you say?" So Joe repeated himself, adding some flavor this time, "Fuck you, you arrogant asshole." Sgt. Butthead said, "I've got you now!" and left. Joe knew he had done the unforgivable, and he figured the price of this burden would be heavy. He told himself he would take it like a man. Not much time passed before Joe was summoned by the Top Sergeant. The Top Sergeant looked like Joe's father; in many ways, Joe would have loved to have him as his father, too. Top asked Joe, "Do you realize what you have done?" Joe said, "Yes, sir, but I believe I was pushed into it." Joe promised it would never happen again. Top said he would take care of it, and the matter was closed.

When Joe returned to his post, he heard the Ark. He started pushing buttons as he had practiced for weeks, but he got back too late and missed too much of the signal to be useful. "Bitch, bitch, bitch!!!" he yelled. Banging the table with his fist, he swore by all his life's blood, "I will capture Ark! I will capture Ark! So help me God, if it's the last thing I do, I will capture Ark!"

Joe could clearly see and understand by now that, no matter what, there was always going to be a constant flow of heart-stopping and terrifying experiences. Joe was out cold asleep during the worst electrical storm that ever was. He slept so soundly because that was the effect that rain falling on a tin roof had on him. The shutters had broken open and rain was pouring in all over the floor and bed, but Joe slept on. Yome was upset that Joe wouldn't get up during this monsoon, so she kicked him—she had a habit of giving Joe a kick in bed when she was angry. That always worked. Joe asked, "What???" Just then they both heard ghost-like wailing sounds. The sounds were coming from within the house, too. Joe asked Yome, "Do you hear that?" She said "Yes, and I'm afraid, too. Go and see what it is." Joe told her "You go check it out; I'll be right behind you." She kicked him again, so he reluctantly went. Joe figured trouble was finding him enough without him looking for it. Joe's curiosity was peaked, though, because these eerie wailing and moaning sounds were not going away.

As Joe went again to face the unknown completely unarmed he was thinking, "Goddamn shit; I never have a goddamn gun when I need one! The whole friggin' goddamn Army has guns; you think they could spare one for me!" He was also thinking this is a lot to ask of a coward. Joe followed the sounds downstairs; they were coming from just the other side of the door to the carport. The sounds were real and the "hell of Joe's fear" was real too. It was a dark and thunderous night as again he faced that part of himself that caused his body to become paralyzed and unable to breathe. He would not live in fear of the unknown like this; he would not be forced to face the shame of his own cowardice again. Whatever this wailing, moaning, sad-sounding thing was, it pissed Joe right the hell off, not only for making him afraid but also for disturbing his sleep, which he sorely needed. The crying was still going strong when Joe took the doorknob in his hand. His final thought was, "Whatever it is out there should be afraid now, 'cause I'm the meanest son-of-a-bitch in this valley." With that he swung the door open and gave a blood-curdling scream.

Be damned if the carport wasn't loaded with women and children, all crowded together, some of them crying with fear of the storm, some of them crying with fear of Joe over his gut wrenching attack scream. Joe called for Yome to talk to them and find out what the hell was going on. They said they were hiding in Joe's house from the storm because Joe and

Yome lived in the only secure house in the whole village. The children were crying for fear of the lightning and thunder. Joe surveyed the situation and couldn't believe this pitiful sight. He invited them all in and provided food and blankets; he played with the children, making fun of the storm, causing them to laugh and lose their fear. Joe thought that was a pretty damn brave thing he did—opening that door in the dark in a thunderstorm, completely unarmed. He promised himself never to do anything like that again, as he wondered how many years had been scared out of his life this time.

When everyone's needs were met, Joe decided to go out into the storm, just to feel its intensity. As he was standing there in the pelting rain, the electricity in the air made the hair on his arms stand straight up. Suddenly, a bolt of lightning exploded across the sky and divided itself into five separate strikes, hitting the ground on the horizon. Joe was fascinated by the beauty and energy of the storm, and how the five streaks of lightning looked just like a hand. In fact, it looked like a giant hand coming down and touching the ground. In Joe's mind he felt as though he had just seen the hand of God. He then realized that he wasn't afraid of lightning anymore, and he wasn't afraid of dying from it either. Joe now understood how his father could sit out on the porch during that thunderstorm in Texas; how he could be cool as a cucumber and laugh in the face of fear. Joe now understood how a man could stand in the midst of terrifying lightning and thunder and not be afraid to die. He understood "what manner of man this was" because now Joe was that man. Now he was standing there as an eternal figure amongst the unleashing powers of heaven. He was feeling pretty good about it, too; he knew he was still a coward, but maybe there was a time and a place for everything, and that was okay by him.

When Joe reported to work the next day he was assigned to hand deliver a confidential pouch to the air base 20 miles up the road. The Army would provide transport to and from the base. After the mission was accomplished, transportation home was delayed. So Joe decided to take a "baht bus," so named because it cost a *baht*, or a nickel, to ride. This was a pick-up truck kind of taxi: you ride in the back on a wooden bench. The truck was loaded with Thai nationals and Joe was the only American. The 20-mile stretch between these two locations was nothing but jungle. This was a world completely untouched by time. You could encounter anything from a Bengal tiger to a spitting cobra. Again Joe was enjoying the scenery, the natural beauty of this place, which was not only tropical, but in many ways it was like how the world probably began. Suddenly, Joe saw something unusual off in the distance. It looked like a thin black line moving across the road, way ahead of the truck. As the truck approached this unidentified obstruction, Joe could see more details: they were men dressed in black. There were about 50 of them, all wearing what looked like black pajamas. Joe had seen the Buddhist monks before, but they always wore orange robes. Joe didn't understand why the people on the truck seemed to become agitated and kept signaling him for something. Joe thought that it might be an oriental funeral he was watching, with people wearing black like in the States. Joe thought this would be something interesting to observe and learn about.

As the truck got closer and closer, Joe could see more details. All those men were heavily armed. They had knives, grenades, and bullets, even two machine guns clamped together for double killing power. Joe then thought maybe this was a gang-style revenge thing, like they do in New York. These men were a bit too heavily armed for that, though. The people in the truck were pulling at Joe's arm and pointing to under the seat. Then it hit him like a bolt out of the blue! Just the day before Joe had had a training class on enemy identification. He remembered that it was the enemy that walks through the jungle in black pajamas, wearing sandals, usually heavily armed. The people on the truck weren't crazy either;

they were trying to tell Joe where to hide. Without hesitation, Joe took up a position under the seat; they hid him with their feet and whatever bundles they carried.

The enemy was now stopping the truck for a quick inspection. The side of the truck had boards that had small spaces between them, and the whole back end of the truck was open; one quick peek would have revealed Joe in all his unarmed glory. This was the real-life enemy, the enemy that loves to kill Americans like Joe. Joe was imagining being turned into a pile of waste in these foreign rice fields.

One of the men was starting to come around to the back of the truck to look in. The people on the truck started talking to the soldier over the side of the truck and were able to hold the man in place. Another soldier was standing directly on the other side of the wall from Joe. Joe could smell his black sweaty clothes through the boards of the truck and was even close enough to see his AK47 assault rifle. Joe was thinking how no one would ever know what happened to him. The people on the truck kept conversing with the soldiers, who seemed to enjoy the diversion so much that they didn't bother to look in the back of the truck. They let the vehicle pass on through. How do you thank a bunch of peasant farmers that don't speak your language for saving your life? Do you simply smile and say *kob kun mak* (which means thank you very much)? God protects small children, cowards and unarmed soldiers.

Joe was becoming tired of walking into dangerous situations with ignorant bliss. He desired to regain control of his personal experiences, so he figured that if he planned an event himself then it would be under his control, with little chance of enemy intervention. He had heard about this crazy sounding place called "Monkey Village." This was a place where you could experience nature up close and personal. Now getting up close and personal with nature was not Joe's forte. So he invited his friend Bill and also brought a native guide along just to insure there would be no further mishaps. Then Joe and Bill set off to find the secrets of Monkey Village.

It was really quite an interesting place. The entrance had an iron gate surrounded by concrete walls that enclosed hundreds of acres of abandoned land. To the far rear of the property was a large and secluded mansion that looked as though it could have been an old oriental palace. All the walls were completely overgrown with vines. There was waist-tall grass all over the place and the trees reached high into the sky, creating a wide canopy.

Now the guide suggested they buy some bananas at a nearby fruit stand. The idea was to take the bananas into the center of the grounds and hold them high above your head. When Joe and Bill did this, the tops of all the trees started moving like the wind was blowing. Then hundreds upon hundreds of really cute monkeys started to climb down the trunks of the trees. Joe was amazed at seeing so many monkeys not in cages. There were big ones and small ones and mother monkeys carrying baby monkeys. More amazing was to see all these monkey heads bobbing up and down in the waist tall grass, all heading towards him. Joe held out a banana until one good-size monkey came up and took it right from Joe's hand. This felt like a real civilized communication between man and beast. Suddenly, another one came up and attempted to grab the whole bunch out of Joe's hand and growled with a furious intent. Then other monkeys started growling and showing six-inch long teeth. The whole thing started to turn into a riot and Joe was too close for comfort. One of the more aggressive animals actually sliced Joe's hand with a quick slash of his razor-sharp claws. Then it was like shark-frenzy feeding time. All the monkeys started to fight with the ones that had the bananas and anyone holding bananas was a target. It was time for plan B: throw the bananas as far as you can away from yourself, and run the other way. That worked like a charm and they were able to escape the melee.

Joe swore he would never again trust a cute monkey, and never again trust this alien land, either. As far as great ideas go, hiring a guide did not keep a hazardous experience from happening. You see, the guide neglected to explain the difference between monkeys and baboons. The place should have been more appropriately called Baboon Village. On his way home, Joe thought of how we may have evolved from apes, and how we behave the same as the crazed monkeys in our struggle for survival.

At just about this time, Joe's nerves were becoming a little on edge. So it was damn good news to hear that a really big celebration was coming up. Joe kept hearing about it, but didn't know what the whole thing was about. From the sounds of it, this celebration was as big as Christmas back home. The event was called the "Water Festival." Joe found out that it was a celebration for a good rainy season that would make for a good harvest. The rules were as follows: for three days you could assault anyone with any amount of water. You could walk up to a perfect stranger on the street and let them have it "right in the kisser" with a glass of water. Then you would yell, "Happy water festival!" and hilarious laughter would follow. There were people standing on street corners with buckets of water to insure you didn't make it home dry. Joe himself walked through the door soaking wet from head to toe on all three days in a row. Joe told Yome he was going to get her. Yome said she was too alert and too quick for that to happen.

So he waited until the morning of the third day, while Yome was sleeping like an angel. Joe's hand slowly crept under the pillow to where he had placed the weapon of choice, the weapon that would resolve the challenge and prove that his word was law: a fully loaded water pistol! Joe slowly and stealthily drew the pistol into a firing position, barely holding back the laughter. He couldn't help but notice how beautiful she was, sleeping so peacefully, so unaware of what was about to befall her. He took aim with hands that were trembling from the laughter that was ready to explode into a roar. Then he fired, shot after drenching shot, right into her face, causing her to gasp for air while dealing with the shock at the same time. Joe yelled "Happy Water Festival!" then ran from the room with Yome hot on his heels. She was swinging a vicious pillow and spewing out a flow of Thai verbiage he had never heard before. Joe realized that the Water Festival was really more fun than Christmas. There was real laughter shared by all and the water fights really got out all your aggressions towards your fellow man. On top of that, everyone was really clean when it was over!

Yes, Thailand was a really strange place with a really strange way of life. For instance, time had absolutely no meaning there. The time was always the same: 200 years behind the rest of the world. Joe had just bought a watch at the PX. While walking home he realized that this was surely the biggest waste of money he had ever made. "What on God's green earth do you need a watch for here?" This land was timeless; to wear a watch here would be like wearing a watch in the Garden of Eden. So Joe took off his new watch and threw the damn thing to the four winds.

Some things are still the same, though, but in a different way. A traffic jam is a traffic jam no matter what. But a traffic jam in Thailand is when the water buffalos get backed up on the trail all the way out to the rice fields. It's kind of odd to see a farmer on the back of a water buffalo with no place to go.

The personal habits of the Thai people were somewhat primitive. For instance, they went to the bathroom by squatting in nature or, if home, they simply squat over a hole in the floor and wash the waste through the hole with a bowl of rainwater. Joe had the only house in the village with American toilets. One day Joe walked in on Yome and found her standing on the toilet in a squatting position. It never occurred to Joe that she didn't know how to use the toilet. He laughed so hard that this poor oriental girl turned red. He hugged her while still laughing and assured her everything was okay. Yes, life was so full of surprises. Even when Joe thought he had seen it all, something new, strange and unexpected would always happen.

Another curious thing was the village fortuneteller; this guy was an event all unto himself. This was a very old man with a long white beard and wearing robes. He also had a long walking staff made of wood with a bone at the top. He would go from village to village and for a nickel he would tell your fortune. The fortuneteller would drape a large quilt-like blanket over a fence. This blanket had many pictures on it of all kinds of events that happen normally through out life. All he needed was your birth date and then he would point to the pictures that applied to you. Yome was really excited that this guy was in the front yard one day. She asked Joe for a nickel and his birth date.

To Joe's surprise, this old man told Yome that Joe had two brothers and one sister back home. That was pretty good since Joe had not discussed the subject with her before. So now Joe was intrigued; for the cost of another nickel more relevant information could be obtained. Okay, Joe said; but the second nickel returned a cryptic statement. The fortuneteller relayed the message through Yome that Joe would receive many stripes from the military, but not stripes. Now Joe lost interest right there because he knew the Army's only reward was stripes. Unless "not stripes" meant becoming a civilian. Ahh! What a sweet thought to be a civilian again with no problems other than when to mow the lawn—Joe could almost smell the fresh cut grass.

Joe wanted to break the routine of home and work, so he planned another adventure. He had heard of the "Giant Buddha." This noteworthy construction was located about 15 miles south of the base. Even though it was dangerous to go,

Joe and his friends went in search of it. It was a real "Wow!" too. It was a three-story tall Buddha, all white, that was being built by hand on top of a mountain. When I say by hand, I really mean by hand. They would mix the cement in buckets at the bottom of the mountain, then carry the buckets to the top of the mountain on a stick over their shoulders. Then they would apply the cement one handful at a time to the structure.

When Joe and his friends got to the foot of the mountain, they decided to check out the surrounding area first. They found some huge rocks in a secluded area that were really high up. Bill noticed that these rocks had large holes in them about eight feet deep. Bill wanted to jump down inside to investigate. Joe said, "Are you kidding? There could be God-knows-what down there!" But before he could finish, Bill jumped. "Ah, shit!" Joe yelled, "You don't even know if you can get back!" as he also jumped down into the dark pit. It was amazing! They found themselves standing in a hallway, a long corridor carved through solid rock. As they walked farther they came to a room, lit with candles. There were 12 solid gold Buddha statues in a row. "My heavens!" Joe said, "These are worth a fortune!" Enough gold was within his grasp for a lifetime of wealth. But they both knew what the punishment was for messing with religious artifacts. They would put you in a bamboo cage so small that you couldn't stand up or sit down, and hang you from a tree until your bones fell through the cage. Joe didn't really care for the gold anyway; the experience of discovering this magical place was reward enough. He felt as though he had found the Golden Fleece. He knew he had reached the pinnacle of his own personal summit; all he wanted now was to go home. It was now just a matter of staying alive until then.

They climbed out of another hole that took them very near the Giant Buddha. All the workers were gone now and the Buddha stood alone. It sat with arms and legs folded, and had a Mona Lisa smile. The interior of the statue was hollow and had a rope hanging that led up to the top of the head from the inside. Joe's friends climbed to the top while Joe was bringing up the rear. The first guy up started screaming. As it turned out, the head of the Giant Buddha was filled with bats. This called for an immediate retreat. Joe had seen enough, and with the news of the bats, Joe figured enough was enough and they returned to base. This adventure had left Joe knowing the secret location of 12 Buddha statues made of solid gold, something the very people of Thailand themselves probably didn't know. Another mystery of the orient had been unveiled.

But enough wasn't enough. They returned to a base that was on full alert. Messages had been intercepted that indicated that a large enemy movement was headed towards the base. The enemy was estimated at 6,000 troops and moving fast. "For God's sake," Joe thought, "there are only 1,000 men here, even if you include the cooks." A quick calculation told Joe he would have to kill six men just to break even. My God! They are even handing out weapons! Phosphorus grenades were placed on all the equipment to be destroyed before it fell into enemy hands. The grenades were designed to glow like a thousand suns and the heat would melt right through the metal to the ground, destroying the equipment completely.

It was made very realistically clear that every man was on his own and for himself. Each man was assigned a foxhole. Before Joe could open his mouth, his sergeant yelled, "Go! Go! Go!" With that, Joe ran for his foxhole and took a flying leap over the sand bags. Damn! Joe just hit wrong and injured his back; the pain was filling his mind. Damn it! He thought, just before the biggest and probably the last battle of his life, he was already injured. If it came down to hand-to-hand combat, Joe knew he would be killed. As he lay there with his gun pointed out across a clear killing field, thoughts were racing through his head. "What the hell am I doing here? Why the hell am I here? Could I and would I kill another human being?" Joe thought, "This isn't my country, and I don't hate these people. All I want to do is go home." He knew he really didn't want to kill anyone. He knew that the enemy wouldn't hesitate to kill him. He remembered what his mother told him in a confidential talk before he left home. She said, "Son, you kill every man, woman, and child that it takes for you to get home again." Joe knew that killing was wrong under any circumstances, except to protect your own life. Joe thought of how he had come to love the innocent child-like people of this jungle land.

The enemy was getting closer now and Joe could hear distant sounds. The daylight was starting to fade now too. Great, just great! This obscenity of killing was going to be at night, making Joe blind, too. When a man stands before death afraid, alone, and in the dark, he is in the valley of the shadow of death. Joe was never more afraid and never more alone; he swore if he ever were able to get his ass out of this alive, he would live in peace forever and never raise his hand in anger. But time was running out—Joe had to decide now: kill or be killed. He knew he wasn't going to get any consideration from the enemy for being a nice guy.

The answer came as the mosquitoes were slowly filling their bellies with Joe's American red blood and the dark of night was descending all around him. "All right! I will kill!" He knew he would have to kill without hesitation. He would kill with all the fury of the relentless savage beast he had within him. He would kill all that moved, and he would kill because he was young and wanted to live. He knew he had no chance, being so outnumbered, but he could make them pay by taking as many of them with him as he possibly could. He would have to concentrate on being a ruthless and an effective killer. He figured if he could take out at least ten of them, that would be payment for his own life, but he wanted more.

Joe's senses were becoming keen in the dark. His eyes adjusted to the darkness and he could hear the movement of a leaf in the distance. His insides laughed at the thought that he had never felt so alive just before his inevitable end—so akin was he to the most veracious animal or barbaric caveman or even the devil himself. He had heard the Turkish army eats the hearts of their enemy to gain their strength. Joe was preparing for the same. He felt as though he couldn't depend on anyone for his own life, as he started calculating numbers. Joe was thinking how many could he shoot, how many throats could he cut, how many would the grenades take out? His back pain and fear were replaced by the planning of how fast and how many human beings he could turn into shit. How long does it take for a man to die when you strangle him with your bare hands? He was thinking of faster ways to kill more effectively. This was important because the time would determine the number you could kill. Joe was agile and could move fast through the dark. How many could he silently take out with quick jabs of his knife? Then he saw the moving shadows off in the distant jungle; they looked like ripples on a dark lake. Occasionally he could make out the shape of a man crouched over, walking with a rifle. Joe could hear the many feet pushing down on the leaves. There truly must be thousands of them. Joe thought he would unleash his monster as soon as they cleared the woods; he would then work his way to get behind them. Joe figured the killing would have to be non-stop and way past exhaustion. He would kill past being tired, past being in pain, past being insane. That's what it would take to get him home again, and that's what he would do.

The shadows were moving all right and the night was alive with movement. Their sandals pressing on the leaves sounded like a large river flowing in the distance. Joe cocked his weapon, loosened the knife from its sheath, and set several grenades in position. The first explosive crack of gunfire came from the left. Joe took cover behind a large tree next to his foxhole to get a better look. He could see the shadows of three men running in his direction. He waited for them to pass and leaped out and grabbed the last man from behind by the chin. He pulled his head back and shoved his bayonet into the base of his enemy's throat. The training taught that a man couldn't make a sound when killed this way; the training was right. But the training didn't tell about the smooth skin of a soldier's face that was too young to shave, or the smell of stinky human sweat from someone that had been out in the field for days without a bath. It also didn't tell about the gushing warm blood, or the feel of the tightening muscles that tremble like an electrical shock when the life force is leaving the body. The training didn't tell about how you can feel your own soul being lost at the same time.

All the while, Joe kept his eyes on the other two men; by the time the other two noticed what had happened, Joe had finished with the first. He threw the lifeless body to the ground and then quickly drew his pistol; he kept shooting until he saw both shadowy figures fly backwards. Joe knew others were coming soon, so he set a quick trap that would trip the next one.

He didn't have to wait more than a minute. Another dark figure came running through the night. When he hit Joe's trap, he fell face down on the ground with a thud. Joe jumped on his back and pulled the man's head back as he ran his knife deep across his enemy's throat. Even as the gurgles of blood and air escaped, the bastard was taking too long to die. Joe started plunging his knife into the man's upper back. The man made a low guttural sound and tried to turn over, so Joe just kept thrusting his knife into him until there was no more movement. With each thrust, a geyser of blood came forth. Again it was warm, but this time it had a sickening sweet smell to it. When he was finished, Joe was covered in blood but all he could do was clean his hands on the surrounding wet grass.

The thousands of shadows were not moving in his direction any longer. They were moving south past the base. There were sporadic bursts of gunfire and an occasional blast of a grenade but all noise subsided within several of hours. Enough time had passed for them to attack, and no attack was forthcoming. Was this just tactics and was the camp being completely encircled? Joe thought it was like being attacked by the dogs, so now he had a plan for that too: break a hole through and get behind them. Joe sat silently and motionless all night with his monster, the monster he was now depending on to get him home. Another thought made Joe's insides laugh: how he had really become the meanest son of a bitch in the valley. He knew there was no honor in this, though; the only reward was survival. If you live through something like this, then you've earned the right to be alive.

Come sunrise the next day—the sunrise Joe thought he would never see—the enemy was gone. The tree line was clear of deadly shadows; the leaves lay quiet and were no longer being crushed by furtive footsteps. The enemy's target was Cambodia all along, not the base; they were just passing through on their way there. Unfortunately, they had just come too close for comfort. Joe would never be the same again after having walked through the valley. It didn't matter that they missed the main attack. Seeing the true evil that he carried would always keep him humble. For the rest of his life now, the only thing he would ever really fear would be himself. I swear by all that is true that that crazy bastard Joe would have taken on all 6,000 single-handedly rather than feel one more minute of fear. Then he understood what happened to his uncle who was killed in the Korean War after five acts of bravery.

When the dark cloud of war passed over, there were other things in Joe's life that offered interesting diversions from war. An example of this was the day when Bill walked into Joe's room while he was asleep. Joe jumped up and saw Bill staring at him with a face that was tombstone white in color. Joe could see something was terribly wrong. Joe wasn't really sure he was ready for another shock, but he could see his friend was in real trouble. He asked Bill to sit down and tapped him in the cheek a few times to break him out of his hypnotic stare. "Bill, for heaven's sake, man, tell me what's wrong!" Bill looked up at Joe and said, "I think my girl is a lesbian." With that, Joe let out a laugh that exploded from his lower intestine. "Bill, you have got to be wrong about this." Bill said he had just walked in on his girl in the middle of a sex act with another woman. Joe could tell Bill really believed what he was saying, but Joe insisted that Bill was wrong. Joe secretly was thrilled the problem was about sex and not about an immediate life or death situation. Joe sent Yome into the room to find out what was really happening. Well, what was really happening was that Bill's girl was in the middle of having an abortion when Bill walked in on them. His girl never discussed her plans with him, and she never told him she was pregnant. It was no longer funny to Joe, finding out that this did turn out to be a matter of life or death. Why was it that every damn thing that happened had to do with life or death, mostly death?

Thailand was always good for an adrenalin rush. Thank heavens it didn't all happen to Joe. A fellow soldier was leaving his house one morning and inadvertently disturbed a big resting cobra on his front steps. The cobra rises up before it attacks; Thai cobras can spit poison in the eyes of their victims, making the cobra a little extra dangerous. Joe laughed when he thought about this happening before having your coffee in the morning. He could imagine the look on his friend's face. Fortunately, the only ill effect of the cobra encounter was that Joe's friend lost all the color from his face. Half the village got in on the excitement of trying to capture this snake, as you could make some money with a snake like that. They often had cobra/mongoose fights and the betting was always good. This is an example of everyday events in Thailand, so you had to be ready every day, which meant ready for anything at any time.

You would never think you could get used to snakes, but you can. On the morning walk into work, there was an area where snakes would cross over the sidewalk on base. Most of these snakes were basically harmless with an occasional poisonous one. Hating snakes like he did, Joe would often stomp on their heads. One day a snake dodged his foot, rose up and bit Joe in the top of his Army boot. After that close call, the practice of head stomping stopped immediately. Joe figured he would never get home if he didn't stop taking stupid and unnecessary chances like that. So from now on it was going to be safety first before all else. He often thought about home now and how far over the horizon it was.

On another occasion, on his way to work as usual, Joe saw a little boy playing with a giant scorpion. Joe became very alarmed and tried to warn the kid. This scorpion was black and about three inches long with hair on it. Joe waved his hands in front of the kid saying, "No, no, no!" The kid just laughed at Joe and pointed to the end of this very large scorpion. He was showing Joe that he knew enough about scorpions to pull the stinger off. Joe felt like an ass in front of this child. Of course he knew enough to pull the stinger off—he was a native boy! This was another reminder to Joe that he was the stranger in this strange world.

Another strange thing in Thailand was a grass-like plant that covered large areas and moved on its own. When Joe first walked on it, upon looking back he was amazed to see his own footprints were still there. This grass has a nervous system and folds up its leaves when you touch it; it is very odd to see a plant move like that. Joe felt terribly insecure at finding how much he didn't know and realizing that footprints left on this plant could lead the enemy to you. Joe later found out that this plant was named *mimosa pudica*, commonly known as "touch-me-not."

Joe learned that Thailand offered many surprising and dangerous encounters with nature.

Did you ever experience a day that felt unnatural? A day when the sun is bright but things look dim? When everything seems distant and you are more like an observer rather than a participant? On this particular day, Joe was having just that kind of day. He didn't know what to make of it either. He felt fine, and he was young and strong. He wasn't in immediate danger, and he even checked the mirror to see if he had "the glow" in his face. Joe had seen a "Twilight Zone" episode when he was a kid that featured the glow, which meant that the end was near, very near, for the people who had it. To Joe, this concept was a real thing; he had seen it in several people of different ages in the past. It never failed: they all died within a short period after he saw it. Thank heavens there was no glow in his face! But Joe just couldn't shake the feeling that his luck was running out. It was an eerie, haunting feeling that wouldn't go away. Joe thought he was just trying to cause problems for himself since he hadn't had a life-and-death incident in at least a few days. But the damn feeling was real, and very strong. Joe thought it was silly at first, but as the day passed he became more concerned. At one point he was so sure his time was up that he wrote a letter home and kept it in his back pocket, just in case. It went something like this:

Dear Mom, Chad, Myra & Burney,

> *I am writing this letter to let you know that I have been fully aware that some sort of misfortune is about to befall me. Unfortunately, I believe it's going to be something of a permanent nature that will prevent me from returning home or ever seeing all of you again. I would like you to be proud of me and want to assure you that I have done my best. I want to tell you how much I love each of you and thank you for your love, too. Because when all is said and done that is all that really matters. I pray you don't cry over me*

as life is too short for bad times or tears. There is only enough time for joy, and that is what I want your hearts to be filled with. I miss you now and always.

Love, Joe

Joe carried that letter around for a month and when nothing happened he threw it away. But this was his frame of mind—a hopeless vulnerability to being subject to whatever happened to him.

As Joe was walking home a short time later he thought he saw a "spaceman." From a distance this was a real curious thing. There was a man in a silver suit standing on the jungle road. He was wearing a silver helmet that had a glass face to it; even his boots were silver. Silver material covered every part of him and he even had silver metal tanks on his back. Now tell me that if you ever saw something like that walking around in the jungle you wouldn't think it was a damn spaceman!

Joe walked up to this guy and asked, "What the hell are you?" The silver-suit man said he was spraying the village for a deadly mosquito that was killing the villagers. Joe asked him if the stuff he was spraying was dangerous. to which the silver-suit man answered no. Joe challenged, "If it's not dangerous, then why are you completely covered in that silver suit?" The man said it was to keep the spray from getting on his skin or in his eyes. Joe left quickly but he knew that if that stuff were dangerous then it was already too late for him. In that case, you just have to wait to see what happens next.

Joe and his five closest friends were playing cards one afternoon. Subjects were discussed like, "Would you risk your life for me?" and visa versa. All the men knew that the answer was yes, that they would gladly give their lives for each other. There was a number of ways that a man could die or become tragically injured. That was when the "Testicle Pledge" was taken: a solemn pledge that if any one of them had his testicles shot off, the others would finish the job. This was a hard thing to do, as it would be easier to give your life for a friend than it would be to take a friend's life. It was a solemn pledge, and the one sure thing you could depend on was that not one of them was going home that way. What manner of world is this, in which young men had to make such a pledge?

Talk about no sleep for the weary. Everything has a procedure, including sleeping. For instance, in Thailand it is practically suicidal to sleep without protection from the mosquitoes. Of course, Joe found this out the hard way. He fell asleep without lighting a mosquito coil and without mosquito netting, and without even wearing a t-shirt. When he woke in the middle of the night, his chest and stomach were completely covered with mosquito bites. He had taken enough mosquito bites to bring a large horse down. Great, just great! Now what is this going to do? Malaria, swamp fever, or worse? When he got up the next day there wasn't a mark on him, no symptoms, and no repercussions at all. Was this another close call or was this something that would come back to bite you in the ass later? Well, the hell with later; it was now that mattered and for now all seemed well.

After a short while it became apparent that bicycles were the only real way to get around. During the short ride home one day, Joe and his friend Larry where horsing around by trying to run each other off the road. Larry warned him not to fool around anymore, but Joe being Joe gave it one more try. Larry got real upset and reached over and turned the handlebars on Joe's bike sideways. Joe was moving at a pretty good clip when he did that. The bike stopped instantly but not Joe; he sailed over the handlebars head first with his arms stretched forward like Superman. When he hit the ground his hands tried to break the fall but he hit too hard. Every bone between his shoulders made snapping and breaking noises. Joe's shoulder was dislocated; it was very odd to see his shoulder in the front of him rather than on the side. He didn't feel it right away but 20 minutes later the pain hit. Whoa! Did the pain hit! It filled his brain and left no room for anything else. That's not the worst part: it was Sunday and there was no doctor on base. They packed Joe in ice and sent him to the air base up the road in hopes of a doctor being there.

Joe was singing every song he had ever learned to block the pain, but it was constant and very severe. On top of that, the road to the air base was full of potholes and every time the driver hit one Joe would let out a stream of obscenities directed at the driver. This caused the driver to seek out more potholes. By the time they made it to the air base, Joe had experienced more pain than he ever knew was possible. The doctor asked Joe if he wanted a shot for the pain. Joe replied, "Does a bear shit in the forest? Of course I want something for the pain!!!" The shot was morphine and all of a sudden every square inch of Joe's body was having an orgasm. After many hours of excruciating pain, this was truly heaven. Then the doctor grabbed the broken arm and put his foot on Joe's armpit and pulled straight out. Joe told the doctor it was okay if he wanted to pull the damn thing right off. After this procedure, the doctor asked Joe if he wanted another shot for the pain. Joe was feeling no pain; in fact he never felt better. But that stuff was so great! Joe said, "Yes." He slept for three solid days.

When Joe recovered from his injuries and was able to return to his duties, he found things had changed somewhat. The base had a new commanding officer fresh out of West Point. That meant he was well trained but inexperienced, and inexperience could get you killed in a heartbeat. This new C.O. ordered exercise and extra duty for the entire detachment. This was not quite the right approach for men with high IQ's. All of a sudden, no one could hear any signals and all interception came to a screeching halt. It was a real funny thing, too, because maintenance had checked all the equipment for defects and had found that all the equipment was operational. Still, the men claimed they couldn't hear a thing. The Army had the entire antenna system checked out; the report came back operational—everything was working perfectly. But still the men reported they couldn't hear a thing. When the chain of command was called in to listen, the signals were again clear as a bell. Would you believe that the United States Army finally got the message, and all those extra work details and physical training stopped. Would you believe the coincidence, that the men were just then finally able to hear the signals again? They could fry you if you refused to do your job, but if you said you just couldn't hear the signal, there wasn't a damn thing they could do about it. Well, I guess there are now two kinds of people that you just shouldn't mess with: a person who has nothing to lose and people with high IQ's.

Back on the home front, Joe's time in the country was coming close to an end. A constant reminder of this for Yome was the countdown calendar Joe kept on the wall. He didn't realize the effect this was having on her. Even though he never had intentions of taking her to the States with him, she imagined that that's the way it was going to be. Joe could see the family sitting around the table during Thanksgiving and Yome in a corner kneeling down eating a bowl of rice. Joe thought that taking this natural creature out of her natural environment would be a transgression beyond forgiveness, even though it would mean breaking her heart. He tried to convince her that she couldn't be happy in the United States. But she loved him and she would go anywhere and do anything to keep him.

One day, Yome asked him for a lock of his hair. Joe wanted to know what it was for and she explained that a ritual belief was that if you take a person's hair, wrap it around a copper coil, then bury it in the ground and pray over it, no matter how long that person lives they would have to return to that spot. Joe gladly gave up his hair for the opportunity to offer her some relief from despair and give hope for her future. At the same time, he knew it would not be possible for him to return; he looked at the whole "copper coil" scenario with amusement. Curiously, in his later years, Joe had an intense desire to return to Thailand. One wonders: is it possible?

Something that you wouldn't expect is that even though you live in the jungle you still need organization and general cleanliness in your home. Joe was not satisfied with either of these fundamental factors. So he decided to show Yome how he wanted his house to be kept. While cleaning the only window in the house, the pane of glass fell out and the corner of it stuck into the top of Joe's foot. When he pulled it out, blood shot up like he had just struck oil. It was a gusher! Yome offered medical assistance through the village witch doctor. Now Joe thought this was somewhat of a novel idea. To Joe, a witch doctor was a guy with a painted face, dancing around the room doing voodoo and chanting, and passing a wand over the injury. He was really curious to see how a witch doctor was going to stop this profuse bleeding. A few moments later, a woman showed up with a medical bag. Already, this was a surprise. This woman pulled out a horse-size hypodermic needle and went for Joe's foot. Whoa! Joe yelled, "You are not going to stick me with that thing!" So she pulled the needle off the syringe and poured the substance over his foot. Then she went into her medical bag and pulled out one red plant and one green plant. She broke open the plants and dabbed the wound. Now this was more like what Joe expected. It was truly unbelievable to see the geyser-like blood flow stop instantly. The wound closed up right away and the skin stuck together like glue. Joe was amazed at this instant remedy so unlike the stitches he would have received back in the states. He didn't suffer any discomfort from this procedure or have any lasting consequences, but for a long time his foot did ache each time it rained.

Learning was the focus of Joe's life now; Joe was learning something new everyday. You may have heard of the oriental custom of the woman walking behind the man. How about the one where the man eats before the woman, or that a woman is never to interrupt a conversation between two men. Well, all this is believed to be out of respect for men, which American women would never accept. In reality, the woman walks behind the man so that the man finds the snake first. The man eats first in case the food is bad. This is all actually done out of respect for women. It occurred to Joe that women never interrupt two men talking because the men obviously live a shorter life!

He learned that the strange cross he saw in the sky was a normal thing. At first Joe thought it was a cloud formation, but when it was bright at night and still there for several days he didn't know what to make of it. Joe thought it was very strange; it looked just like the cross that Jesus Christ is associated with. It was white and very large. Later he found out it was a common phenomenon called the "Southern Cross" and was caused by light. Sailors had seen this from the beginning of time.

In Thailand, they can do almost anything with rice. Rice was the mainstay of the diet. They would goo-it up and put it on a stick, puff it up like Rice Krispies, and even make spaghetti or flavored deserts out of it.

Some of Joe's learning experiences were a little more meaningful. He learned that the cost of an American life was $15 dollars and the cost of a Thai life was $25 dollars. He learned that you could get sent to jail for stepping on a coin; the coins had a picture of the king on them, so it would be like an insult to the king and his people to step on his image. Also you could not raise the bottom of your feet higher than someone else's head. For instance, if someone was on the floor and you raised your foot to a higher point than his or her head, it was the same as saying "you are lower than the bottom of my feet." He learned that you could get shot dead for stealing, as he so witnessed on the street when a policeman shot a suspect in the back while he was running away. There was no arrest, no reading of rights, no trial, just immediate retribution.

In Thai, there are five different tones to the word *mai* and each tone has a different meaning. Mai could mean mother or it could mean dog. Joe learned this when he inadvertently called someone's mother a dog. That went over like trying to float a brick. A friend saved Joe by explaining that he was not familiar with the language. Yome taught Joe that if a man has both arms and legs then he has no right to be a beggar.

He learned the meaning of *falong mai*, which meant "foreign dog," as a neighbor had once referred to him. Joe didn't let on that he knew what the guy said, and simply returned a friendly smile instead. It is better to know who your enemies are, without them knowing you know. Joe learned to walk opposite traffic so he could spot the large baht bus that had a horn louder than a train. This bus would travel very fast and you couldn't hear it coming until it was right up on you. The drivers got a kick out of scaring the shit out of soldiers with that horn. That added a new dimension to Joe's already-developing nervous condition. Joe's reflexes would cause him to hit the ground every time the drivers blasted that damn horn at him.

Joe also learned not to go anywhere alone. Bill and Joe were going for a night out on the town. A taxi would take them to Udorn, the nearest thing to a major city. There was only one road and it was a straight shot all the way. But the taxi driver took a right turn onto a dirt road. Bill pulled out a knife and held it to the driver's throat and ordered him back to the main road. Joe yelled, "Bill, what the hell are you doing?" Bill told Joe it was commonplace for these taxi drivers to take an off road where others were waiting to rob the passengers. Joe realized again he was being oblivious to the dangers that were all around all the time.

On another occasion, this lesson would again reveal itself when Joe was feeling claustrophobic. He just wanted to take a walk in the jungle to get out of the house and get some fresh air. He walked a good distance into the jungle feeling as though he was being watched the whole time. That was mainly because he was really being watched: Yome had sent a boy to follow him, to warn him of any unexpected danger. Joe forgot the feeling of being watched when he saw hundreds of flashlights moving through the woods ahead. He was going to investigate when the boy ran up to him and told him the flashlights were enemy soldiers. Joe lost interest in the walk and the fresh air; he wondered how long it would be before his stupidity would cost him his life. He learned his life was just saved by a village girl's love and an innocent young boy.

A small group of the guys Joe went through school with were also doing something really stupid. They would sneak up to the Chinese border to take pictures of the Chinese communist guards. They asked Joe to go but he said no. He had come too close for comfort too many times already. On one occasion, they guys crossed the Mekong River and went into Laos. They were drinking with the villagers on the other side when a communist patrol caught them. The Reds took them back to the Mekong River and threw them in. The Reds told them it would be a death sentence if they returned. Why they weren't killed is still a mystery to Joe.

A young man who was Joe's neighbor taught him never to underestimate anyone. Joe was giving a boxing lesson to this young man. They were standing face to face and Joe took a boxing stance. This young man decided to give Joe a lesson first: he reached up and slapped Joe across the face with his foot. Joe was taken completely by surprise. In Thai boxing they use their hands and feet. Another example of underestimation was a playful rock fight Joe had with some village fishermen. Joe bent down to pick up a rock and when he looked up they were gone. There was really no place for them to go as the lake was to their backs and there was nothing to hide behind anywhere. Nonetheless they disappeared in a split second! Joe found out that they had completely camouflaged themselves with fishing nets and moss that was on the ground.

With these small lessons Joe knew he could live or die at their discretion. He also knew that we could never win a war against these people unless the Army developed the same tactics. But the Army was far too arrogant with brute force to learn anything. The Army's tactics were to justify funding from Congress through body count, be it yours or theirs. Joe thought this method to be unsound and not particularly in his best interest. He wondered why the American Army didn't try to survive on a handful of rice a day or use tunnel systems of its own or use the AK47 assault rifle that could put a hole through an elephant at 300 yards without failing. Instead of traveling lightweight and moving fast through the forest like the enemy did, American soldiers carried a heavy backpack, a helmet, and a rifle that jammed if you sneezed on it. What all this amounted to was to make an American soldier a slow moving target.

When Joe went to work one day, atmospherics made interception the best he had ever heard. In fact, he was able to pick up a signal from the other side of the world. "Oh, my God! It's New York!" Messages were coming in from his hometown. It was like getting mail from home. Mail was very important because it was the only link to reality. The message went like this: ......*Reuter's news flash: Across the New York metropolitan area today college students were participating in a new form of activity called "streaking." Streaking means to take off all your clothes and run around naked on campus......* (End of message.) Joe wondered if he had made a big mistake by not going to college. It appeared as though people back home had gone completely berserk. If all that other people ever heard about the United States came only from the news, it would make the country seem like a lunatic asylum. Nevertheless, Joe was starting to miss it.

The last mail he got from home was a little strange to say the least. Joe had written that he missed having a big hamburger from one of the big fast-food places, and he asked his mom to send him one. When he got a box from home, he thought, "Oh, boy!" Upon opening the box he found a pair of sneakers and an empty burger container with a note from Mom. The note said that the sneakers were for running when the going got rough; the burger box was because she couldn't send a burger due to restrictions but the box still had the smell of a hamburger in it. Oh well, what the hell; it was mail after all and the hamburger box really did smell like a burger.

Well, when things got slow—I mean life and death slow—it would be time to seek out a new adventure, preferably of a non-lethal nature. Bill and Joe had heard about a tribe living in the mountains that had never seen a white man before. The mountains were within eyesight but you really couldn't tell how far away they were. So Bill and Joe set off to find this tribe. All they needed was water for the trip. Thailand can get to be a really hot place. There is no humidity so you can't really feel the heat. But the heat is there all the same. Once in a while it can get too hot even for cacti.

They walked for hours and weren't any closer to the mountains than they appeared from the village. Everything was okay until the water ran out. Great, just great! They had drunk all the water on the way out! Now the mission had to be abandoned and our two heroes had to make a hasty retreat before sunset. The water situation was pretty serious but getting lost in the jungle after dark was unthinkable. Every few miles they would find these grass huts made by the Thai people for temporary shelter from the sun; they just had a wood floor and a grass roof, and no walls. Joe thought it was a good idea to hole up in one of these until either it was cooler to travel or a better idea came along. Bill wasn't interested in spending the night in the mosquito-infested jungle, so they continued their trip back. They ran the risk of walking right by the village if it got too dark.

It was one hell of a walk, too. The sun beat down on them until they couldn't walk straight anymore. Joe had doubts about being able to last too much longer. Bill was starting to weaken quite a bit also. Fortunately for them, a rice farmer appeared riding a two-wheel oxcart that was being pulled by a water buffalo. It was unbelievable to Joe to be rescued by something right out of the 16th century. But at the same time, that oxcart was the best thing since man invented cold beer. The driver knew his way back to town, too. Joe learned a new lesson that day: an uneducated, poverty-stricken, bad-smelling, rice farmer was saving their asses—how many more different ways were there to learn how to be humble?

The danger would occasionally give way to routine. That is what Joe was really beginning to like best, routine. So it was back to work and life with his Yome. Just when Joe thought he had Thailand under control, Sgt. Butthead, who was still seeking revenge for the previous breach of military protocol, came to Joe with a smile on his face. Joe knew instantly that he was in deep doo-doo. Sgt. Butthead told Joe that the captain wanted to speak to him ASAP. Now, to be called by the captain ASAP meant that life, as you know it, was going to change and not for the better. But Joe promised himself to take the punishment like a man; after all, he did commit the crime: insubordination and failure to follow the orders of his superiors.

When Joe opened the door to go in, all the company clerks stopped typing, stopped talking, and stared at him. This treatment was usually reserved for those about to be shot for treason. Then Joe knocked on the captain's office. The encounter went something like this:

"Sir, Specialist 4th Class Joe reporting as ordered, sir."

The captain said, "Specialist, when was the last time you wrote home?"

"Sir?"

"You heard me, specialist. Now answer the question."

"Sir, I can't exactly remember, sir!"

"And just why is that, specialist? Don't you know your folks are worried sick about you? That your mother has written to the Red Cross and has been trying to locate you?"

There was only one real acceptable response, and that was, "Sir, yes, sir!"

"Well then, specialist, here is a room with a table, chair, pencil, and paper. Specialist, you are to consider yourself under arrest and are not permitted to leave this room until that long overdue letter is written."

"Sir, yes, sir!"

Joe sat down and wrote the letter, after which he was released. Oh, brother! Talk about having the shit scared out of you. Joe was amazed that his mother was able to put his ass under arrest from the other side of the world. Oh brother!

Sometimes the strange things you never expected came right to the door. Joe thought it was pretty strange when someone knocked on his door, only because they lived at the edge of the village and, as far as Joe knew, Thailand didn't have any door-to-door salesmen. When he opened the door, Joe saw an old lady and a very young girl standing there. The old lady started talking a mile a minute and Joe didn't understand a word. "Yome!" Joe called, "There is an old lady and a young girl at the door and I don't know what the hell they want." After Yome talked to her for a few minutes, the tone of the conversation started to get a little harsh. Then Yome slammed the door in the old lady's face. Joe had never seen Yome treat anyone so rudely before. Joe yelled at her in a surprised and shocked voice. He didn't understand how an old lady like that could do any harm to anyone. Yome explained that the old lady was trying to sell the child. Bewildered, Joe asked Yome why couldn't they just give the lady money and make the child a gift back to her. Yome said the woman would take the money and sell the child somewhere else anyway. Joe was shocked by all this, but realized that he couldn't criticize this behavior when he knew that a similar practice of slavery took place in his own country just 200 years ago. And Thailand was just about 200 years behind the United States.

Well, with all that had happened and all that was happening, mental and physical shocks were commonplace. In fact, Joe would become disappointed if he wasn't shocked on a daily basis. Thailand would never let him down in that department, though. But the epitome of barbarianism was still to be unveiled. When Joe was again on his way to work he noticed a small crowd gathered at a ditch on the side of the road. Joe wondered what new attraction would hold such interest for so many. Naturally he had to check it out. When he saw what it was, something very bad happened to Joe's insides. His stomach twisted like you would ring out water from cloth. His heart broke and his brain rejected all visual accounts of the incident. If he told himself it didn't happen, then it didn't happen. As it seems, it is common practice that should a child be Amerasian, or if the mother was not financially able to care for it, the infant would be thrown into a ditch and the wild packs of dogs would devour the problem. What manner of world is this?

Joe had enough; the only logical answer was to do some intensive research into alcoholism. He was absolutely sure that he could drink that experience right out of his existence. The experiment failed with the unexpected interruption of a girl named Vien. This girl was a noteworthy interruption because God himself had endowed her with the largest breasts in the Far East. She sat next to Joe at the bar.

Vien was a woman of the evening more sensitive to human suffering than anyone else. Men surrounded her all the time, offering her whatever she wanted. Joe was finally drunk enough to say something stupid to this magnificent creation. He said something that would put him on the same level as all the other tongue-hanging-out fools: "I want to take you to bed and make love to you." He thought the act of love would be a good treatment for what tormented his soul. Joe knew the jig was up when she replied "Why?" That was the kind of response you give when you're stalling for a no. This caused Joe to think of why he really wanted to go to bed with her. He was drunk, and tired, and recovering from a recent shock. But he thought, "She does have the biggest tits in the Far East." So he told her what he thought. "I want to make love to you because you have the biggest tits I've ever seen on an oriental girl." With that she took his hand and they went to a motel. Joe was somewhat put off by seeing two single beds. He couldn't figure out this problem in his drunken state. Fortunately, Vien put the beds together, and oh, what a night! After they made love, she asked, "Do you want to again?" Joe said okay. This routine went on until the sun came up the next day. Joe knew he would have some tall explaining to do with Yome later, but figured he could get away with it by telling her he was on base the whole night.

Joe asked the taxi to let him out at the edge of the village so it would appear he was going home alone. But Yome had gotten the word of his transgression before he walked through the door. Believe it when I tell you that the word gets around faster by mouth in a village than on the six o'clock news. He found her crying hysterically in the bedroom. Joe had never before seen someone so completely destroyed. He then realized how much she truly loved him. He felt as though he had committed his first real sin. A sin he knew he would surely pay for in this life or the next. So he grabbed her trembling body up and held her tight in his arms, and swore never again. He held her as her tears soaked his shirt completely wet.

Yome was never really the same after that. She was more solemn and less happy. She became absorbed in embroidering some pillowcases for Joe's mother. Every day, when Joe came home from work, that's what she'd be doing. Joe thought nothing of it—other than she was being a little obsessive about it—until she was finished. It was amazing! The pattern was definitely oriental, and it glowed with all the colors of a rainbow, all on its own. It was as if she had sewn all the love of her soul into it. Joe has not since seen a rainbow with colors that can compare.

During this time, Yome began to feel ill. Her color faded, she stopped eating and Joe was getting very concerned. He tried to get help from the clinic on base, but they refused. There was some sort of rule about not using American medical supplies to treat the foreign nationals; besides, Joe could lose his security clearance if it were found he was living with one. Everyone lived with a foreign national, but as long as it was undocumented it was okay. But should your name be associated with them in an official way, it would be the end of your career. Joe bribed an orderly and, after describing the symptoms, was able to get some pills for her. The instructions were for two pills every four hours. Somehow the instructions got fowled up and she was taking four tablets every two hours. For a short period she bounced out of bed with zeal, then got seriously sick from the medicine. She accused Joe of trying to kill her. After that, the trust they had between them was over and so was their relationship. After they broke up, Joe went from woman to woman to woman, never really finding anyone that made him as happy as Yome did.

Around this time a newbie showed up at the base and was assigned to Joe's crew. This guy had "new" written all over him. He had stark red hair and had taken a few Kung Fu classes. Joe named him Kung Fu Idiot. He wasn't in town but a week and three men tried to rob him. Instead of handing over the money like any sane person, Kung Fu Idiot took a Kung Fu stance and yelled, "Ha!" After they stabbed him three times, they took his money.

One day while Joe was at the bicycle repair shop, he saw a couple walking together hand in hand. It was Yome and Kung Fu Idiot! Joe yelled out, "Yome!" She stopped and walked up to Joe; he asked, "You took that idiot as my replacement?" With that, she slapped him and walked away. They would never see each other again.

Nothing was going too good for Joe or his friends. As it seems, bad news follows bad news. Case in point: Sam. Sam was a seasoned veteran and a true leader of men. His sense of humor could belittle any serious situation and could also be used to enchant women. He was a robust and healthy-looking young man with an extremely high IQ and good looks to match. Like most other soldiers, he had found the perfect woman for him. Early on in their relationship, his girl became pregnant. To her, having his child meant a sure ticket to the United States. But Sam had other plans. When his tour was over, he was going to catch a quick flight out of town before she knew he was gone. Somehow, she got wind of Sam's intentions.

The day finally came and, instead of leaving right away, Sam stopped off at a bar to have some farewell drinks with friends. While there, Sam's girl walked up behind him, tapped him on his shoulder and, as he turned, slashed the entire length of his face with a razor blade, leaving a deep bleeding gash of a wound from his forehead to his chin. This of course delayed his immediate departure. Scarred hideously for life, Sam went into a deep depression. The laughter was gone, and he became completely introverted. This incident taught Joe that danger came in all shapes and sizes and that it was important never to sit with your back to the door, as he never did again.

No matter what the hell was going on in his personal life, Joe still had to go to work everyday. The pressure was starting to show on Joe's face. This day, he slapped on his headsets and prepared for another eight hours of mindless noise passing through what was left of his sanity. Then out of the clear blue, and for the third time, there was Ark! Joe started pushing buttons fast as he had practiced for months. In an entire tour of duty only one or two men had ever even heard the Ark before, and no one ever captured it. This was Joe's third time at bat; after dropping the ball twice before, he was feeling like a real loser. But he was ready now. "That bastard Ark is mine," he said. In a split second, Joe was on the horn to Korea, the Philippines and Taiwan. Ark was chirping away like a little birdie with a big long song. The Ark even stayed up longer than ever before. When Joe saw the tape recorders receiving good signal for over ten seconds, he screamed, "I got you, you dirty bastard! I got you!"

Joe knew this was big, I mean, really big! This was going to turn a few heads all right. First there had to be verification by the National Security Agency. So when the signal finally ended, he packed the tape up and away it went. Days went by with no response; Joe figured they probably couldn't believe it was the real thing either. This was the biggest discovery in the Far East since rice.

About a week went by when the base commander showed up in Joe's section, requesting to shake the hand of the man who captured Ark. Joe was put in for the highest non-combatant award the Army had to offer. You should have seen the faces of all around when a man from the National Security Agency traveled half way around the world just to speak to Joe. He brought 100,000 dollars worth of the most sensitive electronic equipment and put Joe in charge of an entire new section devoted to just the interception of Ark. He was now also in charge of training all new incoming personnel in the further capture of Ark.

When Joe first arrived in Thailand they had one page of information on Ark. Now they had volumes on it. But the military honors and the medal were not approved thanks to Sgt. Butthead and his want for revenge; he stated it was just a matter of luck. Joe didn't really care about the medal—all he wanted was the recognition. Now it was all his. Not a damn thing Sgt. Butthead could do about that.

Sgt. Butthead wasn't through with Joe, though. When Sgt. Butthead again showed up with another glowing smile, Joe was really puzzled. Joe knew he hadn't done anything wrong. "Joe, you are to report to the captain's office ASAP!" When Joe opened the door to the clerk's room, again all the typewriters stopped and all heads turned to look at him. Joe didn't know what the problem was but this had to be the deepest shit he ever stepped in.

Joe knocked on the captain's door and reported as before. "Joe, the captain said, "I have some very bad news for you; maybe you better sit down." Joe figured that probably Sgt. Butthead was finally able to make his charges stick. The captain said, "Someone in your immediate family has died." Joe's eyes bugged out; at first he didn't say anything. Then he made an odd request. He said, "Captain, I would like time to have a cigarette before you tell me."

Not a word was said as the cigarette slowly burned away. Joe was taking this last chance to remember his loved ones and say goodbye to each one of them in his own mind first. Joe thought goodbye to his mother first, then Chad, then Myra, and last Burney.

When Joe put the cigarette out, he said, "Okay, captain, I'm ready. Who is it?" The captain said, "It's your father, Joe." When Joe heard that, he let out the biggest sigh of relief he ever made. The captain—being a father himself—was greatly shocked and angered at Joe's response. "Oh, Captain, I never knew my father; I only met him for one day when I was ten years old," Joe said. "I have not seen him since. My immediate family was my mother and brothers and sister. I am sorry for my response sir, but I can't be upset about loosing someone I never knew." The captain came around to understanding and they had a nice chat about what the next step should be. He asked Joe if he wanted to go home. Amazed by the question Joe was speechless, but after considerable thought he said no. Why he said no was beyond even his own understanding. After all, that was honestly the only thing Joe really wanted more than anything else in the whole world: to go home.

The captain suggested Joe call home before making his final decision, and Joe agreed. It was a radiotelephone call halfway around the world; that was pretty good for back then considering satellites weren't in use yet. Joe could barely hear his mothers' voice. What he could hear was the suffering she was going through at her son being so far away and in a danger zone. Joe's year in Thailand was coming to an end anyway so he agreed to go home. All he could think of was, "I'm going home, I'm going home, I'm really going home! Oh my God— I'm going home!!!"

When Joe was returning to his barracks to pack his things he could see a rainbow in the southern sky. A rainbow always represented the promise of a bright new future, and that's what it meant for Joe, too. At that moment, a phantom jet came out of the eastern sky and was heading west right over the camp. Joe couldn't help but notice that sleek aircraft appearing to be gliding without resistance through the wide-open sky. The pilot did something Joe would never forget: he made a left turn towards the rainbow as if he could see it too, and then threw on his afterburners and shot through that rainbow like an arrow headed for a bull's eye. Joe was impressed by this free-wheeling spirit and figured that signaled the end of his Thailand adventure.

Joe had already put in his request for his next duty assignment; he requested to be sent to Korea. He wanted a fresh start on the oriental scene. Figuring that Korea was a different part of the Far East, he was curious about the differences. The orders were approved before they left the captain's desk. This was never done for anyone before. Joe could feel the influence of Colonel Green; that would be the only way this could happen. Joe had come to think of him as his guardian angel. It had to be the Colonel, like an all-seeing-but-never-seen entity, who was controlling the scene from behind the scenes. Joe often felt the Colonel favored him maybe because Joe reminded him of a fallen buddy or something like that.

All that mattered now was going home. Joe was packed and on a truck to the air base in minutes. Thoughts of how these people and this place had changed him and how the changes were permanent raced through his mind. It was funny to think that after spending a year of your life in one place and having a home there, you could just board a plane and never see the place or the people again.

He was going home on the same type of aircraft that he arrived on: a C130, the plane that had a roar like the devil. But now he was used to it and didn't even notice the sound. He rested his feet on the cargo and let all his cares go free. When they landed for a short stop in the Philippines the cargo was checked. The long silver box Joe had his feet on turned out to be a refrigerated coffin. It had the remains of a pilot that crashed a jet fighter. They opened the coffin for inspection and pulled out a small plastic bag and shook it. That was the entire inspection. That was all that was left of the guy. Joe felt sick to his stomach and at the same time lucky that it was not him.

As they approached California, Joe was feeling good that he was coming home alive and in one piece. The sounds of American voices and music on the radio were the first signs of home. The pilot announced that they would be landing soon. The sky was overcast with a thick blanket of clouds and when the plane hit them it bounced off them as though the clouds were a solid object. The pilot momentarily lost control of the plane, causing it to turn upside down. Joe thought how ironic it would be to survive all that went before just to die on the doorstep of his homeland. There was dead silence from everyone on the plane—no screaming or hysteria like you would imagine, just a planeload of frightened souls. Fortunately, the pilot recovered control of the aircraft. When the wheels touched ground, Joe felt that the death that had been stalking him had failed one more time. Finally, safe at home plate!

After being confined to an airplane seat for so many hours, all Joe wanted to do was stretch out in bed. He bee-lined it to the nearest hotel and went straight up to his room. He immediately ran over to the radio and turned on the sound of American music and voices. This seemed like such an awesome experience after hearing oriental sounds for so long. As soon as he got into bed, he noticed a strange mechanical device hooked up to the bed. It required a quarter to find out its purpose. Joe's curiosity was peaked to the max. As he inserted the quarter, the bed began vibrating like an 8.5 earthquake, causing Joe to break out in unleashed laughter. How wonderful Americans are, that they can make a bed do such a thing! It was no matter anyway, because Joe realized that he couldn't sleep on the bed, as he was now accustomed to sleeping on the floor on a mat. He woke up the next morning and was startled and disoriented by his surroundings. This was not the jungle and there was no smell of distant campfire. He could not remember where he was; then he saw his Army uniform and realized his direction would become clear soon. Somehow, he was suffering a momentary lapse of memory, but he was not concerned. When he found his airline ticket, everything came back to him.

Joe's original purpose in coming home early was to attend his father's funeral, which was taking place in Texas.

Not only was Joe not interested in flying to Texas but he was not interested in attending the funeral of a stranger with the title of father. Instead, all he could think of was home, blessed home. He remembered always wanting to see the other side of the world, now all he wanted was to come home from the other side of the world. He decided to take a non-stop flight to New York. He had a little money in his pocket and chose to take a first-class flight.

For a while during the flight the vista was an incredible view of the Rocky Mountains. Joe listened to beautiful music while seating in a spacious and comfortable seat. The stewardess was beautiful, too, and treated Joe like a king. The food was American food and tasted really great; even the butter had a sculpted shape to it. All of a sudden Joe started to cry, and he didn't know why. Joe tried to cover up his emotional outburst but the stewardess saw it. She asked him what was wrong, to which he could only reply that he had forgotten that life could be so good. He told her, "Look, even the butter has a fancy shape!" She seemed to understand and handed him a hot towel to dry his face. Imagine a tough and hardened soldier being brought to tears over a little first-class treatment. How embarrassing!

As the plane got closer and closer all he could think about was having a normal life again: houses in rows, home-cooked food, family and friends. Half his heart was exploding from the emotion and the relief he felt over being able to come back home, and the other half of his heart was crying over all he had been through. Five hundred miles an hour was not fast enough! Joe pushed the seat in front of him in a vain attempt to make the plane fly faster.

After arriving in New York, and while passing through New York City, Joe stopped in a restaurant for a cup of coffee. He went to raise the coffee to his mouth and his arm started shaking violently. His arm shook so much that the coffee spilled all over the place. Joe was slightly embarrassed but just figured it was an uncontrolled reflex, and should be no further problem. When he raised the second cup to his mouth the same thing happened. Wow! What's going on here? Well, this is a problem that I'll deal with tomorrow, he thought, 'cause I'm going home now. Joe apologized for the mess he caused, paid the check and left in a hurry before becoming a further spastic nuisance.

You want to hear something funny? Joe was home a month before having to go to his next assignment. For some unknown reason he doesn't remember a thing about the whole month he was home. He did have a problem with loud noises; the backfire of a car or the slamming of a door would cause him to "hit the deck" or assume an immediate combat stance. It was odd for his family to see Joe sleep on the floor. But it was the grocery store that really scared Joe the most: the bright lights, the bright colors, the cash registers going like machine guns, and a loud God-like voice that came from the ceiling shouting that fish was on sale for a reduced price. The jungle was a very quiet place where you could hear sounds at a long distance, where all the colors were the same, and a loud noise meant danger. Joe felt upset that his own country was now strange to him, but he was never so determined to bring his mind back home, too.

The last thing he remembered before going off to Korea was saying goodbye to his mother. She had lost a brother during the Korean War and now her son was going to the same place. As he was leaving the door, she called him back in an urgent way. Joe stopped dead in his tracks and asked, "What?" She had nothing to say; this happened three times in a row. She had a look on her face that said dread and danger at the same time. Joe smiled at her and said; "Don't worry, I'm indestructible!" He meant it, too. Joe wasn't that worried about his new assignment, mainly because there was no fighting going on in Korea since the early 1950s. That meant Joe could do his job without interruptions and unpleasant interference from the enemy. Not having a gun should be no real problem there either.

ONE YEAR IN HELL

WHEN JOE ARRIVED in Korea he found himself at the air base in Seoul, Korea. It was a place that seemed ready for anything. It was completely decked out in that special military decor. There were machine gun nests and jet fighters parked in combat-ready positions. This was where each man got his assignment to report to different sections of the country. A top sergeant came and announced that every one in the room could forget their previous orders. He yelled in the usual sergeant manner, "You troops are all going straight to the DMZ!" This is not what Joe had in mind. Besides, the last place for a coward is on the DMZ. Life on the "Z" was cold and hard. The men stationed there were the first men to meet the enemy if attacked, and they were really mean, tough men.

Joe realized he would again have to take matters into his own hands. There had to be an Army Security Agency detachment in this country somewhere. Once he connected with his own men, they would get him headed in the right direction, mainly away from any misunderstandings or unfortunate circumstances that the DMZ had to offer. Just then a man yelled, "Bus leaving! All aboard!" Not knowing or caring where the hell the bus was going, Joe slipped out the back door and boarded that bus so fast that he made the doors flutter as he went through them. Any place was better than the DMZ, and if that sergeant wanted Joe for the DMZ, he would have to catch him first. After all, the front lines are certainly no place for a coward! Just by a miracle of chance that bus was going straight to Camp K6 Humphreys, exactly what was on Joe's reassignment orders.

The bus went south through the countryside to Joe's new home. There were mountains with small trees everywhere. Each house he saw had a neat little garden. There were rice fields—of course—and fields of ginseng growing everywhere.

The mountains had large sand pits in them; Joe would later find that they were the holes left from phosphorous bombs that were dropped some 25 years ago. Also, the reason for the small trees was because during that war all the trees were leveled.

Finally the bus pulled into a small town. All the buildings were made of adobe. There was a big sign at the end of town that read "Camp Humphreys." Joe got off the bus and walked under the sign expecting to see an Army camp. There was no camp! There was a huge open field with nothing on it. Great, just great!!! After traveling half way around the world, now he was expected to spend a year in a big open field on the ass end of nowhere. Then off in the far distance he saw the glimmer of a small white building. It was about a mile down the road. Joe walked to it and saw the familiar antenna associated with his job. Well, it wasn't much but it was certainly better than the DMZ.

After getting settled in, it was time to explore the surroundings. Joe ventured into town and found a number of places for entertainment. He noticed what a strange-looking place this was. The streets were muddy with red clay for dirt and there was a feeling of uneasiness everywhere. It was hard to describe, but there was a certain callous attitude about the whole place and the people too.

There were living areas called compounds where the people lived. They had about four or five rooms in a row, surrounded by a tall wall that had embedded glass chards with barbed wire at the top. There was one restroom shared by all across the open common area of the compound. The alleys between the compounds were very narrow. The roofs over the rooms hung low into the alley; they were plenty high for the Koreans but Americans could surely suffer a serious concussion if they ran into the roofs, especially at night.

Each single room in the compound was a kitchen, bedroom, dining room, and living room all in one. Each room was a family's home, no matter how big the family. Each home had a small coal-burning stove to keep warm in the winter; you placed two bricks of coal in the stove at a time that lasted about three hours, then the cold reminded you to put fresh bricks in—especially at night. The stoves had a piping system that carried the fumes to the outdoors. God help you if the pipes had a leak because you could easily get poisoned by carbon monoxide and die in your sleep.

Not having soil available, rice was grown in red clay. Joe later found out how they can grow things in clay: they carry the contents of everyone's cesspool out to the rice fields and spread it around. In the summertime, the smell would rise about six feet above the ground. All in all, you would swear you were in hell. All in all, this wasn't the kind of place where you would want to spend the next year of your life.

It was hard to believe that anybody could ever adapt to this place with any measure of reasonable comfort, but many did. Joe would simply do as he did before: imitate the success of others. He would find himself a one-room house and would then start shopping for a moose (moose being the name for a Korean girlfriend). It was certainly a strange thought to try and build a life for yourself in hell, but that was the task at hand.

This new duty station was a helicopter base and there was always some large object flying through the air being carried by a helicopter. Joe's job was fairly routine: to surrender himself again to the interception of never-ending radio signals. The idea was to maintain the status quo by regularly monitoring and intercepting hostile communication. Joe was no longer seeking to test his heroism or seeking recognition for his accomplishments. He was simply trying to survive within the confines of a hostile environment. Even the men he had served with had changed and had a kind of morbid morale. That is what happens to men that have been away from home too long and miss their loved ones. Even the Army was aware of this because they asked the men what they missed the most besides family. A lot of the guys said they missed the large-sized hamburgers. So the Army invented their very own large hamburger. Joe was mighty surprised to find the damn thing was pretty damn good.

On another occasion, Joe got a craving for strawberries; that was unusual all by itself, mainly because he didn't even like strawberries as they made him breakout. In fact, he hated strawberries and never ate them. The very next day they served strawberries in the mess hall. Joe wasn't the only one with a strawberry craving because all the men went through countless vats of strawberries and still they wanted more. So they kept serving strawberries until all requests were filled. Joe had over ten full bowls of strawberries. The odd thing was that he would never eat another strawberry again. Joe had never really seen an example of the Army trying to make a place more pleasant to live, which just goes to show how bad things really were.

Joe could readily see that this Korea experience was not going to be an individual type of experience. Whatever happened to his unit was going to happen to Joe, too. There was an exception that comes to mind right away: when Joe finally hooked up with a moose. Her name was Kim. In fact, all the Korean girls were named Kim; that was good because if you ever cheated on your girl you would never get in trouble by calling her by the wrong name! Anyway, this Kim was nothing special as far as looks go but her personality was that of a loyal woman. She would serve the purpose of keeping Joe company and being his woman too. On this one day, they were going to enjoy themselves at a kids' park. This was just a playground for children, with swings and slides and everything else you would expect. Joe's favorite was the merry-go-round, a large spinning wheel where you sit on after starting it manually. This merry-go-round was the biggest one Joe had ever seen. He had his moose join him for a spin. She sat on the wheel while Joe got a good running start and jumped on. This wheel went far faster than Joe had ever experienced and this was completely unexpected. The centrifugal force was almost too much for Joe; when he turned to look at Kim he could see she was losing her grip. Joe yelled, "Don't let go; hang on!" At that very moment she let go. Kim went sailing into the air, turning her into what now could be called a "flying moose." Joe was amazed to see her whole body leave the ride and fly backwards like that. She landed on the concrete about ten feet away, not very gracefully, looking like a gooney bird with no breaks. Her landing was like a hit-bounce-and-roll acrobatic move. After her body stopped rolling, she looked like a broken rag doll. The whole thing was so surreal that Joe couldn't help but laugh. Joe was finally able to stop the merry-go-round and ran to Kim's aide.

When he helped her up he could see her face, arms, and legs were covered with road rash. Fortunately, there was no serious injury. Joe was eventually able to get her to laugh about the whole experience. Joe helped her limp back into town and back to the "hooch" or house. As they were entering town, several Korean men started to look concerned when they saw her. It must have looked like Joe had spent all day beating the crap out of her. A small crowd of men formed around Joe looking kind of hostile towards this unwelcome American brute. Since Joe never had and never would hurt a woman, it didn't dawn on him what could be the problem—but that small crowd had every intention of beating the very life out of Joe. When Kim told them the truth of what had happened, they seemed to be kind of disappointed that they had lost their chance to kick the stuffing out of an American.

Joe had made a small group of friends by this time; one was named Smitty. Smitty was an average red-blooded American guy. He was the type of guy that made for a good friend. Smitty had a moose named Cho. Cho was a very attractive

Korean girl. In reality, she was a living ball of fire. She had more life in her than a dozen other women combined. If you ever saw two people more in love, it was Smitty and Cho. Occasionally the Army would declare the base off limits to Korean nationals, and Smitty and Cho would spend the night on a hill alongside the helicopter pad. They would fight off mosquitoes, cold, and dampness—and avoid the occasional helicopter—without minding a bit, just to be together, wrapped up in each other's arms until morning.

For as hard and cold as Korea was, Smitty and Cho set the example that love can exist anywhere. As they loved each other with all their hearts, they would also fight with each other with equal intensity. Cho could also be compared to a class-five hurricane. On one visit to their hooch, Joe was making a right turn into the alley where they lived. All Joe could see was Smitty pinned up against the wall by debris flying at him through the open door of their home. All Joe could do was turn around and abort the visit.

It all started one night when Smitty and Cho had one of their famous break-ups. Cho was hanging out with Joe and some of the other guys at a local watering hole. All Joe had in mind was getting drunk as usual. Over the course of the night the other guys slowly went their own way. Cho and Joe remained sitting alone with each other. Joe figured this would be a good time to get to know Cho a little better. But before Joe could speak a word, Cho asked him if he wanted to return to her place. Joe asked, "What about Smitty?" She said they were broken up and he didn't matter anymore. Joe said okay.

Joe had not seen a Korean woman that really sparked his interest, but Cho was different. She was a spark of life that kept a man interested, no matter what. Joe knew she was special and if Smitty couldn't make her happy then he would. Joe was thrilled that now he was going to love and make love to a woman he knew he would always remember. A woman he really wanted, and even more, wanted to keep.

First they both went to a bathhouse. It seemed to be the custom to bathe each other first. Cho taught Joe that this could be a very relaxing preamble. When they got to her hooch, she locked the doors and windows, and they started making love. They made love for two days and three nights in a row, only stopping for a quick snack to keep their energy up. Sure, Joe had had marathon sex before, but never lasting that long. When it was over, he felt as though he had experienced some kind of renewal of life. She had satisfied him and made him happy at the same time. Joe was already thinking about the next time he would see her. He started thinking about different ways to make her happy, about how he finally had someone he really cared about, which sure gave meaning to life again.

Joe was walking back to base feeling the sun on his face. It was a long walk, but what the hell; it was a beautiful day for walking. The sun was shining and happy wonderful thoughts filled his head. Off in the distance Joe could see a figure coming towards him. It took a long time but finally Joe saw it was "Tall Pine." They called him that because he was a big farm boy. Kind of strange for a farm boy to be savvy in the ways of the big city—but he was. Joe greeted Tall Pine and asked what's new? The first thing out of the bastard's mouth was, "Did you hear that Smitty and Cho got back together?" Joe replied, "Can't be true—I just left her." Tall said, "It's true" and kept walking. Deep down in his heart, Joe knew it too, because no sane man would ever leave a woman like Cho. She was exciting and knew how to make a man feel alive. Without her a man was just living. But to know her and then lose her was a really special kind of pain. So not only did he have to be in Korea, but now he felt as though his heart had just hit the red clay beneath his feet. He waited until he could hear the last sound of the last beat of his pitiful heart, before what remained of him could continue his zombie-like walk back to the barracks.

The very next day Joe ran into Smitty on the same road. Smitty told Joe that he knew what had happened. The two men discussed the situation in a manner that was befitting their friendship. Joe knew he wronged his friend and did the best to explain what happened and why. Joe told Smitty that he loved Cho. Smitty responded in a way that proved he loved her too. He forgave Joe, and to prove it, he invited Joe to dinner that night. Joe wasn't sure whether to attend the dinner, but was compelled by curiosity to learn about forgiveness, to see if it was really possible, especially in this instance. Joe also wanted to see her again, to look into her eyes and feel the full measure of exactly how wrong he was about his own feelings.

Joe was glad that he accepted the invitation; it was a very enlightening experience. Cho behaved as if nothing had happened between them, Joe finally saw how his illusions of happiness betrayed him in full. Nevertheless, the three of them had a delicious dinner and warm and caring conversation. Joe was humbled by the entire experience and knew he would always remember these friends. If the day ever came for Joe to be the one to do the forgiving, he would do it with the grace and maturity that was shown to him.

The only good time left for Joe was a drunken time. That's the way he stayed as often as possible. One night, Joe returned to the barracks from town after a night of drinking. The guys were having a poker game and invited Joe to join. He really shouldn't have because he was "three sheets to the wind." Joe could barely see the cards, never mind what was on them. After losing three month's pay to Tall Pine, he called it quits.

The next day Joe realized he couldn't pay, mainly because half his pay went home to family. This was a real problem because bad things would happen to people that didn't pay Tall Pine. Like broken arms or legs or whatever would befall them. So Joe approached him with a deal. Joe said he would pay back half the money and work his own shift and Tall Pine's for a month. The offer was accepted with one addition: Joe had to agree never to gamble again. That's the way it was for the next month: Joe worked two shifts, 16 hours a day. It really didn't matter much, because if you live in hell you might as well be at work.

When the sentence was paid in full, Joe resumed his life of ill repute. On one occasion he convinced this working girl to have sex with him in exchange for his dog tags. He told the girl the tags were as good as a credit card, and if he didn't pay she could take those tags to the Army and get reimbursed. To prove his honesty, he pointed out the name and serial number on the tags that identified him. For not having any cash, Joe seemed to be able to take care of his needs very well. Joe thought the guys back at camp would never believe this one. But things didn't turn out as he planned. The very next night Joe was out bar-hopping again and ran into the same girl. She was as pissed off as a Korean girl could get. She followed Joe to every bar and told everyone what a cheap skate he was.

Joe was doing his best to avoid the girl and he thought he lost her a time or two. But no! There she was again. Half the night went like this. Joe got the idea he was going to have to put this girl's lights out. He was going to let her follow him into a deserted ally and then he would deck her with one punch. The plan was going well; she was following him everywhere. He went into the ally and she followed without hesitation. He then turned around and grabbed her by the scruff of the neck. He pulled back for the punch and stopped. Joe was disgusted to see the contemptible beast he had turned into. He saw it and the shock of it was enough to get him sick. He let the girl go and started back to camp. She followed him and turned him into the military police at the main gate. They arrested Joe and he found himself standing before a really tall desk, like in court. The desk sergeant came out and read the charges. He looked down at Joe and asked, "Did you really get laid for your dog tags?" Joe stared upward and replied, "Yes, sergeant, I did." The sergeant asked, "Why don't you just pay the girl?" Joe replied that he didn't pay because the girl had made him angry. The sergeant said, "Pay the girl and get out of here." Joe complied and the matter was dropped.

Joe was still shocked by the change he saw in himself. He was afraid this would be a permanent change for the worst. He knew he had been able to stay the "beast from within" this time, but what about the next time? Would he or could he ever cross the line that separates decent behavior from that of an animal? He became so afraid of what he could do as evidenced by what he had attempted to do that he buried the entire experience deep within the regions of his most unobtainable psyche, as though it was his worst sin and it had to be hidden.

In Korea, you had to be off the streets by 12 midnight or get a rifle butt in the head by the Korean police. Because of this, the guys would get together and chip in to rent a bar for the night. That way you could get drunk and not worry about curfew. Oh, my God! The things that would go on behind closed doors were akin to the lustful cravings of Barbarians: sex, drugs and rock & roll everywhere, naked dancing girls on all the tables. These parties were called "body-count parties" mainly because sometimes during clean up they would find someone buried under the leftover debris. Joe had attended his first body-count party, which meant that you were on the "accepted and trusted list." When the party ended the next day and the doors opened, Joe was completely spent. The first glint of sunlight sent Joe's eyes back into the farthest recesses of his head. Every sound seemed to be emanating from a giant gong. This was not good since he had to be on the job in twenty minutes. It was especially not good because the North Koreans had been acting up lately.

North Korea had sent an envoy to China to request support for a second invasion of South Korea. Joe knew that if

China agreed to this, then everyone's ass would be in the wind, including his. The job was sure getting a little tense, mainly because Korea is the last place where you want to fight a war. There wasn't a damn thing to hide behind, not even a tree, and nowhere to run, either. It was probably a similar scenario that got his uncle killed 20 years before. Although his uncle distinguished himself valiantly, Joe knew he wasn't made of the same stuff.

When China said no to the North Korean request for support, Joe breathed a sigh of relief. Now he could just finish his time and get the hell out of there. But the real scary shit wasn't over yet. North Korea then sent the same request to Russia. Joe could see how much the North Koreans wanted to take the South and he didn't want to get in the way, for good or bad. If Russia said yes, then it would be "asses in the wind" all over again. When Russia said no, too, Joe knew he would live to be an old man. Maybe his Uncle's sacrifice did make a difference in the long run. It's funny to think that a world leader in another part of the world—whom Joe had never met and who probably couldn't even speak the same language—could have the power of life or death over him from a distance. Then again, maybe it's not funny at all. "No!" Joe thought, "It is absolutely not funny at all!!!"

Joe was learning just how crazy the North Koreans really were. He was wondering what their next move would be. They used up their trump cards, but Joe knew not to turn his back on such a determined and relentless people. Joe knew his only weapon was a radio, and that's what he would use. Maybe they would make a mistake and reveal their next plan by a "slip of a lip." Most people are unaware that code-breaking radio operators made major contributions to the winning of World War II and every war after that. Sort of like the saying, "The pen is mightier than the sword" or "For loss of a message the war was lost." With radio, it was like a hide-and-seek waiting game. You had to be patrolling the airways and be in the right place at the right time. You had to be able to identify origin and type in a split second.

But it only took one hit of a highly classified signal to make the difference. Sometimes the enemy would throw you a curve and hide a signal in or around regular radio music or plain carrier tone. In fact, Joe was intercepting a strange carrier tone at this very moment. Okay, if this was a carrier tone then all he had to do was wait until the station came on line, then he would know all was well. It only takes a few minutes for a station to warm up and get on the air anyway. Most interceptors wouldn't wait around, figuring it was a waste of time. Joe only stayed because he thought he had heard a waver, which may indicate a hidden signal. He could have his suspicion verified as being unfounded and unreliable by just staying on that frequency. The tone continued without variation; why was the station not coming up? Who in hell would send a carrier tone with no message? Joe turned his equipment on and decided to take a sample for further investigation. The sound could be photographed and areas of sound beyond human hearing could be detected for variations.

Joe took all the samples he needed then turned the matter over to his supervisor. It was later determined that the sound was not a radio signal at all. It was what drilling equipment sounds like when picked up by a radio operator. This drilling equipment was being used by the North Koreans to create large tunnels through the mountains for a new invasion route where they would be least expected: in the mountainous region on the eastern side of the DMZ. Listening poles were placed in the ground and the tunnels were located through cross triangulation. Pictures were taken of the tunnels and presented at the United Nations. This was naturally a very embarrassing situation for the North Koreans. It also enabled President Ford to have approval from Congress to send small nuclear weapons to Korea. The funny thing about the whole affair was that everything went really quiet after that.

Well, it was time for another body-count party. Joe was feeling out of sorts and really didn't have the kind of energy it took to survive one of those things, so he told the guys to count him out. It was a lucky thing for Joe too, because the party was busted. The MP's, the C.I.D., and the Korean police were there; in other words, everyone and his mother. They kicked open the door armed with sub-machine guns and lined everyone up against the wall. A lot of Joe's friends got away but a lot of guys got arrested, too. Naturally this cast suspicion on Joe as being a ratfink because he wasn't there. The other men questioned Joe but he told them the only thing he knew: that he was from New York, where the penalty for ratting is death. They believed him and there was no further problem. That is, there was no further problem until the next time.

About a month later another party was scheduled. Only the in-crowd was invited, which included Joe. Only this time a program called "M.A.S.H." was coming on television and Joe wanted to watch it. The show was about soldiers in Korea; Joe thought it was a novel idea to be in Korea as a soldier and watch a show about it. He was also writing a letter home. At some point, he got up to go to the latrine and came back to find his letter missing. There was no evidence that a letter was ever being written. But he was sure that he was writing one. He checked the floor and the desk and this was truly an unexplainable thing. Who would want to take a letter to his mother and why, he wondered. The answer came the next day when a spy was caught with letters from many soldiers. The enemy would use personal information to blackmail or bribe soldiers into giving up classified information. This spy—who worked in the barracks—was turned over to the South Korea Army because they had no mercy; they readily shot him. Joe could not believe the enemy was in his room, and that a man got shot dead over a letter to his mother.

Anyway, Joe had told the guys he would join them at the party after the show. That's not what happened though. Joe was tired and went to bed instead. Again, the party was busted. Again, it was MP's, C.I.D., and Korean police. Again, a lot of Joe's friends were arrested. Again, Joe was asked if he had turned informer; he told them he knew nothing about it. Joe and one other guy were the only ones that did not attend both parties. This other guy was not an accepted member of the group and suspicion was running high against both men. Dylan, one of Joe's friends, told Joe they were going to find the informant, and when they did, they would cut his throat from ear to ear. Again Joe swore by all that was holy that he was innocent. Dylan looked at Joe with a cold glassy stare and said, "Joe, if it is you, friend or not, I will kill you myself." Then Joe knew how much trouble he was in.

While on his way to the mess hall later on, Joe passed a friend and said hello, but the friend did not respond. Joe just thought maybe the guy just didn't hear. The same thing happened several times in a row with several others. Joe thought maybe there is something wrong with his voice, but he could hear himself clearly. After getting his food, Joe saw a table where most of his friends were sitting and he went over and sat down. At that moment, everyone at the table got up and left. Joe then realized he was getting the silent treatment. This treatment was reserved for unconfirmed informants. This angered Joe to no end; what kind of people convict before all the evidence was in? Joe knew from experience that this was the preliminary treatment before a possible death sentence was pronounced. Joe had seen before how informants were treated and how they turned up missing or dead. In Joe's mind, if you were an informant then death was too good for you. Joe believed that slow torture, then death, was more appropriate. Now he was on the other end of the stick. He knew there was no way he could prove his innocence, but he had to turn things around before it was too late. Joe certainly didn't want to end up a casualty of friendly fire. Also, because he was one of them, he knew they weren't kidding.

A plan was needed. Joe figured that if he went straight to the barracks from work every day, and stay there until work the following day, this would eliminate him from further suspicion as he wouldn't have any knowledge of other parties or happenings. It was a mighty hard thing to do, to stay locked up in a small room with no human contact. Since not a soul on base was talking to him anyway, it didn't make much difference. Now all he had to do was find a way to keep entertained until the real informant was found. So he bought a thousand dollars worth of stereo equipment and listened to music every night, night after night. More body-count parties were held and of course Joe was no longer being invited. After several weeks, Joe's actions were being noticed. Dylan stopped by and told Joe to keep doing what he was doing and soon all would be okay.

After so much silent treatment, Joe really didn't care for anyone's company anymore anyway. More time went by; in fact, three months had gone by without a single word being said to Joe for anything. But at least he was still alive, even though it was hard for Joe to keep this up. One day, Joe was headed back to the barracks after work as usual. He couldn't believe his ears when another soldier said hello to him. He thought it must be a mistake and continued walking. Then someone else said hello and Joe wondered what the hell was going on. Shortly after, he found out that by taking himself out of the picture the others had time to find the real informant through the process of elimination. The bastard was found and it was no surprise to Joe when he turned up missing.

Joe was welcomed back into the fold, but he had changed now. He no longer needed the companionship of his peers. During his next and last association with his so-called friends, Joe lashed out. He berated each one of them, one at a time, to the full measure of their scum-sucking existence. He told them that at one time he thought he had something to learn from each one of them. He couldn't believe that they could turn their friendship on and off like a faucet. His so-called friends had threatened his life. He was wrong to think that they had something to offer or teach him. All they did was insult each other on a constant basis. Their behavior had disgusted Joe, and he didn't want to have anything else to do with any of them.

Back to the goddamn job again because that was all he had. If listening to signals all day wasn't enough, now they were asking for volunteers for a dangerous mission. There was a mountain on the DMZ with a monitoring station at the top from where the Army could monitor the build-up of enemy troops. Our side owned the mountain, but the enemy was at the bottom of it. The soldiers stationed up there had to be eventually replaced. Joe knew the first rule of being a soldier was never to volunteer for anything. Especially when he found out that the first two helicopters that tried to get there were lost, one from high winds and another from sniper fire. This trip would be the third attempt to replace the men. The sergeant pointed at Joe and said, "You are a volunteer." Joe thought, "Shit, shit, shit! Now I'm going to get my ass stuck on a top of a mountain in the danger zone until hell freezes over." They would take you up there, leave you there, and promptly forget about you. Well, at least he wouldn't have to leave for a while; the mission was scheduled for the following month.

Finally, after his self-imposed solitary confinement, Joe was able to go out again; he went to town to buy a new shirt. The Korean tailor measured Joe's neck. In fact, he measured Joe's neck three times, each time saying "No, no can be." Joe thought this Korean was sure acting strange. When he got back to the barracks, Joe did notice that his neck was quite a bit wider. He just thought it was the military training making him look like a leatherneck Marine. He also started to get these tremendous headaches. No, not just headaches; they were super migraines. The headaches were so bad he had to hold his head to keep from screaming in pain. This had never happened to him before, but if it continued happening Joe knew it was a sure sick call for him. Well, it happened again and again and again. After about a week of this pain, Joe was left in a completely weakened state. Not able to even do his job, Joe reported for sick call.

When he got to the hospital, there was a line out the door and in the snow; it looked like the whole camp was sick. He stood in line, in the snow, as long as he could. As he reached the door of the hospital, he felt like he was losing consciousness so he grabbed the top of the door to steady himself. He was hanging onto that door for so long that the entire line went by. It must have been hours when, finally, a doctor who was leaving the building stopped and asked Joe what he was doing. All he could say was that he was sick. The doctor examined him and concluded that it was mononucleosis—the kissing disease. Joe was relieved that it was not serious and took the antibiotics the doc gave him. But the next morning, while he was combing his hair in the mirror, he noticed a large, golf-ball sized lump on his neck. Wow! He thought, "This is the largest pimple that I've ever seen." When he touched it, it was hard and solid. This was no pimple, and this was certainly not a case of mono either. This really pissed Joe off that this doctor was wrong and now he would have to go back to the hospital.

When he saw the doctor again—who happened to be a major—Joe did three things. One, he pointed to his neck and said, "If this is mono, then I'm Red Chinese." The second thing he said was, "You're fired!" And the third was, "Find a replacement for yourself immediately." There was no hint of military courtesy or respect for a superior officer. Joe was only a corporal, which was even less than a sergeant. But one thing Joe could not abide by was an incompetent officer. "Those dumb bastards get people killed," is what he always said. At least this dumb bastard saw the resolve in Joe's eyes and heard the meaningful message in the tone of Joe's voice. Fortunately for him, he did exactly as Joe had ordered.

The replacement doctor was not even three steps in the door before he diagnosed the problem and started talking about sending Joe to the 121st Evac Hospital in Seoul, as they had better facilities there. Joe asked him what the hell was the lump in his neck. The doctor said, "That's why we are sending you to Seoul, to find out." Joe could tell that this doctor knew more than he was saying; that's when Joe stopped asking. If this doctor didn't want to come out and tell him what the problem was, then Joe didn't really want to know. Maybe it was best leaving things alone until absolute proof could be obtained. "Ignorance is bliss," he thought. And he needed all the bliss he could get, so there was no need for further questions. Besides that, this meant that Joe could get out of this God-forsaken shithole, and anyplace else is where he wanted to be.

The joy of being transferred overcame any fear of illness. In fact, he felt as though all of a sudden it was Christmas and Santa had just filled his wish list. The more he thought about it, the harder it was to keep his insides from exploding with screams of joy! But just to be sure, Joe asked the doctor again in a low, unsuspicious tone of voice, like he didn't really care. "Do you mean I can leave here?" The doctor said, "Yes." With that little yes, Joe sat calmly and quietly as every fiber of his being started celebrating his liberation from hell. If this doctor knew what was going on inside of Joe, he would have had him hospitalized for joy overdose. This also meant no mission to the DMZ! They could take their dangerous mission and stick it where the sun doesn't shine. "I'm still alive," he thought, "and now I can stay that way."

Yahoo!!! Joe ran back to the barracks to pack. He figured it would take a couple of hours, with stereo equipment and all. Then some fellow soldier came into the room and asked, "Are you Joe?" "Yea, what's the problem?" Joe asked. "The truck's outside and you've got five minutes to get on it." Five minutes! He had no choice but to ask the houseboy to send his stereo equipment on, but Joe had to give up a suede leather jacket to get cooperation from the little thief. Joe was ready in five minutes—nothing was going to stop his ass from getting on that truck.

As the truck was headed for Seoul on the main road, Joe took a moment to admire the scenery, the small trees, the bomb scars in the mountains left over from the war 20 years ago. Just then those little trees started moving. There were thousands of South Korean troops pouring out of those trees. They swarmed over the valley like locust and rolled over the next mountain like an unstoppable green tide. Joe knew again he was caught off guard; even though there was no war, this was inexcusable. You don't get caught off guard ever!!! You be stupid, you be dead! Joe realized he was far too stupid to be in this dangerous part of the world. That meant it was time to go home and get the hell out of Dodge. To further emphasize the danger, the truck Joe was in was on the outside of a wide turn. Up ahead of the turn, Joe could see an overturned truck on the inside right lane. At the same time, a bus was coming from behind Joe's truck on the right lane. The bus didn't see the overturned truck in time to stop. "Boom!" The bus hit the overturned truck and glass and people went flying. Joe yelled, "We've got to stop, maybe we can help!" The driver said, "We can't stop; this is a Korean matter and we are not authorized to lend assistance." Joe wondered what kind of world this is, that people don't stop to help each other.

Arrival at the 121st Evac Hospital in Seoul was finally accomplished. Joe had some time to kill after settling in. He went around to meet the other guys in his room. Most of his fellow patients had been shot up on the DMZ. Either it was the enemy that was shooting or it was friendly troops shooting each other in the dark. Joe didn't think getting shot was as bad as the marine with a rash. This marine was on a mission in the mountains and came back with a small rash. This rash became progressively worse and was beginning to cover his entire body. It was a red, bumpy, baby-like rash that itched with no relief. Unfortunately, the doctors didn't have a cure. Joe made the conversation short because the last thing he needed was an incurable rash.

That's when the doctor found Joe and gave him an exam; he told Joe they would have to give him a biopsy. Joe thought a biopsy was a pill, and when the doctor explained that they actually had to operate on his throat, Joe yelled, "You're not going to cut my throat, buddy!!!" The doctor reminded Joe that he was government property and really didn't have a choice in the matter. Joe realized that he really didn't have a choice and requested that at least the resulting scar be a small one—he didn't want to be left with railroad track stitches all over his neck. The doctor reassured him that it would be okay, and the operation was scheduled for the next morning.

After the surgery, when Joe regained enough strength to walk again, he happened to pass by the doctor's office and saw him sitting there. Well, why not stop in and say hello. Joe swaggered through the door and jokingly asked, "Well, doc, is it a matter of life and death or what?" The doctor turned to Joe and said yes. Joe asked, "What the hell are you talking about?" The doctor replied, "You have a form of cancer, but we're going to have to send you back to the States to determine the type." All Joe heard was "States." He knew that meant the United States of America. He knew that meant he was going home. Any reason to leave this place was a good one for him. Within 24 hours, he was on his way. He was glad this Korea bullshit was finally over.

What a long ride it was! It didn't matter, though, because Joe would have kissed the devil's ass to get home. He landed in California, from where he flew to Washington D.C. on a Learjet. It was the middle of the night when he arrived and the air was warm. Again, there was no welcome-home parade. As Joe entered the air terminal, the sweet smell of a woman's perfume caught his attention; it reminded him of a promise he had made to himself, to kiss the first American girl he encountered wearing perfume. Unfortunately, the woman turned out to be an armed immigration guard; Joe approached her and told her that he had just come from the worst-smelling country in the world and he needed to fulfill a promise. She was amused by his story and agreed to help him carry out his pledge. They kissed. That was Joe's welcome home.

THE GREATEST BATTLE YET

JOE WAS TAKEN by ambulance from the airport to Walter Reed Hospital. Upon leaving the ambulance, Joe found himself standing on a dock-like platform. As he was straightening his hospital pajamas, a woman's voice came from a dark corner. The unseen person asked, "Joe, is that you?" Joe's reflexes made him jump into a military defensive stance and said, "Show yourself." It was Myra, his sister! They hugged, and he couldn't keep himself from crying. He couldn't believe his entire family was waiting there for him. Everything was going to be okay now. Joe made it back alive despite all the close calls, mishaps, and insanity. If anything were going to happen now, it would be on American soil, where there were no land mines, enemy patrols, snipers or friendly fire. Little did he know, but the real war was just starting.

Joe had discovered that a hero in one circumstance can be a coward in another, and that a coward can be a hero, too, under the appropriate conditions. He had learned a lot about the truth of his own strengths and weaknesses. But Joe no longer cared about such trivia. He realized that to win the game you had to live, that's all; just staying alive means you win! If you survived in one piece, then you were the grand champion of all time.

The first day in his new hospital home there was a morale-building party going on. There was music and even a belly dancer. Joe really needed this, too; it was a chance to relax and forget for a short while. Any good time was a time worth having, especially now. The belly dancer even coaxed Joe to join in. This was obviously an inopportune time for the new doctor to meet Joe. The doctor was a tall, thin man who was mostly bald. He stood in the door with a stern stance and a stern tone in his voice. He said from across the room, "I'm your doctor, and you don't look sick." Joe had enough of doctors that knew everything but still diagnosed wrong. Joe told the doctor it was impressive how he could misdiagnose from across the room. As this doctor began to speak again, Joe cut him off. In a loud voice, Joe yelled, "You're dismissed, and find a replacement for yourself!" Joe felt that the first rule of medicine should be to respect the patient and he would not accept less.

The very next day a staff of 40 doctors, like a herd of white coats, descended down on him. They all stood in line to poke and prod Joe, each one doing the same tests. It was determined that the biopsy that was done in Korea would be needed to take out some of the guesswork. Well, that was just fine with Joe, because he didn't want anything to do with guesswork either.

He had a few days to wait before any treatment could begin. After spending the last year in a place where the normal decor was human waste, where a human body could freeze solid, where the silent, odorless gas of carbon monoxide could leak through a pipe and kill you while you slept, where you could get your throat cut by a friend, all Joe was interested in was having a good time. Of course having a good time in a military hospital after the Vietnam war proved to be somewhat of a challenge. They did have a recreation room, and you could go outside and get some sun on a bench, but that was it.

It was during one of those days of sunbathing on the bench when Joe woke up from a nap and saw something. He couldn't make out what he saw because his eyes were still groggy from sleep. But it was large and white and had many sections to it. It was moving at ground level, and from a distance appeared to be wavy patches of moving white snow. Upon clearing his eyes, he saw what the image really was. Yes, he could identify it, but believe it? No! He looked away real quick, and then looked back just to insure a mirage or illusion could be ruled out. It was real all right: real women, hundreds and hundreds of them!!! Is God good or what? There was a nursing school on the hospital grounds; they were all nurse trainees dressed in white, all going to the mess hall.

Now being the good soldier Joe had become, he was able to size up the situation and determine that both backup and reinforcements would be needed. He really wanted to attack on his own, and why not. But this was different. Joe had made a couple of friends in his short time at the hospital, so he ran all the way back to his room to get Boli, his roommate. Boli was a tall, blonde-haired guy with fair skin. You couldn't tell he was tall because he was always in bed. He was there for a heart condition.

Joe tried to appear calm, cool, and collected when he got back. He asked Boli, "What is the only thing that would get you out of that bed?" Boli rolled over and looked at Joe with a timeless groggy stare and said one word, "Women." Joe couldn't hold it back any longer; he told Boli about what he saw. Now every soldier knows that you do not lie or joke about finding women. This is a subject of complete reverence. Boli took a long look into Joe's eyes and asked him, "What have those doctors been doing to you?" Joe said, "Boli, I swear! I know I saw this! Please come with me to be sure. If you see them too, then I know I'm okay."

Boli reluctantly crawled out of bed and grabbed his pajamas. Joe said, "We have got to find Nate, I think we're going to need all the help we can get with this." Nate was standing in the door and asked, "What for?" Joe told Nate about his unbelievable discovery. Nate asked Joe, "Are you okay, man? What would hundreds of women be doing in a military hospital?" Joe said that it looked like they were going to lunch. The three headed for the mess hall to get verification. It was a long walk and Joe secretly doubted his vision the whole way, but didn't say anything. When they got to the mess hall, the three of them peeked around the door like Moe, Larry, and Curly. When they pulled their heads back, no words were said, but their eyes were all bulged out in disbelief. It was true, they were real! Joe took a sigh of relief because he knew now that he was really okay.

It was Boli that called for an immediate retreat. He was the true thinker and natural leader of the group. Joe argued, saying, "We are here now, we should attack!" Nate agreed with Boli, saying how a plan was needed first. Boli told Joe that if you just jump in, they will scatter and you will come up empty handed. Joe finally agreed and the three set off to plan their strategy. They observed the targets from a distance to determine when and where would be the best application for success. They decided to wait till the next day to take action. A plan was developed where the three would be casually talking as the "herd" was approaching. Then, when they were close, the three would fling open their pajama shirts, exposing their t-shirts that would read "Ward B, Room 343. Come up and see me!" The plan was put into action the next day. Joe was surprised to see how it made the women laugh, and be dogged if some of them didn't seem interested! Now all that had to be done was wait for a visit.

In a short while, Joe lost interest in his natural pursuits as his condition began to get worse. More swollen lymph nodes had appeared and Joe couldn't help but notice how he was becoming weaker. For the first time, he really felt as though he was dying. It was a sensation like being flushed down the toilet and there was nothing anyone could do. You would slowly get weaker and weaker as the doctors increased the testing. One test called for a doctor to dig holes in the top of both of Joe's feet. A radioactive dye was injected and then x-rays were taken. Joe's lymphatic system lit up like a Christmas tree, showing the true extent of his decline. Another test was for a doctor to stand on top of the bed as he used the entire weight of his body to shove a thin pipe through Joe's hip bone. The test was so painful that Joe's body rose three inches off the bed with the doctor sitting on his back.

As bad news became the theme of his existence, what did he next get more of? That's right, worse news. The doctors told Joe that the Korean biopsy was lost and another one was needed. Joe asked in complete shock, "Do you mean you want to cut my throat again?" Great, just great! Since it was even more apparent now that something had to be done, Joe had no choice but to agree. The operation gave a name to the true enemy that was killing Joe. It was called "Malignant Histiocytic Lymphoma, diffuse stage 3b." Death takes place at stage 4c. It was a terminal cancer with no medical treatment and no cure.

Joe was still living in ignorant bliss until his sister Myra came to his room. During a casual conversation, she asked Joe, "How would you feel if you only had ten years to live?" Joe replied, "Ten years is good; that would be fine." Then she asked, "How would you feel if you had five years to live?" Joe replied he would rather have ten, but five years was a long time and anything can happen in five years. Then she asked about three years. Joe stopped replying, and asked her not to go any lower. He got the point and a nauseating fear came over him. Joe requested a meeting with the head of hematology. Now he wanted a medical answer, the truth and nothing but the truth.

The doctor told Joe that no one with his illness makes it past five years even with medicine. He said the usual life expectancy was two to three years. Joe asked, "Do you mean there is nothing you can do for me?" The doctor said there was a new experimental treatment called "chemotherapy." This was an extremely dangerous treatment that could itself cause death. It seems they didn't have the dosage figured out for the height and weight of an individual. They needed volunteers for testing to get the right answers. Actually, this life-altering decision was really somewhat easy to make for Joe: the choice was no treatment and you die, or become a guinea pig and come what may. Well, it was "come what may" for Joe. He took the chemo treatment.

The day came for his first dose. There were many different colored and rather large syringes that were all injected into one tube that went into Joe's arm. A cold sickening feeling went through his veins and right to the gums in his mouth. Then they said that was that. All they had to do now was sit back and watch the effects. Joe thought this isn't too bad—no extra limbs were growing, and all seemed apparently well. But not for long.

Once a month, he was injected with "bug juice," the nickname used for chemo by the other patients. As the chemicals saturated all his tissues, the side effects kicked in. He ate for the sake of eating because nothing stayed down anyway. He watched his hair fall out and clog the shower drain and also cover his pillow in the morning. Losing his beautiful, wavy jet-black hair—what he thought was his most attractive feature—made Joe feel naked and freaky-looking. As long as he didn't look at himself in the mirror, he was okay, but the shock in other people's eyes as they looked at him was a constant reminder. To avoid being noticed, Joe started wearing a baseball cap. No longer being able to hide behind the confidence that his hair gave him, he had to find confidence elsewhere. After searching his soul and estimating how hopeless the situation really was, he realized that all he had was himself, and he would not dishonor himself by being less than the man he really was. So his new confidence now came from within, a confidence that was not interested in hiding—a real man's confidence. He only wore the baseball cap to help the onlookers.

What was upsetting Joe now wasn't the treatment but that they transferred him from a two-man room to a ward. The ward was called the "assembly line" because that's what it was. It was a long hall-like room with windows on one side and two rows of beds going down the full length. Joe was amazed at the number of soldiers that had cancer. Why were so many soldiers coming down with cancer? There was one guy in a bubble room. He had leukemia, and even the air could kill him. This guy had just gotten married when he found out he was sick. It was really something to see the way his new wife would touch his hand by pressing up against the plastic that separated them. Chemo and radiation treatments weren't going to help him; he had a ticket and that meant he was going to leave soon. Married or not, his number was up and he knew it.

Then there was the gatekeeper; he was an old man in the bed just before entering the assembly line. Most of the time his curtains were kept closed. He had a large stomach, and was always asleep. Joe became curious about him and would look at him in passing. The gatekeeper slept as much as Joe needed peace in his life. So Joe considered this man to be sort of an anonymous friend. When Joe went by he would always say "Hi!" or "What ya dreaming about?" The gatekeeper slept on, though. Most of what you saw in the assembly line was the end product. At the end of the line you would lose your hair, have some kind of operation that puts stitches from your abdomen to your chest, or have grid lines painted on where they shot you with radiation.

At this point Joe was living deep in fear. He could see the truth in everyone's eyes. So he stopped looking into other people's eyes. Day after day he could feel the fear that hid in his chest and made him want to run away, but to where? You can't run from yourself. One night, Joe had a nightmare that all of his hair fell out. Imagine waking from a nightmare to find that it was true. Joe was losing weight, too; he was like a dissolving bar of soap. Reminders were everywhere. All he wanted to do was end this nagging fear that gnawed at his very soul. It seemed logical to die like a man rather than a dog. If killing himself would kill the fear then he was open to the idea.

Joe noticed that one nurse had a habit of leaving the medicine cabinet open in the nurses' station while on rounds. He waited for the right time to make his move. He rushed into the room and started looking through the medicine chest for something that would do the job quickly. He had just found some possible cures for fear when the nurse came back. When she confronted Joe he said he was looking for an aspirin and left abruptly. The nurse didn't let on but she knew what he was planning. She was a pretty woman and Joe couldn't help but think that maybe in another time and place they could have been a couple. She reported Joe for attempting suicide. They sent a priest to talk with Joe. Nothing the priest said really made much difference, except when he said that no man is an island. When the priest told Joe that he had cancer too, that was the last straw. Joe thought that God didn't even take care of his own priests so what good would it do to ask Him for help?

One day, when he was returning to the ward, Joe noticed the Gatekeeper. The curtain was open wide and the gatekeeper was glowing. Really, his whole body was glowing with a bright golden light and it was really beautiful. It seemed to be coming from within him. First Joe made an off-the-cuff remark: "I see you've got your good clothes on, got a hot date?" Then he said a solemn goodbye because he instinctively knew what the light meant. The next day the gatekeeper's bed was empty.

Joe learned that you couldn't live with constant fear on a daily basis. The human spirit simply would not tolerate that. He remembered something his sister Myra said to him as a kid. She had read this and repeated it to Joe. "A coward dies a thousand times before his death; the valiant dies but once." Being a coward, Joe wanted to reduce the anxiety of dying a thousand times as he did every day, waking and wondering if today was the last day. To resolve this problem, he decided to take control of the situation and choose the day of his own death. He decided that December 3rd would be the day. It should be a day of no particular or previous consequence. That way no holidays would get in the way and he could miss the worst part of winter. Not a bad idea, huh? Problem solved; he would not die before or after that day. This way he would have to live a thousand years to make his sister's lesson come true. Each year on that day, he would concentrate on being extra cautious while preparing himself for the inevitable, and if it didn't happen he would grant himself another year to enjoy.

Fear was his enemy and it lived inside of him, traversing his mind and body to the point of cringing his muscles. If the real enemy came from within, then that's where Joe had to go to fight it. Joe got the idea to put a pillow over his head to block out all light and sound. He would remain like that, searching his soul until this hidden malady showed itself. He was sure he would know what to do when the true reason for his fear was found. First the truth had to be identified and then the cure would be forthcoming. He searched relentlessly through his pitch-dark internal universe and nothing. Then he decided to be still and let the answer come to him. When the brain could no longer take the absence of sound and light, it started to give up its most sacred secrets. It was the grenade incident! He never really had time to deal with what had happened. He had suffered a nervous breakdown thinking he had killed two men. The Army had broken him; his sanity broke knowing it was better to die yourself than to kill another. To protect his sanity he had put the whole affair away, deep in his mind. Several years had gone by, but he had never come to terms with the fear he experienced back then. He was sure that this was the truth because he felt so much better. For the first time since he could remember, he felt good inside. Even the thought of dying of cancer didn't scare him anymore. He saw his only responsibility now was to party like it was 1999. A smile of eternal relief and confidence came over his face.

So how do you celebrate the liberation from fear in a damn hospital? There was death and suffering all around him there. It was time to shed the grief; the plan was to go to town and get drunk and get laid. Going AWOL was the only way. He would wait till a change of shift, and then go over the wall. Not a bad plan, huh? The plan was going off perfectly: he accomplished the first part of going over the wall. The second part went well too; of course, getting drunk was kind of easy. Now it was time for a woman. Sure as the good Lord understands men, there she was. She was a Nubian goddess with flawless skin and a shape that commanded awe. Their eyes met and even though no words were spoken, she took Joe's hand and led him to a cheap hotel. When she took her clothes off and stood before him, Joe had never imagined a woman's body could be so perfect. She put every woman in every playboy magazine that Joe had ever seen to shame. Only God himself could have created such awesome beauty. She had an hourglass shape with full rounded breasts and alluring satin brown skin. Her hair was long and black, which accented her soft brown eyes. Joe knew this was going to be one of those moments he would cherish into old age or whatever age he made it to. He relished the moment with reckless disregard for time or military punishment.

Now it was late into the night and he was long overdue for return. He thought if he could make it back without being caught, it would truly be a perfect night. Joe made it back over the wall and through the creaky ward door. The only light on was coming from the nurse's station; he detected movement there. If he could make it past that door, he would be home free. Joe crept up to the door and peeked around the corner. A tall guy with white hospital clothes was taking some kind of inventory. Joe waited until the guy turned his back before attempting the crossing. In mid-stride the man turned and said, "Joe, do you know you were AWOL?" Joe simply replied, "So what are you going to do, send me to Vietnam? Besides, it was worth it and you can't take that away." The orderly began to berate Joe, but Joe interrupted and said, "Listen, I've had a long night and I'm really tired. I'm going to bed now and if you've got a problem with that, then take it up with me in the morning. Goodnight."

The next morning Joe was woken up by the usual parade of trainee nurses practicing the taking of vital signs on the patients. But this time it was different: there was an angelic-looking girl with golden blonde hair in the group. She also had pure blue eyes that seemed to look into your inner feelings. All that and in a pristine white nurse's uniform— exactly what you would hope to wake up to in the next life. Even though Joe was still tired from the night before, he wanted her. So he memorized every fiber of her being and fantasized about making wild passionate love to her while they stared at each other. His fantasy was so real that a satisfied smile came over his face. She saw the expression on his face as he lay back against his pillow. Joe could easily tell that she became very curious about his thoughts. But the herd of trainees was moving on and she had run out of time to investigate. That was okay with Joe, though, because he could put his memory on instant replay and see her again in a moment's wish.

Days had gone by and Joe had forgotten the incident until he saw her again at lunch in the mess hall. Joe had lost most of his hair by then and started to look like the radiation patients. But the baseball cap he wore constantly held off the curious stares of the bystanders. She was headed right for Joe's table. Could my luck be changing, he thought. She again stood before him, this creature of beauty. Joe was as speechless as an asshole could be. Just as he began to move his tray so that she could have more room, she turned and headed for another table. Joe thought he understood; he didn't blame her for not wanting to sit with a freaky-looking, bald-headed being like himself. Just then she turned and upon seeing that Joe had moved his tray, she came back and sat down. A very pleasant conversation took place. Joe mentioned that he had not really talked to a woman for so long and he had forgotten what it was like. Her name was Angelica, and she was from up north. She was attending Army nursing school and would become a lieutenant when she finished. Joe didn't say it but he was not thrilled about that news. Not once during the entire conversation did he think about death or dying. He just knew he wanted to see her again. In her eyes was peace, in her smile there was joy, and in her touch there was love. She casually possessed everything he needed.

After meeting Angelica, Joe was starting to at least feel normal in some respect and he began to explore his environment again. On this particular day, Joe took the elevator to the basement. Be dammed if there wasn't another ward down there! Why in hell would someone put a ward in a dark and dingy basement? All Joe could think of was, "This must be where they keep the dead people." Joe thought it would be a novel thing to see a dead person; besides, they couldn't hurt you. So he went in to take a look. As he entered and stood on the other side of the door, he saw beds with patients just like anywhere else in the hospital. But in each bed there were the last portions of what a man could be and still be alive. Some had no legs, some had no arms, and some had neither. As the quiet exchange of stares took place, a wheelchair came barreling up to Joe. In it was a head attached to a pair of shoulders. This guy was controlling it by guiding a stick with his mouth. He pulled up to Joe and stopped. He had long hair and a beard but you could tell he was a young man about Joe's age. Looking like a wild thing, he started yelling like one. He yelled, "Have you seen enough of us freaks yet? Get out! Get out! Get out!" Joe left fast all right, but the shock of what he saw—what war could do to valiant young men—would stay with him like the wounds they suffered. They didn't know Joe was under a death sentence himself, but at least he would die as a whole man in the sunlight.

You've heard the saying, "There is always one in the crowd." Well, that orderly that caught Joe going AWOL was one. He actually pursued the charges of AWOL against Joe. This could mean a dishonorable discharge from the military. For some strange reason, Joe seemed to care about this. In his own mind he imagined he would die a soldier under honorable circumstances, not be drummed out of the corps because of a long overdue night on the town.

Now Joe had to get a military lawyer (J.A.G.), go to court, and defend himself against the charges. Well, at least Joe had something else to worry about now besides dying. While waiting to speak to a lawyer, Joe could hear the lawyer making arrangements for a game of golf with the orderly that was bringing the charges against him. Is there no justice in the world? After much consideration, Joe realized that if he were going to get out of this mess, it would be through his own initiative. Joe would go down fighting. He would write and present his own defense. After all it was the Army that created the man and now they wanted to prosecute their own creation. Joe had it in his mind that if the Army wanted to know why he went AWOL he would tell the truth, the whole truth, and nothing but the truth, which most of the time should not be a matter for the record.

The day came and Joe stood before the military tribunal. He presented his written statement to the Judge. The Judge didn't finish reading the first page of Joe's defense before throwing the case out. Joe had described the hopeless situation he was in. The discerning judge realized that when you are facing death, all other matters pale in importance.

Joe once again felt like celebrating—having removed this legal monkey off his back—and returning destiny to its normal course of events. Joe was talking the idea over with Nate when it hit him: the perfect way to celebrate! Joe told

Nate he was going to cleanse his soul by taking a swim in the hospital fountain. There was a giant fountain in front of the hospital. If caught it could mean another Article 15 or a trip to the psych ward across the road. But with the constant medical testing, living with the fear of death, and his contempt for the law, Joe felt as though he needed a kind of baptism, to clean his mind, to clean his heart, and to clean his soul. He talked Nate into going with him.

When night fell, the two intruders waited for the interval between military police patrols. Then they both made a screaming dash for the Olympic-size fountain and jumped into the pristine waters. It was deep enough to swim underwater, and cold enough to shrink any man's privates. As soon as they jumped in, another MP patrol car came by and circled the fountain. Joe and Nate had to stay under as long as they could. They stayed close to the sides, and took a breath only by letting their mouths touch the surface. By the time the MPs left they had enough fun to cause laughter from deep within their guts. It was the cure for a mind in pain, a tortured heart, and a depressed soul. Joe didn't know if Nate felt the same way, but he felt as though he had just been baptized. Completely rejuvenated, our two soggy heroes went back to the ward with one major difference: they were washed clean of despair as they climbed the stairs arm in arm laughing, leaving a wet trail behind. No matter what tomorrow may bring, they could at least face it with an undeniable optimism.

The next day Joe was shooting a game of one-man pool in the recreation room. When he looked up, she was standing right in the door looking straight into his eyes. It was Angelica. Her blue eyes engulfed him, her smile disarmed him, and her presence left him motionless. They talked and as the conversation progressed he tried to hide his need for her, as she could easily see through him. They agreed to meet again and Joe knew he was going to make the most of it. She made him feel like a man again, not like the lab rat the Army had turned him into through constant experimentation.

After that, they saw each other every chance they got. They would go for walks, movies, and do all the things that bring two people together. One evening he visited her at the nursing school dorm. He walked up the stairs past the great white pillars that solemnly guarded the entrance. She was playing the piano in the lobby and she played beautifully. Later, while sitting on the love seat together, she took his hand. That gave Joe all the confidence he needed. They took a short stroll across the street to where the cherry blossom trees were. It started raining when he took her in his arms; their kisses were passionate, inspired by her glistening wet skin. The white cherry blossom petals were falling all around them in the rain. Joe grabbed her from behind, pulled her close, and whispered in her ear, "I love you, will you marry me?" He could hardly believe his ears when she said no. In every romantic movie that he had ever seen, the woman had never said no. Joe turned her around to look at her straight in the eyes. He said, "You know we love each other, and we were meant to be together. You know you're the only one for me and me for you. I know you love me! I know you love me—then why?"

She told Joe that when she finished Army-nursing school, she would have to serve six years as a lieutenant nurse to fulfill her contract. She didn't know where they would send her and she didn't want to start a marriage that way. Joe felt that might not be the whole truth. Part of him feared it was because he was a terminal cancer patient and she knew it. He couldn't blame her for that, because of course she was right. But that didn't stop his heart from aching. First was the shock, then disbelief, and then his mind and body went numb. How strange it was to feel his heart die in his chest, while the rest of his body still moved. He let go of his grasp of her, turned and walked off into the pouring rain. He realized he lost his last and only chance for happiness. Maybe that was because being "terminal" meant he lost the right to be happy.

Nate and Boli knew that Joe left to propose to Angelica. They were waiting for Joe's triumphant return to start the celebrations. When Nate saw Joe he asked, "Well, what did she say?" Joe looked straight into Nate's eyes and responded, "She said no." Nate was shocked. "You're kidding me—right, Joe?" "Nate! She said no, dammit!" Joe told them the whole story and his friends were supportive, but all Joe wanted was to be alone. You could tell that Nate was afraid that Joe was going to harm himself. Joe was getting used to that crap, too, so he just outright told Nate, "I'm not going to do anything to myself, Nate. Now get the hell out of here." Besides you really can't do injury to yourself when you've already died inside. It even hurt just to think a simple thought, so he gave that up too.

For the next three days Joe would sit on the balcony of the ward and watch the crippled and wounded veterans go by. It seemed to him as though all the pain and suffering he was witnessing still didn't match his own. He thought that if he saw more pain than what he was experiencing it would make him feel better. Life again fell into a hellish routine of medical testing, eating, sleeping and all the other things that had no meaning. Again he would no longer look into the eyes of anyone else, because that is where he saw the truth. The truth was that "malignant" meant there was no cure, and this could be seen even in the eyes of the professionals.

About the only good thing left for Joe to enjoy was having lunch and lying out on the grassy area in front of the gardens. The grass was soft and the sun was bright and warm. Sometimes while sitting on the bench, the smell of flowers would carry his mind away to better times. Joe would report to the garden every day, to the same place at the same time, as if it were a duty instead of his only pleasure. His idea was catching on, as others started having lunch there too. On one occasion, Joe noticed a young nurse who had spread a small blanket on the ground and was having lunch. She was at a distance, but close enough for Joe to study her without being obvious. The sun lit up her white nurse's uniform to a bright glow. Her hair was long and black and her skin was tan. She had laid out her belongings around her and appeared to be an island unto herself. There were several times when their eyes met, but Joe would look away so not to scare her away. She was the only one Joe didn't mind sharing his little piece of heaven with. In fact, he felt comforted by her distant presence. He didn't approach her for fear of having his illusions changed or ruined. He needed to keep her just the way she was—just a fantasy that could not hurt him, disappoint him, or otherwise crush what life he had left.

Even though the time to enjoy the outdoors was short, going there every day seemed to help Joe somehow. Every scrap of good was good and Joe was living on the scraps alone. Now he would have an added pleasure: to see her. She would give his garden visits a tone of mystery, not knowing anything about her or even if she would return the next day. This made every nanosecond in her distant presence a timeless event that Joe oh so needed.

The next day Joe went to the garden early; somehow he was sure she would be there. He waited for her, but it soon became apparent that he would again be denied even the simplest of pleasures. As he lay across his sun-drenched bench, he fell asleep while picturing every detail of her. If he couldn't enjoy her in reality then he would leave it up to his memory to help out. This couldn't possibly be considered cheating on Angelica because he had not even met this girl.

It was important not to sleep too long because he had to attend a medical appointment and if he missed it his name would be mud. The penalties could range from sarcasm to missing the vein 12 times. On this particular day he did sleep too long. He rose up in a panic, still groggy. While looking at his watch, he realized that even if he ran he would still be late. He stood up, pulled the string tight on his blue military pajamas, and off he went. While still clearing his eyes, he could see a light-covered area, on the ground, coming up in his path. Opening his eyes fully now he could see it was her, the girl he shared his garden with. Joe was moving so fast he almost ran completely over her. He realized then that this was an excellent opportunity to obtain more detail for his fantasies. He expected to be disappointed by seeing her up close, but he wasn't. She was beautiful in a seductive way. He found himself standing before her while she was reading a book. He stood above her, staring down at her, feeling he deserved every moment of her beauty because he was starving for it.

When she finally looked up at him, Joe was speechless for what seemed an eternity. He was confused by why he stopped to begin with, and confused by why he stayed. His own behavior was beyond his own awareness. For some strange reason he felt obliged to meet her. "Hello, my name is Joe. Please excuse my interruption; I was just passing by and felt compelled to introduce myself. Well, now that I've done that, I guess I'll be on my way." Surprisingly, she invited Joe to sit down and join her. In Joe's mind, this took priority over any lab-rat experiments or any abuse he would receive for being late. He didn't care about his medical appointments; he would deal with the consequences later as they arose. Besides, one moment with a beautiful woman was surely worth a little abusive sarcasm or even a dozen stab wounds with a syringe.

She seemed lonely, too, and much in need of a man as Joe was in need of a woman. After a few words, she asked, "Joe, why are you a patient here?" Not wanting to get into the details, Joe just said he was taking part in an experiment. Now was as good a time as any to announce that the side effect of the experiment was the loss of all his hair. He warned her about it and asked her not to run away in fear. In response, she asked him to take off his baseball cap. Removing his hat was like standing naked before the world. But he did it anyway, mainly because he had to know; he had to know if he could see his own death in her eyes, too. Her look was very revealing, as it showed shock, pity, and disappointment. As she looked away, Joe quickly put his cap back on. He now felt as though he should never remove it again. He then made a joke about the glare from his head blinding passing aircraft. When she looked up again and smiled, Joe forgot the look he had just seen in her eyes as her smile warmed him all over inside.

A very pleasant conversation followed this chance meeting. Her name was Soleum and she was half American and half Filipina. Joe asked about the book she was reading. She became flush with embarrassment and quickly put it away. Later she confessed it was a book on how to meet people. She did everything the book said about wearing light colors and making yourself accessible. She also confessed that she had noticed him and was interested in meeting him, too. Joe thought maybe this wasn't such a chance meeting after all. When they made a date to see each other again, he didn't care if it were chance or not, he was just glad. Angelica could have the Army if that's what she wanted. At least Joe could enjoy a little distraction from his deepest sorrow.

They made plans for lunch the next day, and lunch led to a date and then to another. The two were getting along famously. As they continued to see each other, Joe was forgetting the true situation he was in. The constant testing, operations, and chemo were certainly daily reminders, but when he was with Soleum he didn't think about any of that. Joe was developing some strong feelings for the girl, but he wouldn't let it turn into love because that was already reserved for Angelica. Whether he could have Angelica or not, he felt he had to remain true to that unfulfilled love.

For this particular date, Soleum was to meet Joe at the fountain. Joe was there early in eager anticipation. When she drove up, Joe wasn't really sure if that was the same woman or not. Her hair was up and she was wearing some kind of fancy sunglasses and a very exotic dress. She was a "Wow!" in every sense the word. The pains of the day for Joe were gone, and he was thanking God he was a man today. As he got into the car, his vocabulary was reduced to just that one word: Wow!

Being on a date with Soleum was nothing but fun. They laughed and talked about everything and agreed on everything, too. She mentioned she had an apartment, and asked if he wanted to see it. Joe said sure, under the pretense of getting ideas for his own apartment. No sooner had they entered the apartment than Joe turned her around by the shoulders and pulled her close. They kissed as if they were both starved for affection and happy to find it in each other. Their clothes fell like tropical rain in the midst of their timeless and unceasing kisses. As his animal instincts were emerging through the sight, smell, taste, and feel of her, he lifted her up into his arms and carried her into the bedroom.

As he laid her across the bed, the dim light enhanced her form and shape. His eyes filled with her amazing beauty, as his mind questioned how it was possible for such beauty to exist. When her body rose up to receive him, Joe found himself unresponsive. "What the hell is going on here!" Joe knew he was turned on and desirous of her and yet nothing. Physically, nothing was happening! Joe silently questioned himself; could it be that his body wouldn't permit a transgression against Angelica? Soleum asked about the medicine Joe was taking and if maybe that was the problem. Joe said he didn't know, but he would check on that first thing in the morning. Soleum was all woman, even during these trying circumstances. She made Joe feel as though there was truly nothing wrong, even though deep in his heart Joe knew that something was wrong, very wrong.

The next day, lab-rat testing continued. Joe asked the doctor if the medicine could affect his sexual drive. The doctor seemed surprised that Joe had not been informed. The doctor said, "We are trying to save your life, Joe." Joe asked if his desires would ever return. The doctor told Joe that this treatment was experimental and they just didn't know. "Besides," the Doc said, "sex isn't all that life is about." Joe gave the doctor the benefit of the doubt, but could still not imagine what kind of life he was referring to. How could a man go through life seeing women, desiring them, and fantasizing about them and yet never be able to have sex again? Surely this was an unfair hell beyond the realm of God or the devil. In his mortality, Joe was lost in a raging sea of torment with the question of why. "What could I have done so wrong that I should be denied the right of even being human?"

As each day went by, Joe would notice the beautiful women that passed by. Seeing them or talking to them was like having a long, cold steel sword plunged through his chest. At this point Joe felt as though the only thing that made him human was the option of free choice. To be or not to be, that was the question. Is it better to suffer, just to live, or to end the suffering and live no more? Joe was always an advocate of no suffering and no pain. He thought of a horse breaking a leg and how merciful it was to shoot it. How strange for a dumb animal to receive more mercy than a man. Well, now that Joe had reached the very bottom of the pit, he figured the only way he had to go was up. The world could not be so cruel as to make one more bad thing happen to him. All Joe had to do now was wait, wait for just one good damn thing to happen.

The very next day Joe got a visit from a major; he was a doctor. He told Joe that he could not return to his duties anymore, and then asked him, "Do you want out of the Army?" Joe's heart skipped about three beats. Joe asked, "How is that possible since my time is not up yet?" The doctor said they could release him on a medical discharge. Joe told the doctor an honorable discharge was very important to him. His brother had come home from Vietnam with all kinds of medals. "Besides, Doc, I've only got two months to go before I can get an honorable discharge." The doctor was looking out the window when he said, "You really don't have much choice about this." Joe told the doctor to turn around and look at him. Joe said, "I want you to look me in the eye because I want you to see how much I mean what I'm about to say. Doctor, I have been attacked with a knife, shot at, almost captured, and almost killed a hundred times, mostly without the means to defend myself. I have been operated on and experimented on. I've seen and been through hell! I wanted to be a soldier all my life, and have served honorably. I deserve an honorable discharge, and I will not sign for a medical or settle for less. The Army made me swear an oath upon entry, to God and to country." Joe proceeded to repeat the oath:

"I, Joe, do solemnly swear that I will support and defend the Constitution of the United States against all enemies, foreign and domestic; that I will bear true faith and allegiance to the same; and that I will obey the orders of the President of the United States and the orders of the officers appointed over me, according to regulations and the Uniform Code of Military Justice. So help me God.

"Now, doctor, I will swear my own oath to you, to the Army, and to God: Even though I may not have long to live, I swear I will spend every moment I have left to live, every dollar I will ever earn, and every resource I can ever devise, to fight this decision. So help me God. And doctor, I mean it!"

The doctor could easily see the resolve in Joe's blood-red eyes. In everyone's life there comes a point of honor; you can take the easy road out, or you can ante up and kick in like a man. Funny thing is, Joe really meant the second oath as much as he obeyed the first. If the Army ruled against him, he would declare war against the United States Army, even if that fight was to the death. He had been through too much to spend the rest of his life in humble disappointment over a medical discharge. By the blood that ran through his veins, he would not permit this decision to stand. Joe did not know it at the time, but this was the day of his "point of honor."

Finally, the doctor said he would see what he could do. The doctor returned the next day and informed Joe he was to be honorably discharged. Joe was really glad, but part of him knew he was lying to himself. By now he was a soldier inside and out; he didn't even remember what it was like to be a civilian. But in giving the subject much thought, Joe figured that in the long run this was probably a good thing. Besides, if he stayed in, they would probably put his ass in another danger zone without a gun.

Ha! If he stayed in! That decision was already made now. Joe's only job now was to learn how to die, and to prepare himself to die as a civilian. Funny thing is, in all his premonitions and visions of the future, he had never seen this. He had fancied himself with this unusual ability mainly because all he had seen before had come true. In any case, he wasn't in control, as fate was in the driver's seat. The first place fate was going to drive Joe was home. Imagine that— home! This time it would be for good.

Well, not exactly home. The next and last assignment was close to home: it was a V.A. hospital in Northport, Long Island. The idea was to continue chemotherapy from a hospital close to home as an outpatient. Northport was only 45 minutes away from where Joe's family lived.

First, he had to say goodbye to his buddies and to Soleum. Saying goodbye to Soleum wasn't easy; Joe told her that if it was at all possible he would be back, but knowing in his heart it would not be possible. Then there was Angelica. As long as he was at the hospital, he had felt that there was a distant opportunity for them. He hadn't seen her since the night she said no; her rejection had kept him away. He didn't want to see her because he couldn't believe that someone he loved so much could hurt him so miserably at the weakest point in his life. He couldn't forgive her for that, but he knew that he was leaving her and would never see her again. He felt that saying goodbye to Angelica was more than he could bear; he did not want to risk being hurt again. So he passed up that opportunity.

The processing of discharge papers took an entire day. Funny thing is, it took years to turn Joe into a real soldier and only one day for the soldier to be turned back into a civilian. No good-bye parties or gold watch, no "job well done" or parade; just a paper that said "Honorable Discharge." Joe wouldn't consider himself discharged until he was actually able to leave the base without being AWOL.

That moment came at night; Joe was being driven off base for the last time. When they came to the gate, Joe asked the driver to stop just before the gate. Joe told the driver that he walked into the Army on his own two feet, and now he was going to walk out that gate the same way. When Joe walked through the gate he felt a strange pull—it was something like the tug of a magnet. Then he knew it was over; it was the release. All he wanted to do now was to get as far away as fast as possible. Certain realizations were coming to mind such as "freedom." You've heard it said that freedom is just another word for nothing left to lose. What freedom meant to Joe at that moment was repossession of his body, mind, and soul. He felt like a caged animal that just found the cage door open. Now he cautiously explored the wide-open spaces for the first time. He didn't know how much life he had left, but he did know he would never sell out his life again for anyone or anything else ever again.

Funny thing is, after finally getting the Army off his back, the war was still not over for Joe and there were many battles still to fight. He had to continue medical treatments, which meant more experimentation had to be done, with appropriate follow-up. But first things first: he was going home!

When the conquering hero came through the door, his eyes went straight to seeing his mother. It was an emotional mess of a scene. There was crying all over the place. Then the moment of truth came when his mom asked Joe to remove his hat. Joe told her to be prepared for a shock. He reached up and slowly removed the baseball cap that protected him in so many ways. A look and expression came over his mother's face that showed him the true extent of the pain she was suffering. Joe felt he had just committed an unforgivable sin and quickly returned his hat to his head. He told his mother that his hair would grow back even though he truly didn't believe that. "Mom," he said, "I'm back and I'm alive, just like I told you I would be. Everything is going to be okay now."

Joe truly believed that everything was going to be okay. There were some bumps in the road, though. The grocery store still scared the shit out of him: the bright lights, the colors, the constant machine-gun sounds of the many cash registers, the god-like voice that came from above, often caused Joe to crouch down and cover his head, just like before. Upon any unexpected loud noise, Joe would either hit the ground or take an attack stance in the flinch of a reflex. They were the same problems he had when coming home from Thailand. These problems were caused by a temporary nervous disorder and just required some time to resolve themselves.

Even when Joe returned to his old watering hole and dance spot, things were different. He saw everyone marching on the dance floor in lines. Did the Army get to everyone? Why are people marching together instead of dancing? Wow! Joe was not the only one who had changed: the entire country had changed, too. How was a guy going to ask a girl to dance; did he have to ask the whole line? Men and women don't dance anymore? Joe wondered—did men and women still date, go steady, get engaged, get married? Or did sex go from free love to non-existence? Joe remembered intercepting messages overseas that told of students running naked across

195

campus. Maybe that was the start of a mass insanity that has lead to these present events. "Okay, I may not know what's going on around here," he thought, "but this is still my country and I will find my place in it again."

Joe thought he would get a job where he was out of the way and from where he could watch everything that happened. He still had time before reporting to Northport. He got a job as a dishwasher at the corner diner. Most of the time he was working in the back, but occasionally he would come out front to collect the dishes. It was then that he watched how people interacted. He would listen to conversations as he cleared the tables. On one time out of the kitchen, a customer grabbed Joe by the arm and asked, "What are you supposed to be, some kind of Hare Krishna?" Joe was taken aback by this man's behavior. "How can he think he can put his hands on me? That's it!" He had done nothing to be insulted or manhandled in such a way. Not wanting to make a scene, Joe leaned over and whispered in the man's ear, "I am bald because I have terminal cancer, which I got while serving overseas in the military so that you could go to college and not have to serve yourself. Now I'm going to die soon and have to work this kind of job because there is nothing else left for me, and all this just so you can insult me." Joe went back to mopping the floor again. The man's face tightened with a sorrowful expression of woe and shame as he slowly lowered his face into his food.

Well, too many people that knew Joe were coming in and he didn't want to be seen like this. So it was time for another job. He found one pumping gas at the gas station down the street. There were two islands with three gas pumps each. There was also a side station for a man to stand out of the cold. This way the "gas jockey" wouldn't offend the customers with his dirty gas-smelling clothes. This was okay with Joe because he found a domain—a domain he understood and controlled with determined efficiency. Every day he would find new small ways to increase his employer's need for him. He would pump gas at both islands at the same time, while taking credit cards and cash. Everything was kept clean and orderly. Of course, Joe couldn't help noticing some strange things happening. Like when a lady rode up to a pump on a horse; Joe asked if she wanted a fill-up and in which end to place the pump. Fortunately, she just wanted directions. Or the time when a clown pulled up and twisted a balloon into the shape of a dog and gave it to him. Or the girl that pulled up wearing nothing but two thin shoulder straps.

This was a kind of pattern that caused Joe to think that maybe small doses of radiation were affecting the general public. But the most memorable of all was when a gas nozzle fell out of a car and stayed on. There was a river of gas pouring over the entire parking lot and going into the street. Joe's boss hit the emergency shut-off and the operation came to a screeching halt. Joe had to clean up hundreds of gallons of gas off the concrete. It was like trying to clean up ice in a skating rink. No matter what you do, it was still there. It was shortly after that incident that a new invention was installed, called the "self service" or "automatic pump." There was no need to have a person pump gas for you when everyone could do it by themselves. It was the second time Joe had seen technology replace him. The first time was when he read a newspaper that said they closed a military communication station in Thailand and replaced it with a satellite. It was becoming apparent which way the future was going.

That gas accident happened right after management hired two very attractive women who left Joe somewhat distracted. One was a blonde and the other had auburn hair. You couldn't tell which one was better looking. Each filled out a pair of jeans like they were shrunk to fit their bodies. Not having taken chemo for a while, Joe was returning to the man he used to be and was naturally responding to the visual input.

He ignored the distractions in favor of concentration on his job. That is, until the blonde leaned over the counter to talk to her friend. Right before his eyes was a creation that could distract any man. It was to the point that he had to say something. He said, "Excuse me, but you're not a little girl anymore and I'm a full-grown man, so please don't ever lean over the counter like that again." The girls laughed, knowing exactly what they were doing. Joe was deciding which one he wanted more.

During this time, one particular customer started coming back in a regular fashion. He was a young, well-built, blonde-haired guy. The girls seemed to like him and always had long conversations with him. He even took the time to befriend Joe. It turns out his name was Hansen and he had recently been released from jail. That's probably why he was built of solid muscles; he had had plenty of time to work out. The girls were named Darlin and Christi, Christi being the blonde.

Eventually, Hansen asked Joe if he wanted to double-date with the two girls. Joe said sure; this was a "no lose" situation. Hansen said the trick was to let the girls decide which one of them they wanted. Christi picked Joe and Darlin picked Hansen. They double-dated quite a few times; in fact, every date was a double date. They did it so many times that Joe realized he was falling in love with Darlin; she was an exciting woman, but Joe knew he had a good thing going with Christi anyway. Christi was so good looking that when they walked into a place Joe could hear the men's awe-struck murmurs as she walked by.

On one occasion the two couples were going on a trip to the Poconos. When they got there, they only had enough money for one hotel room with two beds. That night was going to be another life-long memory for Joe. He saw for the first time the body of the woman he was with. Her body was flawless. Joe often wondered how God managed to create such beauty in women. During the love making process, even though Christi was responsive, she was able to make love only once before her mood cooled and further interest was lost. Then, as Joe pretended to be asleep, he heard the deep, passionate moans and the muffled and excited sighs of the woman he truly loved making love to Hansen in the next bed. Joe didn't know what sin he had committed to deserve such a fate, but he knew he just paid for it.

By this time, Joe was ready to go back: go back to the hospital and go back to the chemotherapy. At first sight Northport hospital appeared to be a very serene place with many college-like red brick buildings; the place even had a large golf course. Joe reported in and preparations began to make this his new home. Joe had cancer so off to the cancer ward he would go. But first he would take a look around the grounds to explore his new home.

Upon walking to the buildings in the rear he noticed that their balconies were enclosed in cage-like fashion. You could see many men inside. They all appeared to be crazy in their behavior, screaming and climbing on the cage fencing. Two men in white coats saw Joe and came over to him and held his arms on both sides. They asked, "Now, where do you belong?" Joe said, "I belong in the cancer ward and if you don't let go of me, you're going to be in a lot of trouble." The two men checked his wristband and verified the truth. Joe later found out that Northport hospital was in transition from being a mental hospital to a veteran's hospital. The cancer ward had an interesting set up. It went from a six-man room to a five-man room, then four, three, two, and finally one. The one-man room was the launch pad for leaving this world. Men were being moved about by the gravity of their deteriorating conditions. Joe was placed into the six-man room. There were several other young men there that had strange-looking afflictions. Their legs had large patches of discolored and rotten muscle tissue, and many other maladies were in evidence, including cancer. Some of them had children that had been born deformed.

All these men had served in Southeast Asia, as Joe did. Joe remembered the constant assembly line of cancer patients at Walter Reed; they were young soldiers from Southeast Asia, too. Well, even a blind man with a broken stick could tell there was a much bigger story going on than just Joe's one individual case. It would be years later before the truth about the use of "Agent Orange" would come out. Agent Orange is a chemical defoliant that was sprayed all over Vietnam. It was so toxic that just breathing it could cause cancer. The chemical was on the plants, in the ground, and in the water.

Since Joe's condition was starting to deteriorate, he was moved from the six-man room to the five-man room. When he got moved to the four-man room shortly after, he knew he was in big trouble. Not being able to sleep one night, he got up and went to the front desk for a sleeping pill. The nurse was in the back room, so Joe just waited for her return. The one-man room was across from the desk and the door was left open. Joe could see inside from where he was standing. The man in bed there suddenly sat straight up from a lying down position. His head turned and he looked at Joe with an expression of shear terror. The man didn't make a sound but his color was that of white stone with dark all around his eyes. His entire body was shaking. As the nurse returned Joe pointed to the man and said, "I think he is calling for help." The nurse put out the alarm and doctors and nurses all ran in, pushing all kinds of machines. The next day the room was empty, the bed was freshly made, and the man was gone. Joe was the last person the man had seen before he died.

Joe had gotten used to the constant nausea and didn't really mind the hair loss, but now his eyesight was leaving. While on a walk, Joe tried to read a street sign but it was very blurry. He got closer and it was still blurry. Joe walked right up to the bottom of it and still couldn't see it. Determined to read the damn sign, he started to climb the pole and stuck his face into each letter of the sign. Joe didn't want to live like this anymore and decided to let nature take its course without further intervention. He would return to the hospital and cancel all future treatments, and that's what he did. The doctors informed him that, if he did so, the medicine might not work later and there would be nothing more they could do for him. Joe said he understood but that's the way he wanted it.

Now all Joe needed was a plan for the end game. He returned home and wrote a letter to Angelica in a last attempt to grasp that elusive happiness. He again asked her to marry him—he wanted one last chance to lead a normal life. Besides, even if she said no again, what did he have to lose? It was some time before her reply came, and the answer was "Yes!" Angelica told Joe she had failed Army nursing school and had gone to live in Hawaii. Joe sent her the plane fare to come to New York. He was going to be a happy man, married to the woman he loved, for as long as it lasted, and that's all that mattered.

The day came to pick his beloved up at the airport. Joe waited with child-like anticipation to look into her soft, compassionate blue eyes and to run his hands through her long golden hair. His eyes searched the crowd as many travelers went by. Then he turned to find her standing right in front of him. They locked in a tight embrace, and he whispered in her ear, "My love, is it really you?" She smiled and squeezed Joe tighter. It had been eight months since they had last seen each other; she still had beautiful blue eyes and long golden blonde hair. The only noticeable difference was her figure. Previously, she had a nice, slim figure. Now her butt was half the size of Montana. She was embarrassed to admit that eight months of eating Hawaiian fruits had gone straight to her hips. Joe told her a little exercise would take care of that. "Besides, there is just more of you to love."

Now it was time to take her home to Mom; there was no telling what could happen now. All Joe knew was that all the important occasions in his life always turned out somewhat different than he expected. As Angelica approached the side porch, she made the unforgivable mistake of saying, "I feel like I'm home." Mom, who was waiting at the porch to greet them, responded by saying, "Well, you're not." With that the tone was set.

The next stumbling block for Joe and Angelica was pre-marital sex. Joe's mother had enacted Vatican rules, which meant "no way." In fact, while trying to consummate his relationship with Angelica, his mother interrupted the process three times. That proved to be a definite anti-climax. The final coup de grâce was when a family member opened and read some of Angelica's mail and misunderstood something in a letter. Based on this, Angelica was ordered to leave. Joe informed his mother that if she had to leave, then he too would have to go. His mother said she knew that. So now our hero and his true love were off to Texas to stay with his older brother Chad until they could get married and find a place of their own; at least that was the plan.

As I said before, Joe's plans didn't always go as expected. First, there was the phone call to her parents. It was Joe's first chance to talk to his future in-laws and be welcomed. It went something like this:

"Hello, Sir. My name is Joe. I met your daughter at Walter Reed hospital. We have known each other for over a year and we are truly in love. Sir, I truly love your daughter and we plan to get married."

To which Angelica's father responded, "Joe, you sound like a nice guy, but I understand you are suffering from a terminal condition. You can surely understand why we are concerned for our daughter and against this marriage. When our daughter does get married we would like her to have a long and happy marriage, with children, and to lead a happy normal life. Joe, can you offer her this? Please don't answer the question now, but take some time to think about it. We will trust in you to make the right decision."

"Sir, don't I have the right to be happy too?"

"Joe, we are sorry for the hardships you have faced. We love our daughter and just don't want to see her suffer, too. Joe, if you truly love Angelica, then you will know what the right thing to do is."

"Yes, sir, I do love your daughter and I will consider everything that's been said. Thank you for taking the time to talk with me. Goodbye."

The conversation made Joe realize the only thing he could offer Angelica was the chance to become a widow. He was beginning to realize there were more ways to die than just one. This burden would weigh heavily on his mind. When you're loosing the rights of life, and you're not dead yet—where are you?

All the same, Joe and Angelica were finally living together as a couple. Over the course of the next few months, they learned more about each other's intricate personalities. Romance and passion were giving way to who does the laundry, who goes shopping, who cooks the food, etc. Joe figured his job was to be the breadwinner. His income covered the bills and he left the chores of the home front to the woman, as was the custom of the American way of life at the time. This was cause for quite a few arguments in paradise.

Then there was the infamous "movie theatre" incident. This was at a time when smoking was becoming no longer welcome in movie theatres. In New York smoking was still allowed in the movies, but the law had changed in Texas. Joe innocently lit up a cigarette. Fortune being what it is, there was an off-duty police officer sitting right in front of Joe. This officer turned around and shoved his badge right into Joe's face. He said, "You put that cigarette out now or I will fine you $250.00 dollars." His tone was very hostile and he embarrassed Joe right in front of his fiancée. Joe put the cigarette out and flicked it at the officer but missed. Joe's blood began to boil and he wanted satisfaction. Apparently, the policeman did not know that the one thing you should never do is fuck with a dying man, 'cause the dying man has nothing to lose.

Joe went into the lobby and bought a large soda with heavy ice. While he was returning to his seat, he "accidentally" tripped and spilled the entire drink on the police officer. Oh, my God—it was beautiful! The soda covered the policeman's silk shirt like a point-blank shotgun blast. You could easily see the shock and awe on the policeman's frozen pose. Joe said, "Oh, I am so sorry and I will certainly pay for the cleaning bill." Then he sat down. Mere moments went by and the officer stood up. That sucker was the biggest cop Joe had ever seen. He looked like he was genetically engineered and tall as the Washington Monument. He pointed his finger at Joe and said "Outside!" Joe figured that no matter what happened, he would always have that moment of complete and utter triumph in seeing that asshole cop covered in soda. Now it was time to pay the tab and Joe went willingly.

The affair went into the lobby where the officer took Joe's I.D. and called for back up. The officer stretched out his hand to give Joe back his I.D. But when Joe took it, the officer yelled, "You grabbed that out of my hand" and took a swing at Joe. Joe leaned back and his chin was slightly clipped. Joe then announced to the entire lobby that this man was a police officer and asked for witnesses to the assault. Everyone in the lobby had a frozen look on their face. They were also frozen in their stance like they were cardboard cutouts. Joe could easily see he had lost his appeal to the general public. With a serious word of caution he said, "Today it is me, tomorrow it will be you!" At this point he submitted himself over to the arriving reinforcements. They dragged Joe out and threw him up against the police car while handcuffing him. A woman from the lobby came forward and told a police officer she was going to file a witness report that the officer's treatment was cruel and unusual.

Joe was brought to the police station and they bounced him up against the wall like a basketball. They locked him in a cell too. Joe took a tin cup and began raking it over the bars, yelling, "You dirty rats, you shot my brother." He had seen that done in a James Cagney movie once and had always wanted to do that himself. An officer came back with a billy club and threatened to beat Joe to a pulp. Joe decided not to press his luck any further, especially since he knew he had the upper hand. The arresting officer hit Joe in front of witnesses and failed to read Joe his rights during his arrest. The charge against Joe was "assault on a police officer with a cola." The whole affair caused so much laughter within the police department that they let Joe go free. Joe then filed a complaint that his constitutional rights were abused.

A few days later the police chief made an appointment to speak with Joe. They asked him what would bring a satisfactory conclusion to the dispute. Joe said he wanted the police officer to be fired. They told him the policeman had two kids and one on the way and asked if Joe would reconsider. Joe told them to put a reprimand in his file; he was also to be passed up for next promotion and sent back to police training school. And so it would be done, supposedly.

The highlight of this story is that Angelica stayed at the theater by herself and came home after she finished watching the movie. She told Joe that it was his fight and she didn't want anything to do with it. Joe felt that his woman should have been by his side, right or wrong.

In yet another instance, Joe's image of Angelica was dramatically affected by her behavior. He and Angelica were enjoying a moment of uninhibited privacy and were watching

T.V. in the nude while his older brother was away. Well, it so happened that Chad came home early, and as the front door began to open slowly, Joe yelled, "Hold on!" as he quickly sprinted for the bedroom. Joe was clear across the apartment when he turned to see Angelica still sitting on the couch waiting to be discovered by Chad. Joe returned to her and said, "Let's go!" before getting her to actually move off the couch. Her actions were very intentional and Joe was surprised to see that maybe Angelica was attracted to Chad.

Joe was ready now to call it quits and that's what he did. He sent Angelica home. In doing so, he was coming to understand that even a short-lived happiness is more than a terminal patient has the right to expect.

Now that time and purpose had changed, Joe had to figure out what the hell his next purpose would be. He knew he couldn't stay with Chad; they never got along anyway. Going back home felt wrong, especially since they had asked Joe to leave. Besides, he could no longer take the look of gloom in his family's eyes. He would have left home anyway just to avoid that. This was no position for a 23-year-old guy to be in. At this point Joe only knew a couple of things that made any difference. He knew he wanted to go someplace where he could live the remainder of his days in peace, a place where no one had ever seen his face or knew of his condition. Then it hit him like a bolt out of the blue, an epiphany of staggering proportions: for the first time in his life he was really and truly free! There was no school system taking years of sunny days away, no Army shouting orders at him, no boss demanding more than they gave and sucking the life out of you slowly. This was the best chance he ever had to go and do as he pleased.

DISCOVERING AMERICA

JOE STARTED TO think of how many times he had almost been killed for his country without having really seen it. Well, maybe this was a chance to rectify that. He was also thinking how he was so much in God's hands now. With one pair of jeans, a backpack, and a knife, Joe was going to hit the road for destinations unknown. He would head west and take odd jobs to pay his way. He had heard of an old Army buddy who was living in Denver, Colorado, so Joe was going to make that his first stop on a countrywide tour. Joe really didn't know if his friend was really there, but thought he would give it a try to find him. There was also plenty of country to see between here and there.

The first strange thing happened in the first five seconds of his journey. Joe stepped out to the road and stuck out his thumb for a ride. The very first vehicle to pass was a tractor-trailer, and the driver stopped to pick him up. The driver told Joe he was going as far as Denver. Now, how is that for door-to-door service? That was faster and easier than catching a cab in New York. The ride was slow because this truck was carrying a real heavy load. That was okay with Joe, though, because seeing this country was part of the mission. The truck headed north, leaving Texas and slowly rolling over the plains states headed for Denver.

What Joe saw was wide-open space clear to the horizon. Well, not exactly wide open—it seemed as though every square inch was surrounded by barbwire. This represented the boundary lines for large ranches. No matter how far he traveled it was the same thing everywhere. It appeared as though America belonged to the people who got there first and took the most and surrounded it with wire. It occurred to Joe that you couldn't say a country is free when you could get arrested for trespassing everywhere you stand.

He certainly never connected barbwire with freedom; in fact, quite the opposite.

The driver mentioned that Joe would be impressed by the Rocky Mountains. Joe was far ready to be impressed by something good and was getting somewhat excited. The real Rocky Mountains! Seeing them would be like experiencing one of the Seven Wonders of the World. The driver said, "First we have to cross the foothills and then we'll see the mountains." Joe saw a thin dark-brown line across the horizon, and thought, "That's the Rockies?" He truly hoped this would not be another unexpected disappointment. To Joe's surprise, the closer the slow lumbering truck got, the larger the mountains rose, until they reached a magnificent crescendo of white topped monuments. They were as high, wide, and deep as he needed them to be; in other words, it was worth it.

Upon arriving in Denver Joe checked the telephone book for his friend's name. Would you believe it? His name was there. After being in town for just five minutes, contact was made with a friend. It sure was turning out to be a small world. Luke and Joe had served together in Thailand under life-binding conditions, which made them distant brothers. But in reality they weren't really that close and Luke didn't owe Joe a damn thing. In spite of that, Luke put Joe up until Joe could get an apartment and buy a car, which really didn't take long.

Joe got an apartment on the north side of Denver, a place called Thornton. It was the last apartment complex going north, and there was just wide open space from there. There was nothing to the east; to the west were the Rocky Mountains, with nothing in between. Joe wondered if he would ever get used to seeing a mountain range right outside his front door. The apartment was below ground with windows at ground level. It was strange to see people's legs go by the window. Occasionally when a good pair of legs walked by, Joe would run over to the window to see if he could look up a passing dress. He never really saw anything but it was sure fun trying.

As time went by, Joe filled the apartment with rented furniture and he was all set. This was the first time he ever lived alone. He took to talking to himself to break the silence. Then another woman came into his life. She was nothing to write home about and the relationship was short-lived. Joe had to take full responsibility for that not working out. For you to understand you have to accept the idea that occasionally people have desires of an unusual nature. This girl was fairly thin, and Joe was having an unusual desire for a fat woman. He had never been with a heavy woman before and he was simply curious. Well, as fortune would have it, a fat woman did make herself available to Joe.

On one outing, Joe and the fat girl where driving in the mountains at night. Joe was trying to scare the daylights out of the girl by driving really fast. He shouldn't have done that, especially not being familiar with the terrain. The road was rocky and it wound up and around until they where much higher than Joe ever suspected. He was approaching a left turn and was going way too fast to make it. When he got right up to the edge he could see the lights of the city several thousand feet below. He slammed on the breaks while wildly turning the steering wheel. The car had turned halfway around before it started falling backwards off the mountain. Joe waited until he felt the back wheels hit dirt, then he jammed down on the gas pedal. The car leaped into the air like a gazelle and landed back on the road. The fat girl told Joe that during the entire experience he had a smile on his face. Joe never told her why, but that smile was because Joe was thinking how embarrassing it would be to be found dead with this girl at the bottom of a mountain. This was truly a close call.

A few days later, Joe's girlfriend came over without calling. She looked through the peephole in the door and saw

Joe and the fat girl on the couch together in the nude. Well, that's why it didn't last.

I would be remiss if I didn't discuss the car that Joe was driving. It was a school-bus yellow 1970 Camaro with a 350hp engine. A simple touch of the gas pedal would nail you against the seat. Joe was always trying to get more speed out of it by playing mechanic. In reality, he didn't know squat about cars. On one occasion, he stopped on the side of a hill and tried adjusting the carburetor's linkage. What he really did was separate the linkage to the gas pedal. So when he tried to test-drive it, the pedal went to the floor and stuck there. He got more speed out of it all right! Joe tried to stick his foot under the gas pedal to lift it, but it was like the pedal was being held down by superglue and would not budge. The car was getting out of control, shooting rocks out the back like bullets. He sped headlong towards a cross road, while clouds of dust were billowing a smoke trail like a Boeing jumbo jet. He pushed full on the emergency break to no avail; the car didn't even slow down a bit. If he turned the car off, he was afraid the steering column would lock and he would lose steering control.

Joe could see that the end of the road was fast approaching; there was a barbwire fence ahead and a herd of cows were on the other side. Joe imagined the mess he was going to make out of those cows. There would be enough beef flying around to block out the sun. Joe thought that if he threw the car into low gear at that speed, the transmission would explode into pieces. Only now it was a matter of who was going to make it: the car or him. In a final decision, he threw it into low gear and the car made an explosive boom sound. That slowed the car some while he applied the break and the emergency break at the same time. The car came to rest about ten feet from hitting the fence and the cows. Joe sat in the car for about a half hour while watching his heart move his shirt up and down, then he got out and reconnected the linkage. He never tinkered with his car again.

Several months went by and Joe was making his usual grocery run. When he got to his front door, he noticed a young man that apparently was living in his car in the parking lot. Joe figured he would eventually have to move on. Each day, in Joe's comings and goings, the young man was still there. Joe said to himself, "That guy better leave before the snow falls or he is going to be in a lot of trouble." A person could easily die in the brutal winter of that part of the country. Sure as hell, the snow began to fall and the temperature started to drop to life-threatening lows. Joe thought no one could be that stupid as to try and tough it out in a car. Joe passed by several times over the course of the next few days, and each time Joe thought, "That boy is going to die." Of all the places on God's green— or snow-covered—earth, why in hell does this asshole choose to die right outside his front door? This situation began to haunt Joe. What the hell was going on? Was this another one of those tests that God gives you? Joe couldn't take watching this young man slowly freeze to death. So he invited the helpless idiot into his apartment. After feeding him, Joe found out the guy was out of gas and couldn't move on. He was wandering around lost and alone. Joe said he would try to help him get back on his feet.

After a short while, when Joe sat on the couch, he became sickened by a pungent odor rising up from the fabric. It turned out to be the smell of the young man, who obviously had not bathed over a prolonged period of time. At every place he sat, he left a stink that ruined Joe's apartment and his furniture. Joe ordered the young man to shower right away. When the young man emerged from the shower, the only difference was his hair was wet. The stink had not subsided even a bit. Joe learned that after not bathing for a while, the skin oils become a natural protective barrier against the elements, and it takes many showers for oils to wash off.

For Joe, it appeared that no good deed goes unpunished. Not being prepared to deal with this problem and the apartment in complete ruin, he figured he would just pack up and hit the road again for better horizons. The stinky young man wanted to go with Joe. This was not even a possibility, Joe thought; he announced he traveled alone. Joe also wanted to leave Denver because he was somewhat disappointed in himself for no longer noticing the Rocky Mountains; he had taken them for granted. Besides all that, the damn snow was getting deep, and Joe hated snow.

Back on the road again, Joe figured he would head south until snow was no longer a factor. He would then take the southern route around the mountains and head for California. At one point through a break in the mountains Joe saw a golden, glowing landscape, which had the appearance of what you would imagine heaven to look like. It turned out to be the sun bouncing off the sands of the desert, creating a beautiful elusive mirage.

Joe was feeling lonely while driving on the road. He decided to pick up the next hitchhiker he saw, just to have some company. He picked up a scruffy-looking guy, thin and worn looking, who went by the name of Wiley. He seemed to have knowledge and experience in this part of the country. He told Joe that he knew a girl who ran a hotel in Arizona and she knew how to party. They drove across New Mexico that night; Joe wanted to see what the desert looked like but it was so dark he couldn't see a thing. The next day, they found the hotel where Wiley's friend worked. As he had mentioned, the woman got on the phone right away and put out the party alert. In Arizona, people will travel over 200 miles just to go to a party. As the party was warming up, Joe was already completely wasted to the point where he had to crawl out of there on his hands and knees. He couldn't even climb up in bed and spent the night on the floor. In all his days, he had never found a people that could party as hard as the people in Arizona.

The next morning, Joe and Wiley continued to travel through the state. Joe finally got to see the desert and the mesas—stand-alone mountains with a flat top. They were passing a really large one with a straight face on it that went up several hundred feet when Wiley suggested they climb it. Joe looked out the window of the car and studied the possibility of doing that. He could see the mountain rising straight up like a wall. He turned to Wiley and said, "Are you crazy? That thing is a straight wall with nothing to hang on to." After a minute of pondering, Joe said, "Oh, what the hell!" He figured he would never be by this way again. So, why not just do it? Joe pulled the car off to the side of the road.

They had to walk quite a distance just to get to the base of the mountain. They also had to cross over many good-sized boulders to get there. Wiley warned Joe about rattlesnakes; he said snakes loved to cool themselves in the shade of the larger rocks. This put Joe on his old military-alert status. Every footstep became one of caution.

It took them several hours to reach the bottom of this awesome natural formation. Then they began to climb; at the beginning it was a gradual incline but it quickly became steeper. They climbed throughout the day, all the way watching for falling rocks that occasionally bounced by. One slip and this story would have never been told. Joe started wondering why he put himself into such a difficult position. They were both tired, bruised and had no climbing equipment. It was just about then that they reached the straight up part. Joe took a look back at his car and it appeared to be no more than a yellow grain of sand. Joe was all for turning back, but Wiley found a crack about four feet wide in this sheer, straight-faced wall. He convinced Joe that by spreading their arms and legs to both sides of the crack, they could inch their way up.

This adventure had turned into another obstacle that Joe had to conquer. There was no option of failure. Even though he was overcome with fright, he felt compelled to accept the challenge.

It was late afternoon when they finally heaved themselves over the top. What a strange place this was. It was a beautiful landscape taken out of time, totally flat with grass and trees, high in the sky. Joe and Wiley sat on the edge with their feet dangling off the side. You could see for hundreds of miles in all directions, clear to the horizon. After sitting there a while, just resting and soaking up the beauty, Joe heard a strange, distant, machine-like sound. Now this may sound strange, but Joe thought the sound was actually the earth itself turning in space—and why not? The earth is just another machine part on a scale so grand that it dwarfs the imagination. Joe knew that he would always remember this experience and be humbled by its majesty.

Of course, it was a lot easier to climb down than it was to climb up. Back on the road again, they came to another crossroad. One way led to Mexico and the other led to California. Joe got one of his "I've never been to" ideas. So off they went to Mexico. There was a small border town called Mexicali. This was a real cowboy-type of town. The main road was not even paved and the inhabitants were gruff and harsh in appearance. The men were the toughest looking hombres Joe had ever seen.

After hitting a few bars, Joe and Wiley picked up a couple of girls, figuring this was a sure thing. After a night on the town the girls wanted to go home. Joe and Wiley traveled over the most muddy and pot-holed road in the world to get them home. They expected the girls would be grateful enough for a little payback. But sometimes a guy just can't get a break. The girls ran inside and that was that.

Joe felt as though he needed a little excitement, so he drove the car back to town and gunned the engine to full rpm's and then let it go. In doing so he buried the entire town in a cloud of dust that covered everything. By the time they got to the other end of town, the entire Mexican police force was waiting for them. They arrested Joe and placed him in a holding cell with a bunch of Mexican farmers. A Mexican guard lined everyone up and was walking down the line, just looking everyone over. When he got to Joe, Joe was just pulling out a cigarette; Joe tapped the guard on the shoulder and signaled for a light. The guard slapped Joe across the face so hard the cigarette flew to the other side of the room. Joe knew then he was in the wrong place.

They brought him before a judge who asked if Joe had any money. Joe pulled out a $5 bill and said that's all he had. Actually, his entire savings—which wasn't much anyway—was hidden under the carpet in the car; he was praying they wouldn't find it. To Joe's disbelief, they let him go. Wiley was waiting for him in the car. As they were leaving town, Joe went through a red light and was arrested again. The police again asked Joe if he had any money. Joe pulled out another $5 dollar bill and said that's all he had. They let him go again. Joe was getting the impression that if he had committed murder the fine would have been $5 dollars.

Well, since Mexico was not making Joe feel welcome, he decided to head back to his side of the border. Only now he ran into the border police—at least they were American. When the border police got one look at Joe's hippy-looking friend, they decided to do a strip search. Joe was standing there in his birthday suit, in a room with a glass wall, as female officers passed by with an entertained look on their faces. Joe waved back at them as though he was the main attraction in a parade. After a futile search, the police let them go.

Back to the USA, where Joe said goodbye to the hitchhiker. The next sign on the road was the Grand Canyon. Now, Joe had heard of the Grand Canyon. It was time for one of those detours. But there were so many canyons around that Joe wasn't sure which one was the grand one. Until he happened upon the real thing: it sure was the biggest hole in the ground he ever saw. So that's what he said, "Man, that's the biggest hole in the ground I ever saw!" Funny thing is, all he felt at that moment was hunger, which seemed as big as the Grand Canyon. The savings were running low and there was no time to dally. When you are hungry, big holes are not that impressive.

It was California or bust; he had just enough money for gas to get there. He figured he could find a job or get a loan, just something to get by on. So he pushed on. He kept going until he ran out of land. He had reached the beach in California. There were giant rocks that jetted out over the surf. A wave would slide in under the rocks until it hit the back wall. There would be a tremendous boom, the rock would shake under your feet, and then the water would shoot out from all sides. If you stood right in the middle, you wouldn't get a drop on you. Joe stood on one those rocks watching the sunset over the Pacific Ocean; he watched as other people stopped their cars on the side of the highway to watch the sunset too—that's how beautiful it was.

Hunger was becoming the primary focus of his attention now. First, Joe went to the fishing boats to get a job. He figured he could work as a deck hand. Nobody on the fishing boats spoke English. Then he saw people eating at a cafeteria in a college so he figured he would go to school just so he could eat. They wouldn't take him because he wasn't a resident of the state; you had to live there three months before becoming a resident. Joe figured that in three months he would be a dead resident. Then he thought about joining the Coast Guard. They told Joe there was an 11-month waiting list to get in. Joe wasn't sure how much time he had, but knew he sure didn't have 11 months.

He then went to a bank to try to get a loan against his car; he was running out of gas anyway. That "must be a resident" thing came into play again—in other words, no.

Every night Joe would find a deserted place to park so he could sleep in his car. Every night a policeman would wake Joe up and tell him to move on. Joe also found that as hot as it got in the day, at night it would get severely cold, with the wind coming off the ocean.

Joe was sure getting hungry now like he had never been before. All he could think about was food. His senses were beginning to sharpen. He could smell food from great distances. After trying so hard to play by the rules, now the thought of stealing food began crossing his mind. Funny thing is, Joe thought, this was the richest country in the world and he had nothing to eat. Joe remembered how many times he came so close to loosing his life in the military for this country he did so love. It was then that he made a solemn vow: "I vow to God and all that is holy, I will sooner die of starvation on the steps of the White House rather than steal a single apple." Joe knew that that vow was not only non-productive but also hard as hell to keep. God knew he meant it, though.

Hunger kept gnawing at him like the wild packs of dogs in Thailand. Joe believed that if one wants to work, work will be found. He was young and as willing to work as he was willing to eat. Both his senses and his thought process were becoming extremely acute. Joe remembered he once got a loan from the Navy Credit Union in Korea to buy stereo equipment. San Diego was loaded with military bases and at least one of them had to have a credit union. This idea had better work, too, because he was running out of options and out of ideas. Joe remembered that passage from the bible about the birds of the air, that they do not plant or harvest, yet they are well fed and well clothed; how much more does God love us than the birds of the air? Before he left to apply at the credit union, he thought he'd better have a little talk with God.

"Okay, God, I know I only talk to you when I am in trouble or in need. I know I never take the time to just say hello when things are going well. I ask that you overlook my flaws and help me. I am hungry, and you have to know how I've tried so hard not to hassle you about this. Now, I ask for your divine guidance, and that you grant me sustenance, if it be your will."

Armed with a prayer and overwhelming hunger, he found a credit union. He approached a clerk and introduced himself, stating he wanted to apply for a loan using his car as collateral. Well, at least the clerk didn't say no right away. She shuffled off to check her records. She returned with several other official-looking persons. First they asked what his name was; then they asked him for his identification, which Joe promptly provided. The next question seemed a little strange; they asked why he was applying for a loan. Joe responded by stating he was hungry and needed money to eat. They then reworded the question, "Why do you want a loan, when you have an account already on file with us?" Joe knew this was a mistake because he had never been to San Diego before, and he told them so. The next question from them was, "May we see your social security card?" Joe again complied but was starting to think these people were acting a little strange.

After checking his social security number they returned again. This time they asked Joe if he would like to make a withdrawal. A withdrawal? Joe asked, "Will I have to pay it back?" They said, "No, you have an account already with us." Joe asked how much money was in the account. They said there was $662.15 in the account. He really didn't believe they would give the money to him so he told them he wanted it all. If they were so darn eager to give Joe money then why should he fight it any longer? They gave Joe a check for the entire amount and all he had to do was sign for it. He figured that he would pay them back once they realized their mistake, so this was kind of a loan anyway. This couldn't be stealing because he was totally honest with them. The only real meaning this had for Joe was that he was going to eat tonight. And eat he did: a steak dinner with all the trimmings. Joe had been so hungry for so long that he forgot about his prayer and was not even aware of the miracle that had just occurred. Now how much more human can you get than that?

It wasn't until much later that Joe found out it was his loan in Korea years before for the stereo equipment that had created that account. He had paid the loan in full and thought the transaction was completed. But when you take a loan with the credit union you accumulate shares with quarterly dividends. The Korean Credit Union had to have a link to the United States. That link was the San Diego Navy Credit Union, which Joe just happened to wander into during his time of most serious need.

The immediate crisis was over. Joe had a full stomach, a wad of cash, and a full tank of gas. Eventually it sank in about the Divine intervention he had just experienced. When he realized that his prayer had been answered, he decided to see if God was still listening.

"Hello, God! I would like to thank you for assisting me in my time of need. That was a pretty good piece of work you just pulled off, and I have to admit I'm impressed. Now I've got another matter that could use your attention. I'm alone and far from home with no direction. Would you please give me a sign as to what you would have me do now?"

At that moment Joe started talking to himself; he could clearly hear himself giving himself instructions about what to do. It was his own voice in his own head that started telling him things that he didn't necessarily agree with. One thing that he said was, "Sometimes you have to go back to go forward." Joe asked himself, "What the heck does that really mean?" The answer came immediately: "You are to return home and resolve all the problems you left behind before my plan for you can proceed." For a moment Joe thought he was loosing it, because the last thing he wanted to do was go home. Besides, it was a 3000-mile trip and he wasn't even sure he could make it on the money he had. Somewhat confused by his own instructions to himself, he asked, "God, is that you or is my mind playing tricks on me?" The answer came back, "Did I tell you to do anything wrong or against your conscience?" Joe answered no. "That's how you can tell the answer to your question, Joe. Now heed my word and my plan will become known to you."

Joe got the message and understood that if God chose to talk with him in this manner, then that was that. No further questions were asked; Joe started the engine to head for home. He figured if he went straight through without taking any detours he might make it. Checking a map it appeared as though the southern route was the most direct way back.

Again he found himself crossing the desert, this time in the daylight. The desert was a completely new environment for Joe. It was everything he had always heard: miles and miles of sand. At one point Joe saw something blue showing between the sand dunes. It was not just the color blue—it was a majestic blue of magnificent intensity. Joe concluded it had to be a mirage. It was hot as hell and Joe wasn't going to be tricked by an illusion. He drove on several more miles and the blue color again showed through the sand dunes for a brief moment. Joe thought if he saw it one more time then he would have to check it out. After about a half hour, there it was—the darn blue again. So he pulled off to the side, parked the car and prepared to take a hike over the dunes. He had no sooner crossed over several sand dunes than there it was. It was a river in the middle of the desert. The water had a blue color that could only be compared to the colors you would see in a picture bible. Joe thought it would really be a nifty thing to go swimming in the desert. So he took off all his clothes and jumped in.

The water was colder than a witch's tit. While swimming around, Joe started to think that he really didn't know what danger might exist in this water; that maybe this water came from a nuke plant or worse. He did know he was out of his environment and was taking an awful chance. Common sense began to kick in and Joe thought he better get out before something unexpected happened. That's when he found out that he couldn't climb out of the water. The sand kept giving way and he couldn't get a foothold. Joe thought that it would be just his luck to die from drowning in the desert! After a few minutes of desperation, he noticed a bush on the side bank not far away. He grabbed the bush and was able to pull himself out, but in doing so he fell into the bush—which happened to be a briar bush. Now Joe had a new problem: he spent about two hours picking thorns out of his ass. However, another valuable lesson was learned: never go swimming in the desert! He didn't know what good this lesson would be in the long run. What he did know was that he was going to take better care of his ass from now on! He was also going to check himself after darkness fell to see if any part of him was glowing from radiation.

Later that night Joe still hadn't cleared the desert. It became so dark that the road was hard to see even with the headlights. There was a light shining at him from miles away that didn't make things any easier, either. The farther he drove the brighter this light became. It was a fairly large light shining all by itself. The light was a good distance from the ground with no other lights nearby. Joe's curiosity was still curbed from the river incident. So he couldn't have cared less about this light; he just wanted it to go away and stop blinding him. Then, to make matters worse, there was car now behind him staying at a steady distance. The lights from the car behind made it seem like driving with a blindfold on. Eventually, something had to give and it did. The car from behind turned on his bubble; it was a damn cop! He pulled Joe over for swerving too much. When the cop asked Joe why he was swerving, Joe told him that the light from up ahead and the cop's headlights were blinding him. He asked the cop, "What the hell is that light ahead anyway?" The cop told Joe that it was a train; he then ordered Joe to stop at the next restaurant and get some coffee. The cop followed Joe all the way, too.

If it wasn't one thing it was another; it started to rain. Nothing unusual about this except it was the heaviest rain Joe had seen since the monsoon in Thailand. With his windshield wipers going full speed, the rain was still sheeting over the windshield. When he tried to pass a tractor-trailer, the backwash from the truck made it seem like driving through a dark ocean. No one ever said it rained this hard in the desert before, but it does. The only way Joe could tell he was still on the road was because he could still feel the tires on the pavement.

After getting a flat in Albuquerque, New Mexico, Joe was beginning to feel as though he was fighting an unknown force that was trying to prevent him from returning home. That was okay, too, because he was up for the challenge. This situation didn't help the financial issue at all. By his own calculation, this unexpected expense was going to leave him somewhat short of his goal. While waiting for his car to be repaired, Joe took a look around. Albuquerque was a city in the middle of the desert. "Whoever thought of putting a city here must have had bats in his belfry." Joe took a walk on the desert and was amazed at how far he could see: there was nothing around but the wind blowing in his ears. The only description he could think of was magnificent desolation.

When the flat was fixed Joe was glad to be on the road again. While driving, he would occasionally see a black burnt spot on the side of the road. He didn't really know what caused this but he would soon find out. Did you know that when a person starts to fall asleep while driving their eyes begin to cross first? This cross-eyed effect causes the lanes on a highway to cross also, making a person believe that they are driving in the right lane when they are actually driving into oncoming traffic. Out west, they drive at great speed because of the great distances, so when they do crash they leave behind a black burnt spot on the side of the road. Joe fell asleep at the wheel several times while driving. Funny thing is, he dreamed he was driving on the same road he was on. When the car would start to leave the road, the bouncing would wake him up. After a while he couldn't tell if he was awake or dreaming. That meant it was time to drink enough coffee to make his hair stand up.

In Oklahoma, he pulled off to a roadside restaurant. In taking his order, the waitress noticed Joe had an accent. She asked where he was from. Joe made the mistake of saying New York. The waitress said they considered people from New York to be crude and ill mannered. Joe responded by saying, "New Yorkers think that people from Oklahoma are uneducated hicks." This was not entirely appreciated by the waitress, who went over to a group of real southern hicks and informed them of what he said. Joe suddenly felt very uncomfortable and decided to leave. As he was getting in his car he noticed the entire restaurant was following him. So he stepped on the gas and made for a fast getaway. Those southern boys had pretty fast cars, too, and a chase ensued. Joe reached speeds of over 90 miles an hour but was still loosing ground to their high-powered engines. Joe knew that without another miracle he would be caught. The broken lines on the highway were turning into a solid line as he was traveling so fast. Joe figured he had just about run out of miracles until he suddenly saw and hit a massive wall of fog. The fog was so thick it blotted out everything, even the road. Then he heard a whooshing sound go over the car, which meant he had just gone under a bridge. So he doubled back and hid on the side of this bridge. The chasing cars went by at full throttle. Joe had never been more grateful for fog before.

Those damn southern boys don't give up so easily. At the next town they had set up a roadblock with their cars. Joe didn't see it until the last moment. He couldn't stop, so again he gave it the gas and figured he would plow his way through. At the last second Joe slammed down on the breaks causing the car to go into a spin, while turning the wheel violently. He spun into the middle of the roadblock, then hit the gas again throwing rocks everywhere and spiraled through it without touching a thing. All he could see was the amazed look on the bystander's faces as he sped off. Joe figured he'd better get off the main road and take a detour until he was out of hick country. His adrenalin was pumping so hard that coffee was no longer needed.

By the time he reached Memphis the gas was running low and so were the funds. Joe had bought a typewriter when he was in Colorado—he had plans of writing a book about his adventures—and he figured he could pawn this typewriter for some gas money. They gave him $40 dollars for a $120 dollar typewriter. So onward he pushed.

There were very high mountains in Tennessee. Joe could occasionally see the great height at which he was traveling. It was nighttime and he figured he could save gas by traveling behind a tractor-trailer. The back draft from the truck would pull the car. This idea was doing fine until the truck driver used his CB radio to call other trucks. Before Joe knew it there were tractor-trailers surrounding him in front, back and left sides. Joe thought they would quit this joke and let him pass eventually. What they did was slowly move closer and closer until it was turning into a matter of life and death. The only way out was to jump off the right side of the road and try to pass the lead truck on the grass. But it was dark and Joe didn't know if there would be grass or just a long fall off a high mountain. Even a traffic sign would be enough to finish him. Out of time and no other place to go, he jumped. Joe's car was really hauling ass as he passed the lead truck. The truckers must really respect blind courage because they didn't bother him after that.

From then on, city after city he went through with no problems until he reached New York, the very city closest to where he grew up. Would you believe he got lost and found himself circling the city three times searching for the exit to Long Island? Whoever designed New York City had no intention for Long Island to be discovered. Upon finally breaking through the New York City barrier, Joe made it to Farmingdale, where he ran out of gas in the driveway of his own home. Now try and explain that!

Joe actually got to sleep in his own bed that night, after having slept in his car for so long. He awoke the next day to find that his brother Bernie had borrowed his car without asking and early that morning had broadsided the only other car on the road. The front end of Joe's car was completely demolished but Bernie was okay. After the car was repaired, it never drove the same way again; it had lost that fiery rebellious kick that got Joe out of so many difficult situations. Joe was really upset when he finally sold it to a friend. His friend then painted the car powder blue—what an insult!

Well, it was a good thing that Joe got home when he did. His sister Myra had gotten married, Bernie wasn't working, and Joe's mother wasn't making enough to pay for everything. In fact, the mortgage hadn't been paid in three months. Joe didn't know what he could do about it now that things were so bad. Joe took whatever job he could, but catching up was proving to be impossible. Joe even applied for Social Security disability benefits until he could find work, but several months went by and he hadn't heard anything from them. Foreclosure proceedings were started and his mother didn't tell Joe about it until the appointment day came to meet with the lawyers. The bill was $2,500.00 in arrears and immediate payment was due.

The only plan his mother had was to go to the appointment and let the chips fall where they may. So they all piled into the car and as they were pulling out of the driveway the mailman was coming down the street. Joe asked to wait to get the mail before they left. The mailman handed Joe an envelope from Social Security. In it was a check for $2,500.00 payable to Joe in retroactive benefits. It was amazing how the problem was solved just like that.

Still, more income was needed and Joe was having a tough time finding a job. Bernie told Joe to apply for unemployment benefits; Joe didn't even know what that was. He still went down to the unemployment office to apply. At that time the unemployment office was divided into two sections, unemployment compensation and employment job search. Joe just happened to enter the building through the job search side. They asked Joe if he was a veteran; he said yes. They told Joe that President Carter had initiated a program for veterans to work in offices like this one. Then they asked Joe if he wanted to work in this office. He took a look around, and when he didn't see anything life threatening he said yes. Besides, since his illness had not returned, it was time to find a way to live again. Joe's new job was to assist other veterans to find work. He wondered how he would be able to help anyone else, when he himself had stumbled into this job.

Their plan was to send Joe to the World Trade Center in Manhattan. There on the 86th floor was the office of the Department of Labor. That's where all the training was done. To get there you had to take the Long Island railroad into New York City and the train would enter the complex through the basement. The rest of the trip to work was made by elevator straight up. Joe never cared for the place but felt that it surely deserved some exploration. He would go to the top and look down. When Joe was a kid he went to the top of the Empire State Building. From there, every other building in New York looked like very small bumps in the earth. When he looked over the edge of the World trade Center, it was the Empire State Building that looked like a small bump in the earth.

While looking down, he saw an airplane fly by. This would not be an extraordinary event except for the fact that Joe could see the top of the plane as it went by. One time when he was out for lunch, he looked up the corner of the building to see how straight it was. It was letter perfect to the sky. Joe put his hand on the building and said, "This building will be here a hundred years after I'm gone." He also hoped God would not be angry for man's attempt at creating perfection.

Joe learned a lot about the labor market, business, and every different type of job under the sun. He learned about how labor unions were formed and why: to protect the worker from the greed of the employer. He learned the story of the labor wars of the 20s and 30s; he learned that children were worked eighteen hours a day under inhuman conditions in "sweat shops." He learned that when insanity took over reason the only battle tool of the people was to strike; that strikes led to police intervention; that police intervention led to shots being fired, and that shots being fired led to people dying, not for freedom but for fairness. Every hour of lunch break, every two-week vacation, every benefit he ever enjoyed was paid for in this way. But Joe wasn't interested in the past; he just wanted to find his place in the present.

Be darned if Joe didn't turn out to be quite the job developer; he was very successful in his job. He worked for many years, all the while saving for that little house of his own that he promised himself in Korea. As soon as he had $10,000 dollars saved, he went to a real-estate broker. They laughed at him. "Come back, son, when you've got some real cash," they said. Okay, so that's what he would do. When he saved up $20,000 dollars, he went back. They laughed at him again! It seemed that the price of housing was going up far faster than he could save. At $25,000 dollars, that was the last laugh he was going to take. Joe realized he was actually being priced out of the area where he had lived most of his life.

But Joe was different now. He had seen the world from both sides. He had faced death, fear, poverty, disease, hunger, and still was able to stand on his own two feet, and in one piece too. Nothing had conquered him, nothing. He had valuable knowledge and insight from working on his job. His logistical skills had become highly developed and he would use everything he had for the change he was contemplating. Again, Joe was going to put himself into a position where he was at the end of his resources.

The plan he was developing would require thoughtful concentration and attention to detail. Joe was planning to find his very own peace in a place where the sun was always shining. He would plant flowers over every square inch of this place until his world looked and smelled like heaven; this would also be done in remembrance of the brothers he had served with in Thailand and Korea. As he had previously promised himself, he would never raise his hand in anger again, and his wars would be over forever. Joe knew he had one shot at this effort and it had to go right the first time. Joe was now the five-star general over all his decisions, resources, and timing with regard to this strategic endeavor.

The plan started with a map of the United States and studying the weather patterns over the entire country. Joe would only consider living in a warm place near the ocean. That reduced his options to just California and Texas on the west, and Virginia, the Carolinas, Georgia, and Florida on the east. California was already tried; Joe was born in Texas but didn't want to settle there. Now it was down to just eastern states. Joe picked several target cities and planned to make several trips to survey each one.

With his revulsion for cold weather and snow, Joe decided to start with Florida, figuring that the farther south he went the warmer the climate would be. Now it was just down to which city was best. As it appeared on the map, the best location was a central one. That way a beachhead could be established with easy access to all other parts of the state. That city was Orlando.

SUNSHINE IN PARADISE

WHEN JOE LEFT New York on his first expedition trip, there was gray slush on the ground; the sky was also darkened gray by the exhaust of traffic. There was even gray, wet, cold snow falling. Every place was crowded, cold, wet, gray and miserable. After a two-and-a-half-hour plane trip and renting a car, he was ready—ready for his first attempt to survey an entire city. The information he had obtained before his arrival was that Orlando was the fastest-growing city in the country. The real-estate value was grossly underestimated, too. When he first left the airport, this place seemed to be some kind of wonderland. The sun was bright and warm, butterflies were hopping from one beautiful flower to the next, colorful birds were everywhere. It was one wonder after the next: people were wearing shorts in the wintertime, and the roads were perfectly smooth with no potholes.

After studying a map of the city, it was apparent that the growth was following the direction of the interstate highway. Like a general studying the battlefield, Joe drove completely around the city. In doing so, he got a real-time feel for the atmosphere of each individual section. One curious thing he noticed was that there were groups of houses with walls around them; it seemed to be a commonplace thing. Joe wondered what these people were afraid of—Indians? In any case the city itself was clean and very young. The skyline consisted of just about six tall buildings that didn't even qualify as skyscrapers. This was a baby city and mighty darn cute, too. It was surrounded by orange groves and the smell of orange citrus was everywhere. The rows of trees with big round oranges and grapefruits made the place look like something out of the Wizard of Oz. The palm trees were a beautiful final touch. Of course, the really big selling point was that this place had never seen snow!

Well, this was it; the search was short and now over. This was the city selected as a final choice without even checking out the other targets. Now all that had to be done was to find a place to live and a job.

There were many things to consider when buying the house of his dreams. Joe went to a realtor and was given a list of several hundred homes to check out; he had eleven days to do it before he had to go back to New York. He made a list of the features he wanted in a house and checked it against the realtor's list. That saved him some time by eliminating many houses that didn't match his ideal concept.

House after house he searched—some came close, and some not at all. As the number of choices decreased the anxiety increased. Then he drove to one address that was one of the last ones on the list. Funny thing is, the numbers on the houses didn't match the realtor's address list. He checked his map and realized that the location was right behind him. So he looked into the rear view mirror, and there it was. The house filled the rear view mirror and, better yet, it called to him. He turned his head to get a full straight-on look and again it called to him. Joe could not believe his eyes; he actually felt as though he was meant to live there.

The house stood proud on ground that was a bit higher. It was perfectly manicured and had lots of trees around. The place was on a corner lot and faced south. It also had a double car garage. In fact, it met all his requirements. While he was still looking at it, a family drove up to look at the place as prospective buyers. Joe was amazed: he was going to lose the place the very moment he found it. Well, hell, no matter what, he was going to get his bid in anyway. So Joe drove around the neighborhood to kill time and get a look around. He found a river just a couple of blocks away from the house. Joe remembered the words, "Lead me by the still waters," and was even more convinced that this was where he belonged. While waiting to return to the house, Joe thought a prayer might help; it went like this:

"Hey God, you said you help those who help themselves. You must have seen how I've busted my ass (please forgive me) to get this far. Besides, I believe you made a promise to me in California; something about taking care of my needs if I took care of my family members. Well, I did that. God, if you let me live here I will never ask anything of you again. This place does appear to be heaven on earth as in the prayer. If you let me stay here then I will consider your promise kept. I know you're there and I know you're listening, so how about it?"

As soon as the potential buyers left, Joe made his move. The price was on the high side of Joe's expectations, but what could he do—the place called to him. So Joe accepted the deal right away. Besides, the place had good vibes and, knowing God was involved, how could it go wrong? Only one problem left: Joe couldn't move in without a job.

Joe already had eight years under his belt with the job in New York and with another two years he could qualify for some meager retirement benefit. That might come in handy someday if things got tight. So Joe continued to work for two years in the north while paying for his house down south. So far, some big decisions had been made and plans were going better than expected. This was a first for our hero, too, as calamity and turmoil usually followed him on a regular basis.

Joe decided his best bet for a new job was with the post office, although he had never envisioned himself as a mailman. They paid well and working outdoors seemed like a good idea. Being a veteran was actually going to help him get the job too. After passing all the required tests for the job and finishing up the required time on his job in New York, it was time. It was time to start a new life in paradise and on his own terms. He would live in the sunshine for the remainder of his days and rejoice in his newly found peace. At least that was the plan.

The date was August 8th 1988. Joe moved into the first house he ever owned on his own and started his new job with the Post Office in the same week. Ah, the American dream realized! Now all he had to do was live, work, and be happy.

Everything started out pretty simple: first he had to undergo mailman training and then he would hit the streets. He also had to go through a probationary period of three months. No problem! He could easily handle this. Then he found out what a typical day would be like: For the first four hours in the early morning you had to place stacks of mail into hundreds of pigeonholes. Of course there was no talking to the persons working on either side of you, which made for a very boring time. On top of that, there was a low-hanging walkway from the ceiling with one-way glass; this was so the supervisors could stand right over your shoulders and watch every move you made. When all the mail was pigeonholed, then it had to be taken down and loaded onto a mail truck and delivered. The truck was then driven to a specific area from where the mail was delivered on foot while carrying a very heavy mailbag. In the summer, a mail truck is really a "tin stove on wheels." If the temperature on the outside was 98 degrees, the temperature on the inside of the truck would be like 120 degrees. Not only that, but a training film showed an accident where a mail truck hit an empty wheelchair—the truck disintegrated. And to make it worse, the damn steering column is on the wrong side!

Joe had his first indication that something was wrong when the route assignments were being handed out. Joe's name was called first and he was asked to stand. There was quite a bit of levity over the fact that his assignment was a place called Linda Vista. Joe was oblivious to the fact that he was a New Yorker who had strategically taken this job from a Floridian. Naturally, there was going to be a price to pay for this intrusion. The price was Linda Vista, a minority section of town where nearly everyone owned a pit bull. It was also the farthest section from Joe's house that they could send him to.

Now, this is the month of August, the hottest month of the year in Florida. Day by day Joe would run the gauntlet of flesh-cooking heat, attacking dogs, and unfamiliar territory. After a month or so of this routine, management told Joe he was taking too long completing his route, so they took his breaks and lunch period away to make up time. They also told him that if he wanted to take water he had to do it while walking from house to house. Joe thought they were trying to make him fail. In fact, he was sure of it. The heat rarely fell below 98 degrees; to carry water was out of the question for Joe, as it would make the huge heavy mail sack even heavier. So Joe would occasionally beg a homeowner for a glass of water. Everyday he would go home completely covered in sweat and head straight for the shower with his clothes on; he would then fall out cold asleep still in his wet clothes. The next day he would do it all over again.

Joe began to wonder if he was physically able to perform his duties. But this was not a job he could just give up on. He had a new house to pay for—the only place he had to live. Not having any family or friends nearby to depend on, he had no choice. There was no plan "B" and he had to make this work.

It was after about two months of this continuing travesty when Joe started to feel his brain expanding in his head from the heat. On several occasions he came close to losing consciousness. He was as a candle being melted by the blazing, unrelenting, scorching sun. Day after day, he could feel the pressure of his brain pushing against the wall of his skull, swelling from the heat. Then it occurred to him all at once. It was God! God was punishing him for some prior sin. He believed that it was God because he had come to learn how God works by now. But Joe felt that he hadn't sinned enough to deserve this kind of suffering. So why would God do this for no apparent reason? The one thing Joe did know for sure was that there was a reason for all this unnecessary hardship. He knew enough not to try and outguess the ultimate plan of his Creator. He knew the answer to his question would eventually be presented to him.

By now the existence of God was no longer a question for Joe. He knew the truth; after experiencing so many miracles, coincidence was no longer a possibility. Besides, Joe could always feel a vast presence out there. Now with all the audacity of a curious child, Joe thought, "Why couldn't I meet God without dying? Surely there must be a truckload of qualifications to accomplish this feat and I'm not exactly a good Christian. But I am His creation and I believe I have the right to have this request granted. I want to meet my creator!"

"God," he said, "I will never really appreciate the gift of life you have given me or be truly happy with a gift I don't understand. But I know happiness would be mine if I could meet you and still be able to be alive. God, my faith in you is solid as a rock. I know you can feel this request is made with all my love and from the deepest part of my heart. I request to meet you."

The next day, Joe returned to the office at the end of his shift, again sopping wet in his own sweat. Joe's supervisor was always ready with a demeaning remark like "not everybody is meant to be a mailman." Today it was "You're too slow, I don't know what I'm going to do with you." Joe responded in heroic fashion and said, "Well sir, I'm not ready to give up." Just as his supervisor started to walk away, Joe felt a funny feeling in his stomach. Everything started to get dim. He knew he was loosing consciousness, but it was happening so fast that there was nothing he could do about it. He started to fall to the floor and by the time he landed he was completely unconscious.

What happened to Joe next may defy all reason and conventional thinking. But in Joe's mind he believes this to be a certainty as true as true can be.

Joe, while still in an unconscious state, found himself standing in a hallway alone. He didn't care where he came from or where he was going. Someone walked up to Joe and asked him if he wanted to meet God. Joe asked, "You mean the real God?" The answer was yes. Joe replied, "Yes, I would very much like to meet God." He was led down a corridor; while on the way, Joe saw a plaque that read "Geodesic Orange Dome." The initials would be G.O.D. Joe thought, "Great, just great! What if God turned out to be a machine? Wouldn't that just be the biggest disappointment of all existence?"

Joe was taken to a room where people were standing on a set of small bleachers and in several rows. You could not help but notice these people because they were made out of light; even their clothes were shining with light. Joe tried to approach them but was told not to get near them. Joe asked from a distance, "What kind of people are you, that you are made out of light?" He was aware that they were conversing with him, but he was not sure how, just that he could hear their voices in his head.

After a brief discussion, he was then taken to a very large window nearby. It was like looking out over an enormous—and I do mean enormous—stadium. The only thing he could see was this immense ball of orange fire. It was fantastically huge! The flames coming off it made a wave-like dancing motion. Joe was told not to take his eyes off the fire. As if he could look anywhere else! This was the type of thing that was so awesome that you just don't look away no matter what. As Joe stared at it, he suddenly found himself standing right in front of it. The dance of the flames began to reach out. Several large flares seemed to come amazingly close. Until one really large flare whipped out and around and hit Joe full force. Instead of being burned, he felt overwhelmed with love. Then it hit him: the fire was love! It was as if you took all the love that ever was or ever will be and put it in one place. Joe was completely disintegrated by this pure, overwhelming, all-encompassing, and never-ending love. Joe could now see and understand the meaning of life; even his place in it was made perfectly clear to him. In fact, the purpose of every blade of grass and every grain of sand on every beach was made known to him. It was a symphony of time eternal: all events and every motion, all being conducted by love.

For an unknown period of time, Joe's body, mind and soul were one with the Orange Dancing Fire. For an unknown period of time his cup overflowed with joy and love—as it would continue to do for the rest of his natural born life as a result of this experience.

His next sensation was being held from under both arms and being escorted back to speak with the people of light. As they spoke with him, images began to form in the background, like on a large movie screen. They were images of every low, down-rotten thing Joe had ever done. Images of every time Joe had hurt someone's feelings or made another person feel rejected or caused another person pain. Except this time Joe could actually feel the pain and misery he caused as if it were his own. Joe could hear the people of light talking. It was like a jury trial. They were trying to determine what the disposition of Joe's status would be. It was a question of whether Joe could stay or be sent back. To be sent back would mean to be separated from God's love. That would be a sentence equivalent to being sent to hell. Maybe it was that Joe had sinned to excess or maybe he had just not completed his mission yet, but this was the sentence: Joe was to be sent back. Joe pleaded on his hands and knees with torrents of tears streaming down his face. He yelled and screamed and begged and cried to stay as he felt himself slipping away from God's love, but to no avail.

Now Joe started to hear other voices. His blurry eyes began to open and he saw people standing all around him. As his vision began to clear, he could see he was back at the post office surrounded by his fellow workers. They were discussing whether to call an ambulance. As Joe regained consciousness, all he could say was, "What happened?"

Not yet having regained control over his body after the shock, he heard and felt himself urinating. In fact, in front of the entire crew and supervisor, Joe peed in his pants. This represented the most embarrassing moment of his life to date. A caring fellow co-worker leaned down and assisted Joe with picking up his head; Joe was grateful for her kind and gentle assistance.

When Joe could finally stand on his own two urine-soaked feet, his supervisor told him to go home and return with a doctor's note the next day. Joe wanted to see a doctor more than his supervisor wanted him to. He was amazed at loosing consciousness like that. He thought he might have some kind of brain tumor or something.

The doctor told Joe he had suffered from heat stroke and ordered him to light duty for the next ten days. What a relief, to find there was nothing long-lasting or seriously wrong with him. When Joe returned to work with the doctor's note, his supervisor told him they didn't have any light duty and instructed Joe to turn in his I.D. badge. Not having an I.D. badge meant not being able to get into the building. If you couldn't get in the building, you could not work. And that meant you were fired.

Great, just great! Now with no job, Joe had no way to pay for his new home. He had a small amount of savings that would last about three months, but after that, all his plans for living in paradise would become null and void. Oh well, Joe had years of experience helping other people find jobs. He would just put his skills to use for himself this time.

The search for a new job was intense and very detailed. He ran down every lead from sunup to sundown, seven days a week. He kept written records of all avenues he was following and did follow-up. For three months this effort went on without so much as a return call. Now he got to the point of no return; he was down to his last $100 for bills and food and everything else. He couldn't believe that all his effort was for nothing. His heart was broken now, facing inevitable failure and realizing that he just couldn't make it on his own. It was prayer time again.

He prayed, "Okay, God, I could really use your help right about now. I'm at the end of my resources and things are looking pretty darn grim. I know you have helped me to get this far, and I really don't want to bother you with all my petty mortal problems all the time, but I have tried all I can. God, if you help me find work I promise I won't quit. I will remember these hard times and will never take my job for granted. Please help me, if it be thy will. Amen."

That's when, for the first time, Joe remembered what he experienced while unconscious at the post office. It started to come back to him slowly. At first he thought it had been a dream, but then the full measure of love that he experienced hit him. He realized that his request had been granted: he had met God while still alive! All fear was gone now. In a subliminal way, Joe knew and understood the intentions of his Creator. All he had to do now was trust in Him and let His love be in control.

Right then it occurred to him why he wasn't getting any calls. He was out all day looking for work, and prospective employers wouldn't call at night. He could have received lots of calls but he was not there to answer. Joe realized that an answering machine would solve the problem. But the cheapest answering machine he found on the market was $100 dollars. That meant going past the point of no return because that was the last of the food money. This was the real test of faith: Joe bought the answering machine.

Joe was out one last time looking for work and using up the last bit of gas in his car; when he returned home he found his answering machine blinking. It was probably his family up north; they would give Joe an occasional pep talk just to keep his spirits up. But it wasn't family; it was somebody else wanting him to call back.

When Joe returned the call, it went like this:

"Hello, this is Joe and I'm returning your call."

"Joe, we were very impressed with you during your interview. We would like to know how soon you could start work with us."

Joe remained perfectly cool—mainly because he didn't believe his own ears—and replied, "At your convenience." A date was set. Joe thanked them for their call and hung up the phone.

What ensued after that was a one-man party: there was singing and dancing, complete with a feast of the last peanut butter and crackers in the house. Of course, Joe was so caught up in the joyous occasion that he forgot to thank the One to whom he owed the favor.

EPILOGUE

THE JOURNEY HAD been a long one from that little farm in Texas, from that beautiful sunny day with the smell of honeysuckle in the air, from his first feelings of individuality. He had traveled, had experienced other cultures, had faced fear, and had overcome many adversities. He considered himself a success because he had earned the right to live by making it through the meat grinder; he also deserved to enjoy life and be happy because he survived the assembly line. He knew he had walked the right road because if given the choice he would do it all over again.

Now he had a new world and a new life in front of him, with more adventures to come his way that would help him grow and learn. He wasn't afraid of being alone or not finding true love. Joe was now a man in all his glory and he realized he did have something to offer. He was not the fastest or the smartest but he was armed with good intentions and a tenacious stubbornness that would never allow him to give up. He had found his paradise in a quiet little corner of Orlando, with warm weather, palm trees, and the ocean and beaches nearby to rejuvenate and inspire him. This was his American Dream.

Joe's life now is one of routine, with the occasional misadventures that seem to follow him everywhere he goes. He's still at the same job, and still lives in the same house. As of yet, he has not returned to the deep forest of his childhood in Texas, but still has plans to go there someday. Fortunately, his illness has remained in remission, giving him the time to reflect upon what he has learned from his experiences.

Joe will forever be satisfied with the outcome of his *que será, será*; he had found his place in the world, and as a result had achieved contentment. His "whatever will be" had finally come to be.